ACCEPTANCE

Book One
The Jewel Trilogy

TRISH BENINATO

ISBN-13:978-1973918165
ISBN-10:1973918161

DEDICATION

This book is dedicated to
My husband.
Thank you for being the inspiration for true love.

&

My grandfather
Because he inspired me with books and dreams.

PROLOGUE

THEY SAY THAT everyone is alone when they die. In a way, they're right. In that moment, I felt more alone than I had ever been in my whole life. I wasn't one to wallow in self-pity and depression, but I let both seep into my soul, tasting and fueling the betrayal that tore my soul right out. I sat there thinking about my impending doom. The cell that they held me in was bare and cold. There wasn't even a window. But the starkness of the cell coincided with the numbness of my soul. Everything that I was... or had been... was gone. I wasn't going to fight my fate. I was ready to embrace it. There was no life here for me.

I was deep in my thoughts when I heard the door to my cell slide open. They had come for me, for my judgment. But they weren't *him*. He wasn't coming. My heart ached. It was painful to be away from him. Yet, it was also painful to think that he may have shared my fate, or worse, be the reason I was here. The man I loved, fought beside, and planned to share my existence with had left me to fend for myself. I felt utterly alone, but it made me more angry than sad.

I liked the anger more than the pain, and I welcomed it back into my soul, putting aside my humanity to invite the rage to envelop me like a lover's embrace. The warrior in me reared its stubborn head in desperation once more. I felt the urge to fight, to survive, and to kill. I felt like a feral animal stalking its prey, ready to let the humanity slip from my fingertips. I waited to pounce.

"Come." The voice was familiar and I looked up into the eyes of my brother Deimos. He was here to lead me to my death—or to my rebirth. Either way, it didn't matter. I wanted to kill him before they took me. He was pushing his influence—his emotional control—out over me, trying to inflict fear and terror before he dragged me away. It didn't faze me, as usual, and he quickly became angry with my resistance.

"Stand." He forcefully spoke through gritted teeth as he grabbed my shackled arms to pull me roughly to my feet.

"I'm going to kill you, Brother." I laughed at the thought. Once upon a time I'd wanted him to love me. He and his twin, Phobos, had hated me all my life, though I'd tried to win their approval many times in my youth. Now all I wanted to do was watch the light leave his eyes as I snuffed his immortal life out. Heartbreak had hardened me. I embraced the war side of my nature and smothered the love. As the daughter of Ares and Aphrodite, I was always trying to balance the two. Today, war was everything I wanted to be. They would take me, they would punish me, and they might kill me, but not without a fight.

I waited as he pulled me swiftly down the long hallway. A hallway I used to run happily through as a child. It had been years since I'd been on the Olympus. I didn't miss it as much as I thought I would. The doors slid open to the council room; it was set up in the round, with a center section surrounded by elevated seating on all sides. I was thrust into the middle, the faces of my relatives and a few of the others staring down at me. Their faces were solemn and they glared at me in accusation. I glared back with equally malicious intent. Let them unfairly judge me in order to justify their treatment of me. There would come a day when they would regret this.

I scanned the large, crowded chamber looking for him, searching, holding onto that last little smidgen of hope, yet there was none to be found, only the faces of those who feared me. They feared me, and the only way to be rid of me was to sentence me to whatever hell they devised.

I stood there waiting, watching them.

"Young lady, have you nothing to say?" It was my grandfather Zeus who spoke. He sat there on his throne of sorts, lording over the room, as was his custom. He was becoming fat in the midsection, no longer the great warrior he had once been. He was the one who really wanted me dead. There were those in the room that had sympathy on their faces, those who even feared for me. He was the spearhead of my punishment.

I continued to smile at him, looking demented I'm sure, but it distracted him from the fact that I was slowly sliding my shackles off. I caught them before they clattered to the floor and felt my powers surge through me.

"None, at the moment, Grandfather." I continued to smile up at him.

"Then I have no choice but to exact your punishment." He may have had everyone else fooled, but I saw the gleam of relief in his eyes—relief that he had found a way to dispose of me in a way that reinforced that he was their gracious, merciful king.

"Do tell, what shall be done with me?" I continued to smile, watching as he became a little unnerved. I enjoyed his discomfort.

"I will say that one good thing has come of this." He paused, watching me closely. "Despite your blatant disrespect for our customs and most sacred laws, we have found a way to forge an alliance with our enemies. We have you to thank for this."

"The blatant disrespect for which I am being punished?" My malicious smile changed to that of curiosity as I turned my head to pass my own judgment on those present in the room, careful to continue hiding the freedom of my wrists from the shackles. I was almost ready. "Pray, do tell me what my punishment is."

"As part of our alliance, we must provide help with the testing of new technology. You, my dear, will be our first sacrifice to this new treaty and you will strengthen our agreement." He smiled at me then, without even hiding the glee in his expression. His appearance was older than that of most of our race because he'd already been quite old when immortality was gifted to us. The lines of a middle-aged man grazed the skin around his crystal blue eyes, and his blond hair had a stripe of silver at the temples. It had been that way for a very, very long time. He was staring down at me with those half-mad crystal blue eyes now. There was no mercy in them, only greed and the lust for power. He may have been my grandfather, but in that moment I'd never hated him more.

"I believe you know our scientist?" Set stood next to my

grandfather and gestured off towards the crowd to our left. His raspy voice was hard from his days scouring the desert lands. It caused me great pain to look at him, as if a knife had been plunged into my heart. Just his presence fueled my grief and anger. I felt those emotions overwhelming me.

Just then, the crowded room parted to our left as a man stepped through. My jaw dropped and all my anger dissipated into sorrow. It seemed my oldest, closest friend would be my executioner, a man who I had looked up to in a way I'd never been able to with my own father.

Why?

Determination sat once again in my heart as I looked deep into the eyes of my fate and he looked back at me, sad and full of pity. He glanced at my unshackled hands and shook his head, but I was once again angry and hurt. It was a strong combination, and I quickly dropped the shackles and unleashed my blade of psionic energy. I roared with all the pain, roared with all the betrayal as I leaped for Zeus. He could have me killed, but I'd kill him first.

As I reached him, he pulled out his lightning bolt and blocked my blow. He knocked the chair over and almost stumbled backwards. I smiled, ready to deliver a deadly blow. He'd taken everything from me. He took my soul, the only thing that ever mattered. I wanted him dead. I wanted him to suffer. The others in the room stood shocked at first, then leaped to Zeus's aid. I barely noticed them as I continued to strike at him. He was stronger than me, but I had resilience and determination on my side. I knew it was only a matter of time before they overwhelmed me and took me captive once again, but before they could do that, I wanted to leave my grandfather a present. I sliced into his left cheek, deep enough that even our technology could not fully heal him.

"Now every time you look in the mirror, you will remember your betrayal, your fear, and you'll remember me." I spat at him. It was the last thing I did before the whole world went dark—dark for a very long time.

CHAPTER ONE

4,000 Years Later

I STOOD IN THE rain lifting my face up to the stormy sky. The rain pelted down onto my skin, and I breathed the dewy dampness in deeply. I loved the rain. I loved the feel, the smell, and the taste of it. Sadly, it snowed where we lived more often than it rained. I glanced over at Teddy. He hated the rain. He had his hoodie pulled over his face and a North Face jacket over that.

Today was the first day of senior year for us both. We stood there waiting for the bus, five miles outside of the compound we lived on, Glen Delphi. We'd been driven to the gate. No one was allowed on the compound without authorization.

When we were younger, Teddy and I and the others from Glen Delphi who'd attended school with us were taken there in a large van. After a while, we'd insisted on being able to ride the bus in hopes of feeling more normal. All semblance of normalcy had ended once our friends from the compound

1

stopped attending school, though. Teddy and I were the only ones left, and we were treated like lepers.

"I hate the rain, but I'm glad it's not snow," Teddy grumbled to me as we stood under a tree to gain what little shelter we could find.

"All weather that is not sunny and warm is bad weather in your eyes." I smiled, my face still turned upwards to the sky.

Teddy was, everyone agreed, a borderline pessimist. He would probably even hate a sunny beach after a while. Despite that, he was also loyal, kind-hearted, and even, at times, funny. When we were younger and the kids at school would tease and pick on us, Teddy would be the first to defend me, with little regard or care for what they said or did to him in return. Then on the bus ride home, with his eye blackened from his most recent fight, he would smile and joke about his newest scar, one he was sure would get him sympathy and attention from all the ladies at home. I smiled thinking about how he played it up as soon as he walked in the door, bellowing and sniffling as all the women pampered him and cooed over him like a hurt puppy. I enjoyed Teddy's company, despite his occasionally gloomy disposition. He was my best friend.

"I'll be glad when this year is over and I'll be able to go west." Teddy hated living at Glen Delphi. His parents had moved there when he was a small child, taking him with them. Only, the traits that made everyone on the compound special hadn't been passed onto Teddy, at least as far as he was aware. Most of the other kids from Glen Delphi that had gone to school with us had already activated, and it was no longer safe for them to be in society until they learned to control their abilities. Teddy took great solace in the fact that I was like him, nothing special—or so he thought. But, although I thought Teddy was very special, I was not like him. I had activated at a very young age. No one outside Glen Delphi knew this, and even there, only the people I'd directly worked with knew. My father had insisted we keep it a secret. He said I was important and one day I would understand, but he refused to tell me anything more than that, which was beyond frustrating. Still, I hadn't told Teddy. I hated keeping the secret from him, but I didn't want to lose my best friend. If he knew, things would change between us.

The bus appeared around the bend, headed in our direction; we knew if we didn't move towards the road quickly, it would pass us by. We walked swiftly through the wet grass onto the gravel road. The bus driver had disliked us ever since he was forced to take on the extra route. It was a sizable distance from the school, a large portion of the trip on a gravel road, and it added fifteen minutes to his route. We were the first ones on the bus and the last ones off.

"Good morning, Mr. Finch." I smiled brightly. I'd hoped through the years that I would win him over, and it had worked somewhat—at least he no longer glared at us as we entered the bus. Now we would, on occasion, get a "hello" or a "good morning" back when he was having a good day and a nod on a bad day. Today was a nod kind of day.

Teddy moved to the back of the bus, naturally. I sat across the aisle from him and leaned my head against the window to watch the drops trickle down the pane. I felt a familiar wave of dizziness, and I closed my eyes, knowing a vision was coming. Lately, flashes of images had been flooding me, almost like déjà vu. These flashes always caught me off-guard—one minute I was fine, and then the next it was as if I were someone else, somewhere else entirely. The experience made me feel nauseous and dizzy, but it was always over before I was even able to gather my wits. I assumed the flashes were a part of my gift, but they'd only started about a year ago and had progressively gotten worse.

A scene played before my eyes now: *Getting caught in the rain, running and dancing... I closed my eyes in the vision, but I felt a soft breeze on my skin and the sensation of someone gently cupping my face, then a feather soft touch to my lips. A kiss.*

Back on the bus, in reality, I touched my lips and sighed. I'd never been kissed before, at least not in this life. But then the vision was over and my head began to pound like a beating drum. Something felt different, wrong. I shook my head, only to feel the pain intensify a little. I cringed and rested my head against the cool glass pane of the bus window. The chill helped the pain to subside a little.

"Jewel, hey, are you there? Earth to Jewel." Teddy was trying to get my attention. He'd moved beside me and was waving his hands in front of my face. "Hey, you did that checking out thing again. I've been talking to you for two minutes."

"I'm sorry, Teddy. I left again. I'll try to pay attention." I'd once told Teddy that I had an attention problem to explain when my mind wandered. I knew some of the truth, but I also knew there were some things that were still a mystery to me. Yet I was ready to learn the whole truth about myself, and hopefully soon. There was so much I couldn't tell Teddy. The older we got, the more secrets I had to keep. I felt like I was constantly betraying him.

"It's okay. I was asking you if you thought this year would be better than last year." Teddy's face went red. Last year had been bad for Teddy. He spent more time being shoved into lockers and fighting off the varsity football team than he did in class. Like me, Teddy had an uncanny ability to rub people the wrong way. I called it an aversion. People normally stayed away from me, and I couldn't say I preferred it that way, but it had its advantages. Teddy, on the other hand, would always say things to piss off the popular normal. Last year he'd even tried to befriend the quarterback's girlfriend, which started his swift descent into social suicide. It was better to be invisible; at least I thought it was.

I examined Teddy before I answered his question. He was older looking now; the summer had matured him, and no longer was he the scrawny, baby-faced boy he'd been the previous year. He wasn't what I would call a nerd; he was actually a rather lean yet still muscular, good-looking guy. He had warm brown eyes with long sweeping lashes that ladies would kill for. His face was boyishly round, yet it was easy to tell his features were starting to develop into a prominent jaw and high cheekbones. He also had thin lips and a long straight nose. And his light brown hair, which he always kept long, swept down and framed his face when it fell from behind his ears, tickling the dimple in his chin. Still, despite his good looks, our secret society and the mystery that surrounded us made his chances at normalcy next to impossible. Teddy just wanted to be normal since he couldn't be extraordinary.

On the other hand, most people stayed away from me because they naturally seemed to have some sense that I was different from them. Every once in a while someone would get brave and approach me, often to comment on how stunning or beautiful I was.

I hated it.

Deep down Teddy and I had so much in common: I just wanted to be normal as well.

The girls hated me and the boys dreamed of me. They couldn't help it. They were wired to. My father—my adoptive father, Robert Cartwright—had explained bits and pieces of my heritage to me over the years, but he said he wasn't allowed to tell me everything.

When I was younger, I would have these nightmares; I couldn't remember them anymore, but they would leave me crying and deeply sad. My father would rock me and sing as I fell asleep. He told me the dreams were reminiscences of another life. I asked him once, "Do you mean like reincarnation?" His reply was extremely vague, and it was obvious he was avoiding the question. We didn't speak of it for a very long time after that.

I hoped the day would go by fast, with the hustle and bustle of finding my locker and my classrooms—though I had the same teachers to pour nonsense into my head as I'd had the year before. The town was small; therefore the teachers and students were all the same each year. Which is why there was such a scandal when the other members of Glen Delphi started to leave school. After several of them disappeared, everyone whispered we were a cult that sacrificed our young. I laughed when I heard those rumors. The others were happily inside the walls of the compound. They enjoyed tutors and hundreds of acres that stretched out across the Rocky Mountains at their leisure.

I stood at my locker, quickly getting the combination down and shoving my loaded backpack inside. Standing nearby was a girl I'd never seen before, which meant she had to be new—a strange occurrence for our little school. She obviously hadn't gotten the memo about Teddy and me being weird because she smiled and introduced herself as Allison.

"Hello, I'm Jewel." I returned her warm smile, tucking a loose strawberry blond lock behind my ear.

"Has anyone ever told you that you could easily be a model?" Here it was, the whole worshipful awe, but I knew that soon she'd shy away.

I sighed. "I feel that brains over beauty is better in every way."

Allison was bookish in appearance, with bright blue eyes that were masked somewhat by the glasses frames that were slipping down her small upturned nose. She had slightly pouty lips and she was on the thin side, but she had a unique charm about her that was intriguing.

"Well, I think I like you. We shall be friends," she quipped. She grabbed my arm and proceeded to pull me down the hallway. I was so shocked that I didn't move at first, forgetting my strength. I, of course, didn't budge. She looked back at me. "Unless, you don't want to be friends?" She looked forlorn, her bottom lip poking out.

I gathered myself. "I would love to be friends." I smiled at her and followed her down the hall. Why did I not repel her like I did other people? It dawned on me then—perhaps she wasn't like the other humans wandering the halls. Perhaps she was like me and didn't know it. Either way, it was a nice change. I had another friend.

The rest of the day, I was caught up in running to familiar classes and deciding on important details like where to sit. Before I knew it, the final bell had rung and it was time to go home. I gathered my things and quickly left with Teddy by my side. The day had drained us and we both rode home on the bus, tucked in the back together, away from the other passengers.

When we got to our stop, I got off the bus and then smiled at Teddy as he hopped off onto the gravel. I quickly waved at Mr. Finch as he grumbled and the bus rambled away.

"Race?" challenged Teddy. He knew me so well.

"Uh, yeah! And guess what?" I teased him.

"What's that?"

"You're gonna lose!" I took off, not waiting for him, laughing as the long day was left behind me. I took off past the gate and the waiting van, and then I hopped over tree trunks and boulders up the dirt path towards our home. I didn't look back. I could hear Teddy crashing through the brush behind me. I pushed harder. Feeling free. I loved running. I didn't feel tired as I pushed myself to go faster, but then I realized that I was leaving Teddy far behind. So I stopped, waiting for him to catch up. A minute or two later, he finally reached me, breathing hard and trying desperately to catch his breath.

"Come on, there isn't much farther to go." I smiled at him and winked, and I laughed with him as he fought to speak.

"It's not fair since you run and hike all the time. You know I mostly nerd it out."

I nudged him. "You do. So step your game up." I took off once again, this time slowing my pace so as not to give myself away. The van pulled up near us, but the driver knew better than to ask us if we wanted a ride. We ran all the way home, enjoying the freedom of running together through the woods.

"How was school?" My father stood outside the main building of Glen Delphi. It was a large mansion that contained many underground rooms. My father owned it and he ran the compound. There were approximately 150 people living here. Some came and went and others never left.

"It was good. Same as always until I made a new friend." I smiled as I thought of Allison. She'd dragged me through the halls. We'd learned we had three classes together today. Teddy shared three of his eight classes with me, and one of them overlapped with Allison's schedule as well. He'd grumbled about her, mostly from jealousy, but quickly warmed up to her.

"She wasn't... um... repelled?" I knew he was searching for a different word but had failed to find one appropriate.

"No, she was not 'repelled.' In fact, she insisted on being my friend." I shrugged, used to him referring to the aversion people had towards me in a casual manner. People reacted similarly to him, so the words didn't hurt coming from him.

"Okay, well this Allison concerns me. I'll need to look into her." He scratched his face in deep thought. I knew he would say that. He was not the trusting sort. Especially when it came to me.

My father was a handsome man; he had sandy blond hair and green eyes. We shared so many features that when I was a child I'd wondered if perhaps we were related in some way, even though my father had told me years before that I was adopted. He'd finally admitted that we were related, but distantly. He told me that the genes in our particular family were very strong.

I had strawberry blond hair that, at times, appeared to be more of a red color. My eyes were large and green, but occasionally I would swear they turned blue. My nose was small and straight with a slight downturn at the bottom. My lips, in my opinion, were too big for my face, which was oval with strong cheekbones and a slightly more prominent jawline than you'd see on the typical egg-shaped oval face. I'd been told I was beautiful more times than I could count, but I didn't see it.

What I hated most about myself was that I was insanely tall, like almost six feet tall. I towered over most boys my age, and if being weird didn't scare them enough, my height sure did.

Robert, my father, was tall as well. He was 6'2", just a few inches taller than me.

"Time to get to work," he said. "Has Teddy gone back to his room?" He'd agreed that we should keep my "work" from Teddy, though his reasons were different than mine. I didn't want Teddy to end up feeling hurt or alone because he was the only kid left our age without powers, whereas my dad just wanted to keep my abilities as secret as possible. That seemed sort of futile since I'd worked with so many of the people on the compound, but I didn't bother to argue. This was one subject that my dad wasn't willing to compromise on, and I didn't see the need to push him.

"Yes, Dad, let's get on with it. I can do the homework later; it's pretty simple stuff anyway."

"I don't know why you even bother with going to school anymore." He smiled, though, because I'd told him why a million times. I wasn't ready to give up this life yet. I wanted to be normal, even if it was for just a short period of time during the day. Plus, I couldn't abandon Teddy.

We walked towards the back of the enormous house

until we reached a pantry hidden within a pantry; in the back there was a door concealed by a sliding panel, and through that panel was an elevator. Deep below the mountain were hundreds of secret rooms, so many that you would think we were a secret government operation, but Delphi Glen wasn't anything of that nature. We were, however, "secret."

"Jewel,"—as we made the long trip down, my father turned towards me. His tone was soft and slightly sad— "this will be the last day you'll be working here for a while. Tomorrow I must introduce you to someone. He's going to train you in ways we cannot." I felt a strong emotion cascade off of him before he stopped himself from saying anything further. He couldn't hide the small tear that begged to escape the corner of one of his eyes. "I thought we would have so much more time. But I hope that whatever path you choose, it is what *you* want." He smiled then and kissed the top of my head.

"I don't understand. Why do I need to train?" I thought all the years of putting in extra time down here had been enough training.

"I'll explain some more later tonight, my bunny." Bunny. That had always been his nickname for me. I knew he'd come to love me, even if I was a responsibility forced on him. He'd never lied to me, this I knew, but he'd never told me the whole truth or elaborated enough to appease me either. He always told me that he wasn't allowed to tell me about my past or my family; therefore, I only knew a little about who I really was, and it drove me crazy, as if I were almost always lost and trying to find myself. My father always insisted that it was for the best.

Once the elevator had fully descended, I walked out into the long, lit corridor and heard bellowing. Andrew was not having a good day.

This is going to be interesting, I thought to myself. I quickly waved to my father. It was time to get to work.

CHAPTER TWO

I SHOT DOWN THE hallway towards the noise. Andrew's bellowing was loud as it bounced through the halls. I could feel the power surging from his body. There were others in the hallway outside the room, but they weren't willing to go past the entrance. I pushed past them, no one stopping me as I entered.

Andrew sat in the corner of the room. He had ignited; his body was a blaze of fire and energy. The suit that the technology team had created to help him control the massive amounts of energy that sometimes erupted from him lay on the floor.

Andrew had been the last of our friends to leave school. He was only sixteen. The consensus was that if you didn't activate into an evolved (or an Evol, as we called ourselves) by age sixteen, chances were that you weren't going to.

"Andrew, can you hear me?" The blaze was hot, but it didn't affect me. I moved closer. I couldn't help him unless I was in close proximity to him. That was the hiccup of my abilities. I was a borrower of sorts, a collector. I edged closer. "Andrew, it's Jewel. Can you hear me?"

I was about a hundred feet away now, slowly moving closer. I didn't want to scare him and cause him to shoot energy and fire towards the others in the hallway. The closer I came to Andrew, the more I felt his abilities seep into my body. I was close enough now that I could reach out and touch him.

"Andrew, look at me. Breathe deeply." Fire ignited all over my body, just like it had on Andrew's, but it didn't burn me. It warmed me. I was in control of it. That's why I was here—to teach Andrew to control the power within him.

"Calm down and breathe deeply. Think about bringing the fire inward, inside of you." I pulled the energy within myself in hopes that Andrew would understand.

"Jewel, I can't. It's too much. I just can't do it." Emotion made Andrew lose control.

I'd watched as the overwhelming pain, the guilt, the devastation of his inexorable loss had wrapped its sticky tendrils around his soul and made its home. I had spent months helping him overcome that pain and guilt. Although the loss would always be there, I was finally starting to see those sticky tendrils of darkness melt away, but occasionally they would still burst up in another desperate battle for survival. That was what was happening now. I watched him shudder and close his eyes as he remembered the guilt that held him so tightly in darkness and in pain. He looked down at his hands, watching as the flames danced around his palms.

He hated his ability. It had killed his family.

"Andrew, please look at me." I leaned forward and placed my hand on his face, showing him he couldn't hurt me. My abilities went beyond borrowing from others, but that was a much-guarded secret as well. Andrew began to calm down.

"Andrew, look at me. Listen to my words. Bring it inside you. Imagine the fire, the flames drawing into you. Like you're pulling in breath. Do it with me now."

Andrew pulled the energy inside himself, and it extinguished. The corner of the room was black and burnt, smelling of ash and melted plastic.

"I'm so sorry." He looked around at the destruction around him. "I didn't mean to," he said, curling up into a ball.

Since his clothes had burnt off, I averted my eyes as I walked over to the other side of the room for his heat-proof suit, bringing it to him and setting it next to him.

"Here, put this on. I'll leave as you get dressed." I turned to walk away, but Andrew stopped me.

"Why does it never burn you or your clothes?" He'd asked me this before.

"Honestly, I have no idea." It was true, I didn't. I suspected my father knew the truth, but he always answered me in the same way: "One day you will know why." Did I mention that I hated that answer?

I walked out of the room to give Andrew his privacy. We'd all thought that he would activate with more of a psychic ability. His mother had been a telepath and his father could manifest a whole reality within the mind of another. Instead Andrew manifested energy—massive amounts. So much so that when he'd activated one night a few months ago, it had burned his living quarters down with his parents inside. He was found alive but naked, lying shocked in the charred remains of his home. His mother had reached out with her mind at the end to call for help. We all felt her pain and her death, but no one could get to her in time. Andrew had also felt his mother's painful death. He lived with the guilt every day.

"It's good. You can come back in." Andrew stood in the doorway in his heat-proof suit. It wasn't super fancy or fashionable, but it helped him. It was made of a special black material that absorbed the energy that cascaded from his body. He was still able to activate his powers when needed, but it gave him more control.

"See. Much better. That suit really shows off your cut body." I laughed lightly, trying to pull Andrew out of his misery. Andrew smiled at me and the pain and grief that had been clinging to him earlier was pushed down, as he seemed to shed it like a skin, forcing it to disappear into the background, hopefully for good. He stood there for a moment watching me, and his smile turned to something different. It was warmer and more sensual. All of the darkness had left. It was the biggest triumph yet. Yet, he didn't fool me. There, behind it all, remained a bit of stickiness, and the sensual smile faltered a bit. Still, he chuckled to himself.

"You mean it shows off my larger than life attributes." He winked and smiled deviously.

"You, sir, are in need of a reminder that no one is thinking of your attributes," I shot back.

This had been the way of things with us lately. It helped him to have someone who didn't treat him delicately, and I was happy to be that person. I just wanted to help him heal and move on from his pain and tragedy. I was always surprised that even after a meltdown like the one he'd just had, he bounced back quickly. I just hoped it wasn't an emotional defense mechanism.

I didn't mind the playful banter because, honestly, Andrew

was a very attractive guy. Activating speeds up growth, and Andrew was now a fully matured young man with ripped muscles and chiseled features. His black hair was cut short on the sides, and the bangs were long, sweeping over his thick brows, which framed his dark blue eyes.

"You know,"—Andrew paused and turned a little red in the face—"if there ever comes a time that you do 'think of my attributes'... well, I don't think I'd mind. I mean, they are hard to avoid thinking about." Andrew played it off as a joke, but I caught the underlying suggestion. Lately, it seemed like maybe his admiration had started to turn into something more, and it made me uncomfortable at times. I didn't fully know why, though. It was hard not to be flattered by Andrew's attention. He was now what would be considered a heartthrob. He set more than a few of the young ladies' hearts aflutter when he looked their way. But, to me, he was just Andrew, the same goofy kid who followed me around when we were growing up.

To break the tension, I picked up a charred pillow left over from his destroyed bed and chucked it his way. "I'm flattered, and it *is* very hard to resist such a tempting offer, but I'll have to pass." I threw another pillow, but this time he dodged it.

It was then that the hall gawkers piled back into the room. They consisted of doctors, scientists, and other Evols who either resided here or worked for my father.

"He's good now. We're going to the east training room and we'll work on his control."

They moved aside to create a path for Andrew and me. I knew it was because they feared and respected us both, but whom they feared most was the question.

The rest of the night, till well past dinner, I worked with Andrew, teaching him techniques to control his ability. And then I left him. I hated leaving him, or anyone, down there, but I had no choice. My father said it was for his and others' safety. It still sucked.

I exited the pantry, grabbing an apple on my way through the kitchen. I waved hello to a few of the residents that stayed with us. All of them were here because they needed help and were different. Some Evols were able to function in society. Many blended in and even started families, but many also found their way to us. My father kept track of all of them, helped them and kept them secret. He was the head of the Evols, in a way. He was also one of the most powerful. Which once again brought up the long-debated question: What was I?

I wasn't exactly an Evol. I was something more. My father had fed me scraps of information over the years, but never the full story. But he had informed me that I was not the same as the others. Then what was I? The older I became, the more this question drove me bat-shit crazy. Maybe tonight I would get another piece of the puzzle.

Which reminded me, where was my father?

Just as I was contemplating where to find him, he slipped out of the shadows.

"I assume you're looking for me so we can have our little chat." My father had an accent, one I could never pinpoint exactly.

I nodded my head yes. I was ready and hoping to finally have some answers.

"Alright then, my little bunny. Follow me to my study."

I followed him quietly to the west end of the house. We

reached his study and, since the door had been left slightly ajar, I walked in and sat in one of the expensive leather chairs in front of his massive chestnut desk. I'd always loved his study and used to play on the floor as a child. There was even a telltale burn mark on one of the expensive Persian carpets where I had decided to iron my favorite stuffed animal Jackie's bowtie. My father had been very upset, but I'd insisted that Jackie had to look perfect for our date and the iron had fallen in the process. Jackie was a jackal with a black stripe on his back. I'd begged my father to buy him for me, and I never let him go. I still had him. I smiled at the memory.

"I've been dreading this day for some time. I fear you will not like me after this." He sat behind his desk looking nervous and uncomfortable. I had never in my life seen him like this. I sat up straight and paid close attention.

"As of tomorrow you won't be helping in the basement as much." I was surprised he'd mention that here. We never spoke of what happened downstairs once we were upstairs. Some of the Glen Delphi inhabitants could be trusted only so far. I waited, watching as he wrestled to find the right words. Watching as he carefully contemplated. I thought perhaps he'd suggest something better, some alternative to me giving up my important work to... what? Work with a personal trainer? It sounded like something a bored housewife would do to get her high school figure back. I was still in high school and I was pretty good in the in-shape department.

Instead of waiting any longer I decided to demand answers. "What do you mean I won't be helping as much? That's what I do. That's what I'm meant to do!" I was angry and I felt like I was being punished. These emotions came on quickly as the words rushed out. Even though I wanted to experience as much of a normal life as possible, I still loved that I could help others.

"Calm down, Jewel. Let me explain." He paused as I collected myself. "You will be doing the training we discussed earlier. You'll still be here, but you'll also spend a good deal of your time there."

"There? What do you mean there?" I never left Glen Delphi other than to go to school. Every once in a while I snuck away to hike the mountains and swim in my favorite mountain lake, but other than that I was always here.

"Do you remember when you used to have nightmares and you woke up screaming?" I nodded. "I would tell you a bedtime story. Do you remember the story?" He moved to the chair next to me and took my hand in his. He smoothed my hair back, tucking a wild strand behind my ear. "I've always been honest with you, Jewel, as much as I could be, and I've loved you as my own. But you were never truly mine. And soon you will need to make a big decision. There are three different paths you may choose to take. I hope you take the right one." As cryptic as ever, his gift drove me crazy. My father was able to see and predict the many different paths of the future. He claimed he was a child of something called an oracle.

"I remember a little bit of the story. Something about a war over a distant planet and two people of different races falling in love." I remembered a bit more but wanted to hear as much as possible from him.

"Yes, there were once many different planets full of humanoid life. They were located on the other side of the universe." He stopped talking, a contemplative look on his face. "Actually, some of the planets were inhabited by people who were once of one race, before they had a disagreement and broke away from each other, scattering across the galaxy. The people eventually evolved into different races, with different strengths and weaknesses, but the tensions just continued to grow throughout the millennia. Of course, they weren't the only ones on that side of the universe, but they're the most important for our story.

"There was a disagreement between many of the races. Some had depleted their planets' resources and others were becoming greedy. There was a special technology that all the races wanted. And they fought for it—at the cost of billions of lives. Once their planets were destroyed, they began looking for somewhere else to live." He stopped again, searching my eyes.

"Okay, I do remember this silly sci-fi story you used to tell me, but I don't understand its relevance." I was frustrated and just wanted answers.

"Jewel, listen closely. It wasn't just a bedtime story. It's history from many millennia ago."

"You expect me to believe that aliens existed and wanted to conquer our planet?" I chuckled nervously because his seriousness confused me.

"I expect you to believe your own story and no more." He sounded tired, the kind of tired that came from a heavy burden.

"And what is my story?" This was the million-dollar question that had been plaguing me for so long. Finally, I wanted some answers.

"Your story has not just begun as you thought. And it has not yet even come close to ending." Dammit, he was being cryptic again.

"Just tell me and stop with the riddle crap."

"I know it drives you crazy. And I'm sorry. It's hard to work against my oracle nature, though. I've been living this life for years, to be here for you, but it's still a difficult task to go against one's nature. Do you remember when I told you after one of your nightmares that they were reminiscent of another life?"

"Yes, and I asked you if it was like reincarnation. You said it wasn't exactly but the assumption wasn't entirely inaccurate." I remembered that vividly because it had stuck with me and stumped me. Was I someone else before?

"You want to know who you were, but I can't answer that, because you were never anyone else. Not exactly."

My voice pitched higher in agitation. "I don't understand how you think this is going to help me. All you're doing is confusing me more. Spit it out *directly* and don't talk around the subject."

"Calm down, I'm getting there. You, my lovely lady, are the daughter of two of the most powerful individuals in the royal family of a race that fought in a war to inherit planet Earth."

Well, that shocked me to the point that I shut my mouth and listened.

"I cannot tell you the full story, but I can tell you that you were sent here—to the future—as a toddler to live with me. I'm your cousin, in a way. You were sent here as a means to protect you, I believe. From whom, I am not sure. Thousands of years have changed many of the stories, and our memories do not last that long." He stopped there for a moment, allowing me to absorb the information.

"Since then, the war between the races has ended, and

regions of Earth were given to several of each race's elected members. The tensions that once flourished have dissipated and the races are more cordial. I do not know how best to explain this to you."

"Can you at least try? I'm still full of so many questions. For instance, who were my parents? Why was I sent here, and who were the races and why were they fighting?" The questions rolled off my tongue in one complete mumbled sentence.

"Do you remember reading about Greek and Roman mythology? You brought a book home once in elementary school."

"Yes, and?"

"Behind every story there is some truth."

"So you're saying that I'm... what? A descendant of the Greek gods and goddesses?"

"No, I'm saying you *are* one."

"Shut the front door! Pretending that I believe you—and I'm not saying I do, but since we already work within the realm of the impossible, I must be somewhat capable of believing in it—why would I be here and not on Mount Olympus or something?"

"My dear, the Olympus was a spacecraft that the mountain was named after because the ship hovered over it. The ship and the mountain were named for their people, the Olympians of the planet Olympia."

"So what you're saying is that I'm an alien."

"Yes and no."

"Oh my God, please just straight answers. I'm going to beat my head against the wall!"

"You were the first and last of your kind to be born here,

which was almost a miracle in and of itself. There are others, like me, who are descended from both Olympians and humans, but you are the only full-blooded Olympian who wasn't born on Olympia."

"Okay, how does that make me different from them?"

"It doesn't, not really. It's only that technically your home planet is Earth, so you wouldn't be considered an alien. But you still inherited attributes and abilities from your parents. You have something damn near immortality and you also have special abilities. The difference is, unlike the Evols, you haven't activated. You're starting the process quite early."

"So I'm not an Evol?" I felt the special connection I had to the Evols, the sense of being a part of something, slowly deflate.

He hesitated, but finally responded, "You are the reason they exist."

It was a knife straight through the heart. I thought back to the pain I'd witnessed with Andrew just a little while ago. All the Evols' pain and suffering was my fault? Damn. I felt like my heart would break and the walls were closing in. All this... Andrew, his parents, countless others... it was somehow because of me.

I was a monster.

"I don't want to hear any more tonight." All my questions, I felt like they were no longer important. I wanted to wallow in my pain and guilt.

"Honey, it's not like that at all. It's not as bad as you think."

"Finding out that others' suffering and loss is ultimately your fault isn't all that bad? Are you kidding me? I just need time to process. Please leave me alone for the rest of the night." With that, I stood up and walked out of the study. I walked up the massive staircase to the suite my father and I shared on the west end of the mansion. Once I was in my room, I crawled into bed and searched around for Jackie, my black jackal. I was tired and the stress of the day had seeped all the energy from me. Before long I was snuggled in my blankets, clutching my childhood toy as if I weren't going to be eighteen years old in a few short weeks.

CHAPTER THREE

Anubis

OWN IN HIS study, Robert sighed while sitting at his desk. I watched him from the shadows. I'd stayed hidden throughout the conversation, listening and yearning. I had waited so long for this day. And I found that even still I was impatient. I stepped out of the shadows.

"Good evening, Robert." The oracle jumped. I watched as the shiver ran down his back. Those of mortal, human blood tended to become nervous and uncomfortable in my presence, even the ones that had descended from our races. I was used to it.

"Anubis." He turned towards me. The man had a look of the inevitable that can often be seen on someone staring at death. "How long have you been there?"

"Long enough."

"She's grown into such as strong young lady. I wish I could take credit. I fear that war is tipping the scales this time around."

"No, I think she's becoming more balanced. You've done well in raising her and keeping her safe. I'm grateful beyond words."

"Do you wish to address the rest with her tomorrow after you meet?" Robert looked at me with the eyes of a man who knew his daughter was leaving him but hoped that humanity would sway her to stay.

"Yes. I've spent thousands of years waiting for her; yet, I would still let her make her own decision, Robert. My love for her has been and always will be the one pure thing I have ever experienced. My greatest concern is that she is safe. We train to keep her that way starting tomorrow. She will miss two days of school per week and will spend the evenings with me."

"She won't like this. She's headstrong and outspoken."

"Then she has not changed much." I chuckled as memories crept up at that thought. Others had gone mad due to thousands of years' worth of memories and had stored them away. I held tight to mine. They were all I had left of *her*. Her own parents didn't even know who she was, and that kept her safe. I intended to keep it that way.

"I don't understand why she's still in danger. The war between the races has long been abandoned and a new alliance has been established. There is no more hate."

"But there is fear. And there are still those who remember the prophecy and hold on to the hope that their reign here will begin once again." I knew this to be true because Zeus, Jewel's own grandfather, held onto this belief. He would kill Jewel without a second thought if he knew she was here. And Set, my own father, who had not perished as lore suggested, would happily help him. I would do everything I could to protect her.

"I'll see you early tomorrow. Don't send her to school—we have much to discuss." And with that, I melted back into the dark shadows.

Jewel

I WOKE TO the morning light streaming in through my window. The birds were chirping loudly. What time was it? I must have overslept. I leaned over the bed to look at the clock. Crap, it was 8:30! I had missed the bus. Where was Teddy? He'd normally have rushed upstairs and started beating on my door by now.

The conversation I'd had with my father the night before started coming back to me. What the Cracker Jack had that been about?

Apparently I was a goddess of the ancient Greeks and Romans, but they—er... *we*—were actually aliens... sort of. I seriously didn't think crapola could get any weirder then that.

I rolled out of bed. I'd already missed the bus, so why not enjoy a nice shower? I raced to the private master bath attached to my room and stood under the hot spray of water as I digested all the crazy information I'd been given last night. I was special, possibly immortal. I was apparently born in the past. How long ago, I wasn't sure, but from what I could gather, it was a long freaking time ago. My parents were gods or aliens... again, confused. There had been a war. I may have been sent here to protect me, but by who and from whom?

The shock was over and I was ready for more answers. *Bring it.*

"Jewel, are you in there? Can you come down to my study when you're ready?" my father called up to me. It looked like I'd be getting more answers soon.

Once I deemed myself sufficiently clean, I turned the shower off, quickly brushed my hair, threw on a pair of old jeans and a t-shirt, and bounded down the stairs to his study.

I was in such a hurry that when I rushed through the door I ran smack dab into a mountain. Or at least it felt like a mountain. It knocked me on my butt. I looked upwards for what seemed forever at one of the tallest men I'd seen in my life. He was at least 6'6", if not more. I mean, I was a giant by lady standards but he was at least a half a foot taller than me.

Once my gaze finally reached his face, I froze. I didn't know why, but he was so familiar, it felt like I was in one of my déjà vu moments. I didn't know how anyone could forget a face like his, though. He was pure sex on a hot stick. He was perfection. He was chiseled but lean with a light olive skin tone. His face featured a strong jawline, a straight, perfect nose, thick eyebrows, and deep brown eyes that melted my insides. I had never in my life reacted to anyone this way.

It took me a moment to realize he was offering to help me up. I think I may have even noticed that he took note of my perusal of him, but I was so taken aback and frozen, I can't be sure.

"Jewel." He said my name, and it was like deep honey warming my insides. What was wrong with me?

"I'm sorry, I'm sorry." I refused his hand, turning to get up to hide the redness in my face. He stood there and waited, allowing me to collect myself. There was quiet power coming off of him. I could feel it coming towards me in waves. I looked at my father, who was standing awkwardly off to the side, and then back at the giant of a deliciously sexy man. Damn, I needed to stop thinking of him that way. I could feel my face turn crimson again.

"Jewel," my father finally said, clearing his throat. I tore my eyes from the man and begrudgingly gave my father my attention. "This is…"

"Anubis," the vision of perfection answered.

Wait, what? Anubis? Like the Egyptian god? This just keeps getting weirder, I thought. *On I go down my rabbit hole. Seems appropriate I'm nicknamed bunny.*

"So you're the Egyptian god of death or something like that?" He looked like he could be death. Even with all his hotness, there was an underlying dangerous element that seemed to lie just under the surface.

"Something like that."

My father had moved to the back of the room to shut the door, but I'd stopped paying attention to either of them. I was in one of my lost moments…

Lying under the clouds on a bright sunny day; it was hot but there was a breeze just off the coast. I'd traveled here to learn from the monotheistic people that lived in the neutral lands. They called this place Palestine. It bordered the forbidden lands of Egypt. I lay on the coast, dangerously close to the line that separated Egypt from the neutral lands. There was a man…

But it was slipping away. I tried desperately to hold onto the vision…

It was gone and I was back in the study.

That was when my head began to pound once again. I

stood there as the wretched pain seared through my brain like a knife cutting butter. The room began to spin a little as I tried desperately to steady myself, but between the intense pain in my head and the spinning room, I had to quickly sit where I was. I held my head in my hands as the agony continued throbbing through my skull to the beat of some unknown song. The nausea quickly overcame me, and all I could do was take deep breaths as I waited for it to pass.

"Jewel, are you okay? What did you see?" The man with the deep liquid honey voice was calling me back to the now. He seemed oddly concerned, since he didn't even know me. He even knelt beside me and placed his palm gently to my forehead. His hand warmed my skin and, strangely, the pounding quickly ceased at his touch. I sighed gratefully and realized I was leaning into his touch. I quickly reassured myself and stood, smiling to hide my embarrassment.

"I'm fine now. It was just … it was nothing." He didn't look like he completely believed me, but I continued before he could argue. "I saw the past, or some little bit of it: a coast near Egypt, a breeze and clouds. Then there was a man, but he was gone before I saw who he was."

The sexy god named Anubis smiled, seeming to relax. "You witnessed a small part of the first time we met." He scratched his jaw, lost in memories of his own. "My memories are just as hard to access as your jumbled ones, but that one will always be one of my favorites." He spoke as if he knew me, knew me very well. I wasn't sure if I was thrilled or worried.

"Sweet. Are you here to give me answers, or are we going to stand here all day?" He may have been a hot man-god, but I was done with not knowing who I really was.

"Straight to the point, as always." He turned to my father.

"I shall take it from here." With that, I watched as my father slipped through the door, abandoning me with this huge man.

"Anubis, is it?" I was trying to act casual and nonchalant, but it was difficult after practically passing out in pain in front of him. "What exactly is it that you want from me?"

"What I want"—he paused, pulling me to him and lowering his voice as he spoke in my ear—"is your absolute happiness and safety." I felt the heat of his breath on my skin and it caused tingles to go down all the way to my naughty parts. This man did things to me, dangerous things. I wasn't sure how to act or react, so I stood there dumbfounded as he led me straight into what appeared to be a wall.

Was he kidnapping me? Did I want him to? Before I had time to think any further we walked through the wall. There was a swift feeling of suction and then darkness and the sensation of wind whipping in all directions. It felt like it was grabbing at me. And then it stopped.

I dropped onto my butt again on the other side of the wall. We weren't in the house anymore, definitely not. We were in a room, a very large one, which contained a sand pit in the middle. Around the room, adorning the walls, were various ancient and modern-day weapons, some I had never seen, hanging on clear display.

"What was that?" I was still trying to stand and felt woozy again. Was I about to have another vision? Anubis steadied me as I embarrassingly clutched at him.

"That, my dear, would be what it feels like to walk through a portal." Anubis gestured towards the room. "You are now in my home."

"I'm not sure if anyone has ever told you, but your home

could use a few things, including furniture and an interior designer—perhaps a woman's touch. Maybe Mrs. Anubis should redecorate for you."

He chuckled, as he looked me over. "As you wish."

"Wait, what does that mean? Is there a Mrs. Anubis? If so, please tell her you forced me here so she doesn't get some crazy *Real Housewives* thing going against me." I looked around expecting a crazed goddess to jump out of the shadows at me.

"There has not been a 'Mrs. Anubis,' as you put it, here in a very, very long time." His tone became sad and yearning. In that moment my heart broke for him. I didn't know why then, but I trusted him. Even more confusing, I felt his pain, his deep sadness, as if it were my own. My heart clutched as if I were experiencing actual heartbreak. I felt tears well up in my eyes, and I tried desperately to push these foreign emotions down, yet they threatened to erupt and consume me. I knew in that moment that he had lost someone very dear to him and he suffered greatly because of it. How insane would he think I was if I told him I knew this just after we'd met?

Or *had* we just met? He'd told me earlier I was remembering him in my flash-trance thingy.

"How do we know each other?" I walked over to the pit in the middle of the room. It was surrounded by a bench that wrapped around it, like this was a private stadium.

"Your father just introduced us; I'm going to train you." He waited, obviously checking for my response.

I decided to choose the words of my next question more carefully. "No, I mean before you said I was remembering you. How?" I studied him, and I could tell that he was choosing his words just as carefully. We were dancing. And I needed to be the better dancer.

"Your father told you that you were sent here from the past and that you are of another race from another planet." He was merely repeating verbatim what I already knew. Why would no one spit the whole truth out?

"You're not telling me anything new." I stood there, eyeing him up. My body was tense and my hands curled into tight fists as I tried to politely hide my frustration, only to give in to my baser instincts, as always. "Dude, listen, why don't you stop treating me like a toddler and we can move onto more important things." I put my hands on my hips and stared him down.

He smiled and stood there watching me, not taking the bait, but rather enjoying my frustration. Rather than irritate me more, this had the odd effect of softening my mood.

"I was a toddler when I came here, so how do I remember certain things? Like lying alone on a beach... and a passionate kiss." The last part made me blush as I touched my lips. My earlier frustrations were forgotten, and I hesitantly smiled as I wondered what it would be like to kiss a man like the one before me.

"You were a toddler when you came to this time, but you weren't a toddler when you left the past." He was once again contemplating how much to tell me. I could see it in the strain on his face and hear it in the inflection of his words. I could tell that he was not a man used to watching what he said, or saying much at all, for that matter.

I snorted. It was unladylike and I didn't care.

Unladylike? Where did that notion come from? I'd never described any of my actions as ladylike or unladylike before.

"That's enough conversation for today. I don't want to overload you. The past will begin to come back to you slowly now that you're activating." He once again used his hands to gesture, this time towards the sand pit. He came off to me as a man of few words and big actions. And now was a time for action.

"Fair enough, but if I agree to train with you, you'll tell me?" I was making a deal, possibly with the devil.

"I'll answer one question after every session—if you work hard and listen to my instructions." He walked towards the middle of the pit and stood there, an olive-toned god that oozed sex and danger. A devilish thought came to my mind. *What if I prayed? Would he hear it?*

"You're blushing again, my Jewel." His Jewel. Why did that sound so familiar? It confused me and I didn't like it. Or maybe I didn't like the fact that I did like it so much.

"I accept your deal."

And with that, I stepped onto the sand with him. And my life changed forever.

I STOOD BAREFOOT with the oddly powdery-fine sand between my toes, facing this man. He was a giant beast and I aimed to take him down. I crouched low, ready for action.

I wasn't prepared for the butt-kicking I got, but luckily it didn't last long.

The first few times he rushed at me, he easily threw me onto my back. The air was knocked from my lungs, and as I lay there gasping, I quickly became angry. I was determined to take him down at least once. I had never fought like this before, but I caught on quickly. Almost too quickly. The next time he advanced towards me I was able to match him, strike for strike. I blocked his kicks and jabs, almost like I knew where the next hit was coming from. It became like second nature.

We didn't talk much at first. Then *finally* I took him by surprise as I knocked him off balance by swinging my legs low, perfectly hitting that sweet spot behind his knees and throwing him backwards. I kicked him again in the stomach to help advance his fall. He fell like a ginormous tree in a forest. I almost wanted to yell, *Timber!* I was already dancing with triumph before he hit the ground.

"That's right!" I danced around his muscular body. He was sweaty and so was I, but I didn't care because I'd finally taken his hot ass down. Victory was mine.

"In your face!" I yelled exuberantly. "I too –" I didn't finish because he quickly used his legs to flip me onto my back, right next to him. The air escaped my lungs once again as I lay there processing my short victory and the mild pain of a sore ego—and back.

"Very well done, but perhaps a little less gloating in the future? It's a blow to my self-esteem." He turned towards me and sat up on his propped arm. He was so close. I could feel the heat radiating off of his body. I turned towards him instinctively.

"You are the expert. I mean, I would be embarrassed that a little girl took me down as well," I teased him. I knew I'd just gotten lucky, but I couldn't help but taunt him.

Instead of taking the bait he smiled, but it quickly faded and I felt the same familiar pain as I'd experienced earlier. But he quickly suppressed it, as if he knew I felt his heartache. He stood suddenly, pulling me up with him. I felt as if he was hiding something in that moment, but I knew better then to probe.

"Okay, little girl." He chuckled and winked. "Let's try this again."

I WAS SHOCKED at how quickly I continued to improve and how easily I caught onto the moves he showed me. It was as if I was a natural. Yet, in all my training growing up, my father had never once introduced me to any type of fighting. He said, with my abilities, I would never need self-defense skills. Still, I felt like I'd done this before, that this wasn't the first time I'd fought. It seemed odd to me, but I decided to store that thought for later.

Anubis moved faster than normal people do, but I eventually matched my speed to his. I'll admit I'd never had a better workout in my life. He seemed so serious that I was surprised to hear him laugh as we sparred. It was a deep chuckle that sounded unused and hesitant, as if he weren't used to laughing.

Finally, he said it was time to stop. The time had gone by so quickly!

"Okay, buddy, it's time to answer some questions then," I said with more excitement than I meant to, but in honesty I was anxious for answers.

"Fair enough." His demeanor changed as he became serious again. His brow furrowed a bit and his face looked almost haunted. He was using my very words from before. I should have found it rude, but I didn't. I sat down, ready for our conversation.

"What does activating mean? I thought I already activated, in a sense, as an Evol." I watched his face for any sign of expression. He was difficult to read, his perfect face a mask.

"Activating is different for you. You'll gain near invincibility and immortality." He paused, sitting on the bench next to me, a task that seemed almost impossible for him for some reason. "You're different from most of our kind because your life was reversed. You'd already started the process of activating. It normally takes a full two years to finish the process; however, your circumstances are different."

"How?" I hated when people were vague. My father could be vague, and it drove me insane. And what did he mean that my life had been *reversed*?

"You were almost complete in your activation when you were sent here and your lifespan was reversed, turning you back into a little girl." He ran his hands through his long dark hair.

"I don't understand. Why was I sent away and my life practically started over?" It really didn't seem plausible that there would be a need to do such a thing.

"It was done to spare your life." He drew in a deep breath and slowly exhaled, as if he held the heaviest of burdens. "It was also meant to punish me."

"For?"

"That's enough for today." His voice was full of melancholy. I would never have imagined a god capable of such an emotion.

"Fine." I was not nearly satisfied with our conversation. I wanted to know so much more in that moment, but a deal was a deal. He'd only actually promised me one question, and it was obvious that this conversation was causing him pain. I would have to wait to learn more.

He led me back through the portal—which, I discovered, was merely a dark shadow, almost like an inkblot—through the same whirlwind. This time it led me to my bedroom door. I was taken aback. Had he been watching me?

Creeper. Total loss in brownie points.

"No, I haven't been spying on you."

He read my thoughts. Damnit. He was a telepath. But why wasn't I able to borrow his abilities like I did with the Evols? Must have been some weird alien god thing. Either way, it was too much to think about anymore. The day had worn me out beyond exhaustion.

"Good night, Jewel, and no, I didn't read your thoughts."

And I'm supposed to believe you after that reply? Yeah, no way, buddy. It didn't matter; I was too tired to reply. I collapsed on my bed shortly after shuffling through my door and almost immediately fell fast asleep.

Anubis

I LEFT HER exhausted and more confused than she had been before she'd met me. It had been so hard to be so close yet not able to touch her as I wanted. Several times I'd reached to touch her in a familiar way only to stop myself. I couldn't push it or I could lose her forever. I had endured and waited for so long, I could wait a little while longer.

She'd betrayed her feelings with her ever-expressive face. It was humorous that she obviously thought me a telepath, when in reality I'd simply memorized her every expression and each perfect smile. I knew her... or the old her, better than I knew myself. My hope for this day had pushed me through centuries upon centuries of lonely existence.

I'd felt when her lifeforce had appeared in this time through our unbreakable bond. It had been so long since she'd been sent away, I had almost given up hope. Yet, here she was, and she was almost ready.

I thought about what the consequences would be if she chose not to follow her destined path with me. We were bonded forever. Loneliness had been my partner for so long, but I was unsure whether I would be what she wanted when it was time.

I just pray that she's happy, safe and loved, no matter what she chooses—even if it breaks me.

Lost in thought, I almost missed my destination. I arrived abruptly, as if new to portal travel.

"Anubis, what brings you here after so long." A cruel voice, full of malice boomed with perceived power, a dying power.

"Hello, Father. I've come as the good son to pay a visit." I bowed my head in respect.

"Your visits are so few and far between. I wonder... what is it you want?" As always he was suspicious. I wouldn't have risked coming here if it weren't vital to find out what he and the others knew.

"As always, Father, I'm not here for anything but the company of my family." Lies—but necessary ones.

"If you missed us so much you would have *visited* sooner." This man whom I had once aspired to be just like leaned forward on his make-believe throne. In the battle with Horus many thousands of years ago, he had been badly wounded, almost died. But he'd survived. My mother forgave him and joined him once again.

"My apologies, Father. I was in stasis for a good long

time." This was true, as my father knew. I'd meant to preserve myself in preparation for Jewel's return. They, on the other hand, just thought stasis was a means to punish myself and avoid my 'issues,' as they called them.

"How has the alliance changed since my departure?" The war was never-ending despite the charter that had been drawn up to align the races. There were those who did not wish for peace but craved the war. I asked this question because I knew it would be expected. For the retired god of death, I was forever full of hope.

"We are allied still and work together to sustain peace." Set, the former almighty god, spat out the last word as if it stung his tongue. He hated the alliance and rightly blamed me for it.

"Yet, here you are out of stasis, and you have been for some time, I gather. I've heard that you have been seen here and there over the last decade." I watched as he paused, looking upwards in a pondering gesture and scratching his scraggly beard. "I assume you will not share with me why you decided to join the realm of the living again?" He was asking if Jewel had appeared yet. They had no idea when she would appear. Time travel had not been an exact science when they used it to send Jewel away. Now it had been banned from use, another of my doings.

"No, on the contrary. I decided long ago that I needed to prepare for the possibility that she would never return." It had been a real possibility, a very scary one.

I'd been forced for over a millennium to suffer without her presence; during that time, I'd learned to play the perfect diplomat, peacemaker, and protector. Once my sentence was retracted and forgotten and my job done, I put myself in stasis. Every few centuries I'd awaken to check to see that my work was still in effect.

I'd built my stasis machine—or, I should say, I built it with help from Thot, an Egyptian man-god of great knowledge who supported my work and was one of my very few original supporters. He was also one of the very first of our kind to evolve past end-of-life aging. It was his technology and progress in genetics that changed our worlds for good. He was almost executed for giving the technology to other races, such as Jewel's. But the Egyptonians needed him to continue his work.

"You are finally accepting reality, my boy. The idea that she even survived is next to impossible." I watched his demeanor change; although it was clear he did not believe me fully, he was opening up to the possibility. Which is what I needed him to do.

"I've accepted now that, since she was the first to undergo the procedure and she hasn't turned up after all this time, she more than likely did not survive. I've grieved and moved on."

Jewel had been the first forced test subject, and no one was even sure how far into the future they'd sent her. She could easily have perished or reached a future version of Earth that was already dead. I'd never truly given up hope, but many times I feared all was lost. Thot would pull me back and remind me of my purpose.

"I see. Yet, you are just now coming to see me?"

"It was a long grieving process." I was direct in my words without any sign of sadness, even though it was true that I had grieved while I waited. I no longer had a need to be sad, though. And, since Jewel's return, I had strategically hidden her away, staying away myself to keep her safe while she was vulnerable and young.

"So does this mean you are joining us again?" I had been a soldier, a prince without mercy. That was the sole reason the Earthlings had called me the god of death: I had the ability to take a soul from them easily. However I never paraded them in the afterlife for judgment as their myths insisted. Again, not all stories are true.

"No, I still no longer have a taste for death. I want to work towards reestablishing my relationships, though." With our long lifespans, the times between family gatherings were often very long. Our emotions, ambitions, and personalities (to a degree) changed each time we met. Some of us stayed away even longer. Some became emotionless or bitter as the years marched on. My father had forgotten why he'd been so angry with me, but he hadn't forgotten why he wanted Jewel dead.

"Either way, I am truly glad you are here, Son. It has been too long." He reached out then for an embrace. I stepped up and embraced him. All was forgiven for now and I had earned acceptance. "Your mother will be overjoyed to see you."

"So you two are back together?" I had heard as much. It was hard for our kind once we had bonded to our mates to stay away from one another. It was the one complication of immortality. We needed our other half like we needed water. After too long apart, we became parched. I was far from parched. I was becoming like a dried out hollow of a man who is finally given a small sip of a forbidden life-sustaining drink. It only made me want to guzzle it down, but I couldn't.

"Aye, she has forgiven me my transgressions once again."

"I'm glad to hear it, Father," I said sincerely.

"Tell me, for what other reason are you here?" He knew me well.

"Has progress been made on the restoration of our two worlds?" I spoke of the Olympian planet and Egyptonia. We'd founded the countries of Egypt and Greece here on Earth, which were the provinces provided to us via peace treaty so that we could rebuild after we'd destroyed our planets in the war. We lorded over the humans as their gods. Yet, we were only two races out of many, each taking a piece of this planet to call their own. This was the only planet left on our side of the universe that sustained life and wasn't already occupied by highly intelligent species. When we arrived, the humans were still primitive.

The other races, however, we were not at war with like we were with the Olympians. Instead, they respectfully kept their distance. Some of the other races, such as the Asgardians, had returned to their planets and recolonized them, while others remained, preferring Earth. They'd sought out Earth for reasons that were similar to ours: due to a lack of resources, because their planets were severely struggling or dying, or to utilize some aspect of this planet—and its inhabitants.

I didn't say we were perfect.

"Yes, Horus is about to initiate a plan to go back and colonize Egyptonia. They are working on a serum with the Olympians to help us to once again create life." I had not heard this, and it was a blessing to know. It seemed a trivial pursuit to go back to our home planet without the ability to reproduce, which had been another consequence of immortality. The fact that our people were actively working with the enemy for mutual benefit was something I had not anticipated.

"Good to know. I look forward to the result."

"No, it is not good. We cannot trust them. They will more than likely betray us again. They have made great progress, but not without life-altering side effects."

"What type of side effects?" My interest was indeed piqued.

"The life-shortening kind. We would be reduced back to a normal lifespan." He said this with fear and malice.

Immortality had been reserved for the royal houses and a select few of the elite. Still, the normal lifespan of our people exceeded a millennium or a little more. The same went for those on our sister planet, Jewel's people the Olympians, since once upon a time we'd been one race.

The Evols, who had slowly been secretly growing in numbers throughout the years, were showing considerably elongated lifespans through the generations as well. My father would definitely not be happy about this, as he loved his immortality and he wished to one day rule over all people on Earth. Petty, greedy, and power hungry were the members of my family. And the Evols definitely threatened them enough that my father wanted to see them wiped from existence. The Egyptonians and Olympians thought they'd done as much many years before, but I, with the help of a few friends, had saved them. I did it for Jewel. I always did everything for her.

I had much to think about and plans to adjust now.

"Father, I fear my visit is going to be a short one. I'll return soon to visit with Mother. I bid you good day."

"Do not stay away so long this time, my son." And with that last comment, I nodded my agreement and parted ways with him by creating a portal and swiftly stepping through the darkness.

CHAPTER FOUR

Jewel

I HAD A DREAM that night. *I was on the beach again; it was hot and the sun was beating down on me. I knew I walked dangerously close to the forbidden territory, but I was hoping to catch just the slightest glimpse of the famous triangular structure that was being built tirelessly by the poor enslaved people. I wanted to free them, but I couldn't. Instead I stood on the border between the neutral zone and Egypt, at the coast, and walked towards the beach. There was a man sitting far away on the other side of the border in the sands, looking out across the sea. I felt compelled to do the same. The last few months had weighed heavily on me and I was beyond tired. I walked to the lapping, foaming water. I smelled the salt in the air, and I felt the life stirring in the green foaming waves. I had always felt so connected to this planet in a way that my family never understood. I sat as the man sat, my legs in the sand and water. I lifted my face up to the sun and let its rays warm my face. My skin would not brown the way the humans' did, but it felt good anyway. I lay on my back to look up into the clouds. There appeared to be a storm rolling in. I welcomed it; I loved the rain and the water because they gave me peace.*

I was in this position when I heard and felt footsteps, and I realized it must have been the lone man. He was the only person around for miles. Based on the sound of his footsteps, he was obviously large. I could hear them clearly, courtesy of my blooming activation, which was near its completion. It was wearing me down in so many ways.

Rather than jump up and recede a safe distance as many ladies would, I stayed. There was very little that I feared, but many feared me, even if I tried hard to make it not so. Before I knew it, the man was a massive shadow over me.

"It isn't often I find a woman trying to wash herself away on a beach. Most do so by entering the ocean." He paused as if sensing something. I sensed it too and proceeded to rise.

"But you are not just a woman." His smile was sly, yet not hard as I would expect. It was tired and almost despondent. He was beautiful, as we all were, us self-proclaimed gods of this world.

"Based on the direction you came from and your appearance, it seems as though Death has come for me finally. Alas, I am not ready." My tone was light, as I was not scared but on guard. This man was known for his dangerous escapades. They'd named him death for a reason. Yet, sitting here before him, all I could think was that he was pure beauty. I knew this man. How, at that moment, eluded me, but despite his invasion into my dreams, I trusted him.

"Yes, indeed I have." He was teasing. Death was teasing me. "Why are you here, so close to the border? This courts death,

though not from me." His tone changed then, and darkness was just on the edges. Was he trying to scare me or warn me?

"I've heard of you. Should I worry that you will kill me?" What better way to test him and probe to see if my assumptions about his dream visits were indeed real? I had been dreaming of this man for months, but how much of those dreams was real or imagined I didn't know. Was he actually with me in the dreams? Did he remember them?

Here stood the man who would spark a prophecy and possibly another war between our races, just because he and I were destined to be together. A Gru té mor as it was called in our mother language. Bonded couples were not unique, but true bonds were something of myth and legend. They were supposed to have died out when we took steps towards immortality. Yet, here stood a man that was fated to be my other half. A man who would help me start a revolution. If we chose that path. I wasn't sure I wanted any of it, even if my fate was hard to resist.

"I've heard of you as well. The stubborn, impetuous daughter of love and war who refuses to adhere to her family's wishes. And, it appears, a miracle in the making." There was no more darkness in his voice but rather curiosity, maybe even a bit of respect and even a gleam of knowing, but it was hard to tell. Obviously, I'd misread him. He should not respect me in any way—I was part of a race that was his sworn enemy. Yet, at the same time, there was something hidden in his tone. There was something playful in it, almost respectful even. Did he know me? Did he remember?

"Yes, you caught me. Are you going to kill me?"

The miracle he spoke of was my birth. Although my parents had other children before the immortality serum took away their fertility, I was born afterward, on this planet. I was *the last of my kind and the only alien Earthling. That bespoke my "miracle" status.*

"No, I think I'll do something better." He grabbed me then, but not roughly, and kissed me as the rain began to fall upon us. It was my first real kiss and it was perfect.

BEEP. BEEP.

I woke up, embarrassed by my own dream. I knew what it felt like to kiss the man who trained me yesterday. I knew that it was passionate... and perfect. I sighed. Apparently we knew each other very well. I wasn't sure how to handle this new information. I had to admit, I felt a strong attraction, one that I'd never felt for anyone before, but I'd just met him and I wasn't sure if I should trust him. No, that wasn't true. I felt that I *could* trust him, as if it was ingrained in me, but could I trust myself?

I pulled myself out of bed. My whole body was sore. My body ached from my workout with Anubis. My head was also pounding a little, but not as badly as it had the day before. It was bearable, just annoying. Still, today was going to be tough. I turned the alarm off and debated a shower. A quick one wouldn't hurt. Before long I was slowly and painfully shuffling out the door, clean, fully dressed, and carrying what felt like the heaviest backpack on the entire planet.

Downstairs Teddy waited for me.

"You look like shit... I mean, shit for you. You never really look bad." He reddened and turned towards the door.

"Thanks, I think." Leave it to him to be an honest, blunt jerk. He was lucky none of the elders in our group had heard him curse. However, it might not have mattered; since we were both considered adults—or on the precipice, as Teddy was—they allowed us certain liberties. As for me, they never corrected me. I'd always thought that was because they feared repercussion from my father. Now I wasn't so sure.

We walked out the front door and got into the van that would deposit us at our bus stop. I silently groaned in pain, but Teddy must have read my facial expression.

"What happened to you yesterday?" he asked with concern. "Your dad said you were 'not to be disturbed.' I just thought you were sick."

"My father has me meeting with a personal trainer two days out of the week." I didn't know what else to say.

"Did you activate?" Teddy's voice was a few octaves higher than normal. I knew he feared this. Being left behind.

"No, not exactly. I think he just wants me to learn how to take care of myself. I'm training to fight." That was the closest to an almost-honest answer I could give.

Teddy didn't say anything in response; he just looked at me like he was waiting for me to say more. But when I didn't, he just shook his head a little bit and smiled at me like he knew there was more to the story.

During the rest of the ride to school, I thought about my conversation with Anubis the day before. Why did we call the Evols' manifestation of power *activation*, just like the gods' (or aliens'?) advancement into immortality and significantly higher powers? Were Evols part alien? I felt helpless and ignorant, with so many questions that needed answered. For more reasons than one, despite my soreness, I couldn't wait till tonight when I would see Anubis.

The morning went by quickly, and before I knew it I was in chemistry class with Allison. We were both a few minutes early. She plopped down in the desk next to me and scooted closer, her hair bouncing around her shoulders as she jerked the desk. The teacher turned around to glare at her, at which point she shrugged and stopped where she was. Once the teacher was preoccupied once again, she turned back towards me.

"Hey, Jewel." She paused as she looked around the room.

"Hey," I responded with a warm smile.

She finished her perusal of the room, but she glanced at the teacher, waiting to see if he was listening. "So, what are you doing this weekend?" She turned towards me and smiled as she brushed a stray strand of her dark hair aside and leaned forward in her desk to listen intently to my response.

"I'm not really *planning* anything important. How about you?" I smiled back, happy to have a friend to talk to. Normally in class I was quiet and kept to myself since the rest of the kids ignored me or tried to stay away from me. I acted as if this were a normal everyday thing.

"Yeah, I'm not really planning anything either." She sighed and stared up at the board as if lost in thought before she snapped back towards me and lowered her voice. "You want to ditch this class and get out of here?"

I smiled but shook my head. I wasn't in an adventurous mood today. My body was still sore and I was nursing a mild headache from this morning.

"No worries. I get it." She looked back up at the board where the teacher was writing our tasks for the day but then turned back towards me once again. "So, hey, you were out yesterday. Are you good? Did you catch the plague?" she teased lightly.

I couldn't tell her what I was really doing so I gave her

part of the truth instead. "I had a really bad headache and decided to stay home." I watched as she nodded her head, but not in acceptance. Rather, it was a knowing nod. This intrigued me. "Why do you ask?" I probed her. I knew I was acting suspiciously, but you couldn't be too careful.

"You weren't here to be my partner for the project, duh!" She playfully smacked my arm. We both enjoyed chemistry and had paired up together for labs on the first day of school. "I was stuck with the weird kid over there in the polo." She pointed to Kyle, the school quarterback, who was even now watching her out of the corner of his eye. It was odd—his type was more of a blond cheerleader. Yet, he smiled at the attention Allison offered by pointing his way. It was enough to give him the confidence to slink over to our desks while the teacher was writing on the board with his back turned to us.

"Hey, Allison." He smiled his perfect-set-of-white-teeth smile, and his blond curly locks cascaded over his forehead wildly, making him look like a young Justin Timberlake.

Allison cringed at me before turning a fake brilliant smile on him. "Hey, er... I'm sorry, what was your name again?" She smiled wider and feigned guilt over her poor memory.

"Kyle, it's Kyle." He pulled his muscular arm behind his neck in a nervous gesture, which seemed fairly odd to me. He appeared to be seriously nervous, though I'd observed him talking to pretty much every girl in the school with confidence. I also noticed he cast uneasy glances at me as he gravitated back towards Allison.

"Yes. Kyle." Allison continued to shine her brilliant smile on him before turning towards me. "You know my friend Jewel, right?"

"Yes. Hi, Jewel. How are you?" He had never. Ever.

Spoken to me before. I just sat there dumbfounded, but I nodded my head.

Allison giggled at my expression. "Well, Kyle, good chat, but if you don't mind...." She gestured with her hand between the two of us, waved sweetly then turned her back to him.

He stood there for a second, oddly discombobulated by the rejection and his dismissal before shuffling back to his desk.

"Where were we?" Allison babbled on. "Ah, yes, what were you doing this weekend?"

I shook my head, still trying to process what just happened. I was sure more than ever in that moment she was indeed more than she appeared to be. I had sensed it, but sometimes in these cases it was just an Evol gene that was dormant. Allison was more than that, and I was sure of it now. I liked her but would, in the future, be wary of her intentions.

"I'm taking a martial arts class at home and studying a bunch. I'm already behind from being out yesterday." I couldn't exactly invite her to my place, and my weekend schedule really was pretty tight.

"Oh, bummer." She sighed. "I was hoping we could do something. You know, it's hard being new, without friends to hang out with." She leaned back in her desk, her shoulders slumping back.

"Maybe next weekend or sometime after school we could get together with Teddy and hang out?" I offered this up, knowing it would take an act of Congress to make it work with my new schedule, not to mention explaining it to my father. He was even more suspicious of outsiders than I was.

"Really?" She smiled brilliantly at me. "That would be perfect!" She then proceeded to pass me a note with her cell number scrawled onto it before we were interrupted with the start of class. I tucked the note into my bag and turned my attention to the teacher.

The rest of the day passed by quickly. The same classes with the same material. A drizzle of mundane information to be stored for later, most unneeded in the grand scheme of things. I was convinced there wasn't a need for calculus in the real world, despite how much my teacher tried to convince us otherwise.

BEFORE I KNEW it, we were once again back at the house. My muscles were already less sore. I healed faster than most people, but apparently not as fast as I would soon. I bid Teddy goodbye for the day and told him I'd see him later.

"Hey, aren't you going to hang out today?" He looked hurt but probably thought I was too sore to do anything. Mondays and Wednesdays were normally my days to act like a normal teenager and hang out with Teddy and some of our friends on the compound, but now I'd be with Anubis every day. I decided I needed to discuss those terms with him later. Me being gone all the time wasn't fair to my friends.

"No, I'm sorry, Teddy, but I will soon. On Saturday." At least I hoped this didn't continue on into the weekend. My favorite place was calling me. It relaxed me.

I turned then and went towards my room. I wasn't sure when he'd show up, but I was going to at least take a quick few minutes to finish up my homework. So I trudged upstairs and into my room, plopping down my backpack and pulling out the numerous books and folders. It was easy, quick work. With me missing days of school due to some made up reason my father had given, my workload that I needed to complete at home would be doubling. Yet, it wasn't difficult work. Just the basics: calculus, world history, chemistry and English. Easy peasy. I already knew all the content. Which was good, because I had enough on my plate.

Just as I was finishing calculus, I felt the atmosphere in the room change. A portal opened behind me in the corner. Anubis stepped through, taking up most of the corner with his large and muscular frame.

"Good afternoon, Jewel. Are you ready?"

Ready as I'll ever be, I thought. He smirked as if he'd heard my response. *Damn, I knew it; he's reading my thoughts!*

"Question before we go." Time to see if he'd gained creep status.

"Questions are for after, that was the deal." He was having too much fun with this arrangement.

"No. One question or I'll stay here."

For a moment, he looked like he would just throw me over his shoulder, but then he thought better of it. Why could I read him so well?

"Fine."

"Can you create a portal anywhere, even without having been there?"

He looked surprised, as if he weren't expecting that type of question. "Yes and no. I have to have been to a location to create the portal—or at least know the layout of the room extremely well." He looked guilty. Creep.

"So you've been spying on me?" I wasn't sure how I felt about that.

"I have been in your room, yes. But it wasn't for the nefarious reasons that you've formulated in your head." He tried to reassure me by softening his deep voice. "I've checked on you through the years. "

He'd "checked" on me through the years. Why? Damn it. Just more questions. My brain was beginning to hurt from the constant need to know who I was. Why did I feel this way? The headache that I'd had throughout the day was still persistently nudging me. Although it was milder than the other ones, it was still a pain in my butt—er... I should say, head. Just as I thought about the pain, it intensified and I placed my hands at my temples to massage them in hopes it would ease it. The throbbing subsided a little.

"Don't worry. We'll get you through this. And there's an explanation for everything you're going through; the activation process for our kind can be frustrating." He paused. "Though we fear your activation will be even more so, as two lives become one. No one else has ever been reversed or sent into the future, so it's hard to know how your body and mind will respond, but we know enough to say it will be temporary as you go through the process."

Two lives become one. That sounded like a shit-hole deal. What if I didn't want to be this other person, who was me but not? What if I just wanted to stay the same? I didn't like for this decision to be out of my control. It was mine to make. I knew then what my question for the day was going to be, and I was hoping for the best possible answer—and planning accordingly.

"Alrighty then, big boy, let's do this."

He smiled at me. "Your change in speech will take some getting used to." I snorted at his response. "That, although wholly endearing, will also take some getting used to."

"Whatever, let's just get into training."

And off we went, my hand in his as we stepped into the portal.

We fought harder than we had the day before. I noticed in awe that I was even better today. I scrambled onto the powdery sand, stretching my sore muscles as I went. Anubis followed me.

"What are we practicing today?" I curled my toes in the sand then assumed the crouching defensive position he'd showed me last time, my arms raised to protect my front in fists. I didn't have time to think further as he came at me fast, really fast. But I was able to follow his movements. It was as if I knew what he was going to do. He went to strike my right flank, but I blocked him and then again on my left. He backed up, assessing me. There was obvious surprise on his rugged, dark features. And then he smiled before coming at me hard and fast, even faster than before. I matched his speed as best I could and was able to block his strikes but wasn't getting any of my own in yet. I knew from last time that he did tire, but it took a while. What better way to take an opponent out than to first tire them out? So I waited and blocked his strikes.

"You're better than before." He backed up again and smiled. "Much better."

"I'm a fast learner." I smiled back and decided to test my own strikes, only I used both my arms and legs, something I didn't know I could do. He blocked my punch, but then I swung my leg high and took him by surprise, but not for long. He began to anticipate my moves as I was his, and we became fluid in our movements: kicking, jabbing, hitting, yet blocking each strike or avoiding it with a swift turn of our bodies. Sweat was dripping down my forehead and Anubis was breathing hard.

His body brushed up against mine, and I lost my train of thought long enough for him to knock me down again, but on my way down I wrapped my legs around his and took him with me, only to quickly flip myself up and then straddle him.

"It appears I have bested you once again, trainer." I mocked. In that moment I felt dangerous as I sat there on top of him. We were both breathing hard and we were slick with sweat. I grabbed his hands, pulling them over his head. My face was inches from his, and he held my gaze as I pinned him there beneath me. I felt him go still beneath me as I leaned in close to his face and breathed in his essence. Even through the sweat he smelled amazing and familiar. Like manly, sweet musk, mahogany and something woodsy and wholly delicious, just like the deep honey of his voice. It caused my body to tingle and warmth spread through me, but before I could lean closer to him, he flipped me onto my back and looked down at me as hungrily as I felt in that moment. His brown eyes were dilated and lighter in color, almost hazel and then they actually seemed to flash blue for a moment. He wanted me. And damn if I didn't want him too.

Suddenly, he flipped himself onto his back beside me and began to laugh. The laugh was deep and boomed through the room as he ran his hands down the front of his face to calm his erratic emotions. This seemed to be how all our sessions would end, this tension. I sighed, trying to calm my own labored breathing, and rolled over to face him once again.

"So, you're already done?"

He looked down at me then lay next to me, looking at the ceiling. It seemed odd that a man like him would do that. But then I heard his breathing. He was trying to hide it, but he was breathing as hard as I was. He was just hiding it better.

The sand under my fingertips was rough but soft at the same time. I ran my fingers through it. It felt different than regular sand. It had a more powdery consistency which I had noticed with my feet before, but my hands now explored it with gleeful intent. I looked around the room again, paying closer attention to the details this time. It was dark—all except the middle of the room. The whole room was only illuminated by a soft glow from the center. I wondered where exactly Anubis's home was.

I turned my head towards him, having yet another feeling of déjà vu. I looked intently at the outline of his profile, the angular outline of his jaw, and the thickness of his lips. If a man could have luscious lips, this man definitely did. Gazing at those lips made me remember the kiss from my vision. And with that thought, he turned his head towards me. There was need in his eyes and something that looked like desire. The look was as hungry as the one he'd given me before, only this was different. This was desire for more than just a kiss—or even more. This was some hidden emotional desire. I wondered once again how I could read him so well.

I quickly sat up, embarrassed, and then crossed my legs and faced him. It was time to ask my question.

"I have a request—or a demand—before I ask my question." I sat up straight and sharpened my tone to show I meant serious business, but it was probably more to reassure myself.

"A demand? I am indeed interested." He did that sexy smirk thing again, the cocky bastard.

"I need time with my friends, and for myself, and I need to know if our training spans the weekend as well."

"I wasn't going to insist we train on the weekend, unless you wanted to." He paused suggestively. Again with the cockiness. "However, I'll make you a deal. I'll give you Friday for half your Saturday. We can start the new arrangement tomorrow."

"I don't understand why you need me so much." I may have answered in an overly annoyed tone, but I didn't care.

"I need to make sure you're prepared."

"For?"

"Is this your question?"

"No." He studied me silently. "Fine, I'll ask *my* question."

"Please do, I'm curious."

"What happens…" I paused, thinking my question through once more since I'd managed to get distracted. "What happens to me once this is over? What I mean is, do I get a choice? Will I still be me or will I be this other person?" I tried to hide the slight fear and desperation in my voice, but like all things related to me, he saw through it. It struck me as funny that I knew this after only two days with him.

Then he did something that again took me by surprise. He put his arms around me and held me to him. He felt… good. He felt right. It felt like, in that moment, everything and nothing made sense all at once. He then gently took my face in his hands and turned my head towards his. At first I thought he was going to kiss me. He didn't. Instead, he leaned in towards my ear.

"I know you're frustrated, confused, and worried. You'll still be you. You'll just remember who you were before. That's all." His voice was soft, and my body instantly heated in response. And to my utter embarrassment, I instinctively leaned into him. Realizing it, I quickly stepped back, breaking the embrace and the intimacy.

I felt vulnerable and I didn't like that feeling. He had that effect on me. He made me feel vulnerable in ways I didn't understand. I needed to fight this. I wasn't sure I was ready to be this other person.

I knew my next question, but would he answer it? There was only one way to find out.

"What were you to me?" I avoided his eyes, afraid, not sure if he would answer and not at all sure I was ready for the answer.

He must have been leaning towards "you're not ready" because he remained silent for a long moment. "I believe we've answered your one question for the day."

He wasn't going to answer. Oh my God, this man was infuriating!

"You're an asshole. I just want to know who I am!" I yelled through gritted teeth. I was done with the games.

"Listen, I've already explained that it will come to you soon. I don't want to overload you before you're ready." He looked lost, almost desperate, so much so that my anger dissipated.

He turned then, looking behind me at what looked to be a door. I hadn't noticed it since it was hidden in the dark nook beyond the glow of light. But now I could clearly see it and hear the sound of someone walking towards the door.

He grabbed my arm and all but jerked me through another dark portal.

And again I landed square on my ass.

CHAPTER FIVE

NUBIS DIDN'T SAY much to me after that, but rather left as abruptly as he'd pulled me through the portal, telling me tomorrow we would start again, early in the morning. I hated mornings. I was more of a night person. And I was almost positive that before he walked back into the portal there was a knowing smile on his face. He knew I hated mornings. I had a strong urge to call him the asshole he was, but he was gone before I had the chance.

Grumble. That would be my stomach. I was starving. I suddenly wondered if Anubis didn't need to eat, because I'd never seen him eat anything.

Even all the way from the west end of the house I could smell something delicious in the kitchen. This girl was going to get her grub on. Off I ran to see what was cooking—or being eaten, as it was late.

The menu was chicken and dumplings, southern style green beans, mashed potatoes with country gravy, and plum pie for dessert.

YEEESSSSSS.

I ate three plates full, perhaps too quickly and savagely. Several people were staring at me. Teddy, who was sitting directly to my right, was one of them, but Andrew and few others who'd joined us also stopped to watch as I engorged myself.

With a mouthful of dumplings, I asked, "What?"

Teddy choked on his water then laughed. "Um, is it good? Because I've never seen anyone eat like that before, not even you."

I'd never been a picky, salad-eating, watch-my-weight kind of person. I enjoyed food. I wasn't going to deprive myself for nothing or nobody.

I swallowed and took a drink of water.

"I was just hungry." I realized I may have come across a bit piggish, but I really felt like I hadn't eaten in days. And then I remembered I'd skipped breakfast and I'd eaten very little yesterday—and I hadn't even noticed. I mentally kicked myself. *Don't do that again.*

"What kind of training have you been doing that makes you *that* hungry?" Andrew asked with a grin.

I decided the best way to play it off was to make a joke. "Haters gonna hate." And I flicked a spoonful of mashed potatoes at him. Which earned me a glare, but no one said anything to reprimand me.

Andrew didn't have time to dodge my missile, so the mashed potatoes landed under his eye, igniting explosions of laughter from everyone. I'd managed to divert that question for now.

Before I knew it, Andrew threw a spoonful of potatoes back at me, which I easily dodged before I proceeded to throw more at him. A full-on food fight ensued.

And this was the scene my dad walked into just before a bit of potatoes landed on the side of his face.

We all froze, ready for a lecture and disappointed looks. Instead he sighed, took out a handkerchief to clean off his face, and waited for us to sit down again. I had an odd, strong urge to throw some more at him, and I snickered at the thought, which did earn me a glare from him.

"Jewel." He used that daddy-is-disappointed tone.

I turned and put my head down slightly, holding back the laugh by biting my lip. Then I realized there was still food on my plate and swiftly finished it.

It was good to have some normalcy.

I noticed that all the younger girls in our compound surrounded Andrew. It made sense; he was a very attractive by most standards. Not as attractive as Anubis, but he could easily grace the cover of a magazine or some type of Abercrombie and Fitch ad.

I turned to Teddy. "Hey, I'll be free tomorrow, Saturday afternoon, and Sunday if you want to hang out." I really wanted to hike to my lake, but I preferred to do that alone. I knew that Teddy was feeling neglected and he'd been a good friend. Pretty much everybody else our age, even on the compound, steered clear of me. I'd helped many of them and they appreciated it, but they kept me at a distance. I always thought it was because in some way I scared them.

"I can't tomorrow. I'm not going to school on Fridays anymore. I'm going to start helping in the basement like you do."

"Teddy, you knew about me helping with the training in the basement?"

"Of course. I figured you'd been helping down there for a while. I just didn't say anything because I know it's something you prefer not to talk about."

"Did you activate and not tell me?" I asked this hesitantly, not meaning any ill feelings. Teddy was sensitive about the subject. I didn't sense anything from him, but that didn't mean he hadn't started the process. There were rare cases where I couldn't tell. That's what I suspected might be the case with Allison.

"No, I'm still the same." He sighed. I knew his frustrations. "I was given an offer to work with the tech team." That made sense since he was amazing with computers and all other electronic devices. He wanted to become a coder and had plans to move to California for college.

We employed an entire team of normals, all of whom were made to sign iron-clad nondisclosure agreements. We even went so far as to secure them their own housing community. They were out in the middle of nowhere—30 minutes from the outskirts of a small town, and they had to travel a mountain pass in order to get to the compound. Anytime anyone asked, the employees said they worked at a lab that produced pharmaceuticals. I liked many of them, but some I didn't trust. Only a select few were especially friendly with me. They all mostly tried to stay away from me, just like everyone else did.

"That's okay," I said. "I'll go hiking. Maybe we can get together Saturday night or Sunday." I was actually happier with this plan. I could go hike the afternoon and evening away in my favorite place in the world, my oasis, my little rock quarry lake.

Dinner was over, the pie was all gone, and people were

yawning on all sides of the table. I bid good night to Teddy, waved at the others, and walked around to hug my dad good night. Before I turned to leave he took my hand, gently.

"Bunny, how was your day? I haven't seen you in so long." We'd spent so much time working together down in the basement that we were about as close as we could be.

"I'm okay, Dad. My day was long but not bad." I didn't elaborate, and I knew in present company he wouldn't question me any further either. "We'll talk later, so don't go to bed yet. I've a few things to take care of and then I'll come see you."

"Alright, I'll wait, but don't take too long. I'm pretty beat."

I turned and walked towards the door, noticing that Andrew had stayed back and was waiting near the stairs. I could see he was wearing his heat-proof suit under his clothes.

"May I walk you to your room?"

Why not? It wouldn't hurt, and it was nice to have another friend, someone who didn't try to steer clear of me as much as possible. I nodded and he walked beside me on the staircase.

"So, Jewel, I've been meaning to talk to you."

"Yeah, what about?" I asked, worried at where this was headed.

"First, I just wanted to thank you. I was in a bad place for a while, but I'm better now." He stopped and placed his hand on my arm. "I know that we've been joking recently, but..." He paused, running his hands through his hair and pulling on the long ends nervously. "But I really like you, Jewel. Like, really like you, and I just wanted to ask you, can I take you out? On a real date or something?"

I could tell he wasn't used to this. He'd probably never

had to worry about someone's response to this question before. He had all the girls at Delphi Glen winking and batting their eyes his way. He was used to getting whatever he wanted. He could ask a girl out, and she wouldn't hesitate to bounce up and down in exuberant exhilaration. Before I helped him in his transformation, he'd always been polite to me and friendly, but our time together and his recent change in circumstances had changed him and afforded us an opportunity to better get to know each other on a more personal level. It would make sense for me to date him if I were just any normal (or even slightly more than normal) Evol. But this was just a really confusing time. I wasn't sure of my emotions on anything.

"Listen, Andrew, I have so much going on right now. I'm very flattered, but I think that it would be best if you just give me some time to process a few things and then I'll give you an answer." I knew it was wrong to leave him hanging like that, but I didn't want to hurt his feelings. Besides, I still wasn't sure what would happen in the near future. Maybe once I worked through my confusion over this whole other-me situation there would be a possibility of us dating. But I didn't want to start something with Andrew only to discover that there was something about my past self that would hurt him. Plus, this thing with Anubis, as much as I tried to resist it, it was real and intense. I didn't want to hurt Andrew, and I was afraid no matter what, I was on the road to breaking his heart. It was better for him if I kept him at a distance.

I'd never dated anyone, at least not in this life. And although I couldn't stop thinking about Anubis, I wasn't sure if he was what I really wanted. I mean, I *wanted* to choose my own path.

"Okay, I understand. I'll give you time to think." He nervously ran his fingers through his hair again, pulling on the ends. It occurred to me he hadn't anticipated that answer because he'd never known rejection before.

"I'm sorry, I wish I could give you a better answer," I said, hoping he could tell that I was being sincere. I hugged him in hopes of reassuring him, but he held on a bit longer than necessary for a friendly hug. I pulled away and walked the rest of the way to my suite, leaving him standing there alone. I felt like an ass.

CHAPTER SIX

Anubis

A FTER PRACTICALLY DUMPING Jewel in her room, I walked back through the portal to see who my un-invited guest was. That was a close call. We could have been exposed or worse. I made a mental note to fortify my home even more. However, I was not expecting the person who was standing in the middle of the room.

"Anubis, how good it is to see you. You have avoided me for far too long, and I think you have something to tell me."

There stood the second most beautiful woman I had ever met: Jewel's mother, Aphrodite, though the only reason I thought her beautiful was that Jewel was almost the spitting image of her. Only Jewel's eyes were a tad bigger and green and her hair more strawberry, whereas Aphrodite was blue-eyed and pale blond. I had avoided her through the millennia because she was a constant reminder of my lost love. Despite all of this, I still wasn't sure I could trust her.

"Whatever do you mean, Aphrodite?" I played coy.

Anger flashed in her eyes. So much like Jewel.

"Don't treat me like an idiot. You aren't the only one that lost her." Jewel's mother had been our biggest supporter from the day Jewel and I were caught together. Jewel had been her favorite child, causing many of her siblings to be jealous of their bond. They sided against us and her father was swayed, as war sometimes is.

"I know she returned. She is my child, my baby. I could never forget her or the hole in my heart. I want to see her and now." She raised her voice during this painful admission then lowered it again, aware of the always-listening ears in our world. "Please."

"It's complicated. I must know, how did you find out?"

"I felt her. She must be starting her activation again. Last night I felt her as if she were here again. And I felt her love. Please, I'm begging as a desperate mother. Let me see her." Her voice held the same yearning that I myself felt. We both just wanted her back.

"Aphrodite, she's not the same. She's another person right now. I'm trying to slowly ease her back into our world and keep her safe, but I promise as soon as she's ready, I'll summon you to see her." Her pain cut me deeply. I had a similar pain gnawing at my soul.

"She's lucky to have you. Most would have moved on after all these years, but you, you waited for her. That is a kind of love even I cannot fathom." She reached out and affectionately touched my face. Aphrodite was the goddess of love for a reason.

"You helped grant us such a love. You gave us a gift of eternal, never wavering devotion." I was speaking of when she was able to recreate the *Gru té mor*, gifting it to her last Olympian child at birth. Both races had forbidden it, as such a connection had consequences, but Aphrodite thought it would save her daughter and her from the prophecy told to her by the fates.

"I fear, although intended as such, it was not a gift. It has been your curse." Aphrodite sighed and stepped back from me.

"No, I don't regret any of it. I would wait another thousand years for her if I had to." I meant it.

"You, Anubis, are the only one of your kind. She is so very lucky to have your love. I pray she returns it in her new life." She turned, pushing her pain down once again.

"Aphrodite."

"Yes, Anubis."

"She loved you very much and she'll love you again. I promise. Sit down and I'll tell you all about her new life."

There were tears in her eyes. It tore my heart up. Jewel was so much like her. "Thank you."

I spent the next two hours telling her all about Jewel. How stubborn she was. How much she cared for others around her. How her adoptive father loved her and how happy she'd been growing up. I also told Aphrodite a few stories from Jewel's childhood that Robert had divulged to me over the years. It had been so hard to stay away; I lived for those stories. I felt bad for keeping the truth from Aphrodite.

When I'd finally told Aphrodite everything I could think of, she rose to leave.

"I will keep this secret close to my heart, Anubis. However, do not keep her from me for long. I am not nearly as strong as you." And she turned towards the door and left the room.

Thoth walked in the room shortly after.

"Do you think it wise to include her?" He had lived with me over the millennia, watching over me when I was in stasis. It worked because no one ever suspected that he would be holed up with death.

"I don't know, but how could I say no?"

"She could be working for Ares and Zeus." He wasn't incorrect. The thought had crossed my mind.

"She could be, or she could just be a mother who wants desperately to see her child, as she said."

"I suppose we shall see." With that, he left to go into his workshop, which was in another part of our home. He went back to his never-ending, tireless work—though no one ever knew exactly what that work was.

I then remembered the abruptness with which I'd left Jewel and thought it best to check in on her. I pulled my portal out and stepped through, melting into the shadows outside her room. She stood there in the hallway with a boy who was acting strangely nervous. I listened intently and didn't reveal myself. This boy liked her. He wanted to be with her.

I wanted to roar, "MINE." Instead, I waited, calming myself and observing. I watched as she politely put him on hold. But why didn't she say no?

I knew that this would be hard. And I also knew that I would have to accept her decision, no matter what, but it was unbearable to think that she might decide that she didn't want to be with me.

For the first time in all the years I'd waited, I was unsure. Maybe our bond and our love wouldn't be enough.

Jewel

WHAT A CRAPFEST. I was so ready for bed again.

Every night, I practically collapsed into bed. This time I was about to crumble with exhaustion, but there sat a man who virtually swallowed my bed with his body.

Anubis.

Dude, does he not understand that I need a break? First him, then Andrew, and now here he is again. I was on ultimate stress level one million. I gave him a look that I was sure was full of annoyance. I didn't care.

"Can you get off my bed before you break it?"

"As you wish." He gracefully stood.

"I thought we were going to see each other tomorrow?" I was confused by his presence, but oddly, my annoyance seemed to ease. He had that effect on me.

"I wanted to check on you. I left you so abruptly. I see that you're okay, though. I'll leave." He turned, about to pull out another portal.

"No, stay." I had a strong desire for *him* to hug me. The hug from Andrew had been nice, but it was nothing like the embrace Anubis had given me earlier.

He turned back towards me, his expression not giving away how he was feeling. "Yes, I would love to stay here with you."

"Can you do something for me?" I paused, thinking I was insane. "I know this is highly inappropriate, but can you just lay with me as I go to sleep? I've been having these dreams and for some reason I feel like you being here would help—or maybe give me more answers about them." I lay down and patted the other side of the bed. He stood there as if he was unsure about how to continue.

What was I doing? I was playing with fire, and I would most definitely get burnt.

He lay next to me as quietly as possible. I turned towards him once again, studying the many planes of his perfect face. I wanted so badly to kiss him.

"Tell me, please. What am I to you?"

"You... you're so many things. You're the beat of my heart, the breath on my lips; you are my sun, my moon, and my soul. You are the only love I will ever know." He said it with such passion and sincerity. It moved me. I let all my reservations about him go out the window as I, for once, stopped thinking. In this moment, right now, it was just him and me.

I wiggled closer to him, enjoying the intimacy. I could smell him again. If a man could be bottled into a scent, I'd invest a shitload in his fragrance. I put my arms around him, snuggling closer. He did the same and we lay there embracing each other for a moment. I had a feeling I'd never experienced before, at least not in this lifetime: the want of a man, the *need* for this man. I held him tight as if I were thirsty, and heat crept into my body. It engulfed me. Finally, I turned my mouth up to his, practically begging for my first kiss.

He kissed me. It was hungry. It was desperate. It was passionate beyond sensibilities. It was what dreams were made from. It was just like him, perfect. He broke off the kiss just before it engulfed us both in its passionate fire. I had never experienced anything like that before. No one had ever told me kissing was like that.

"Jewel, you need to sleep." He spoke as if he were in pain. Had the kiss hurt him somehow?

"Are you okay? Are you hurt?"

He chuckled. "I am so much more than okay. You have no idea."

"Is it always like that? Kissing I mean. I mean, I've heard kissing is fun, but… that… that was so much more than fun." My hands were on my lips again, thinking of it. I blushed then, realizing what I'd just done with him.

"It's always been that way for us. Always. I cannot speak for anyone else." He kissed my forehead then, and though I couldn't stop thinking of his words, I turned around, allowing him to continue holding me. I fell asleep quickly in his arms.

CHAPTER SEVEN

I WOKE UP THE next morning feeling refreshed. I'd slept like the dead—no dreams, no tossing and turning, and no racing thoughts. And then I remembered how I'd fallen asleep.

Anubis. Where was he? Had he simply left me? I was annoyed by this and was wondering where he had snuck off to as I turned in the bed, stretching and then snuggling into the soft covers, refusing to leave my perfect oasis of comfy-ness. There, in my corner chair, sat Anubis. The annoyance dissipated and relief washed over me. He was still here.

"Good morning." That deep baritone voice caressed me in my cocoon.

"Mmmm, yes. I'm staying here, where it's warm and comfy. You can go train with yourself." I snuggled deeper into the covers, pulling them over my head. I wasn't budging.

"Then I shall join you." The bed wobbled and creaked as he crept under the covers with me. "I thought perhaps today we could do something else. Something fun. Where's your favorite place to go?" I thought of the rock quarry I loved with the waterfall that cascaded down into the deep waters. I always went there alone, but why not take him along? Maybe it would loosen him up so I could pump some information out of him. We'd call it operation shakedown.

"I like to hike to this place in the mountains. There's a rock quarry with a small lake. A waterfall with a small cave entrance underneath, perfect for using as a diving board into the deep area of the lake. It's my secret, favorite place, but I'll share the secret with you... but only if you answer one question now and one later."

"I accept your offer on the terms that if I don't like the question, I can pass and you'll have to ask another one in its turn." He was clever, this one. How could I not accept his terms when he looked at me like that?

"Deal."

Operation shakedown was a go.

I popped out of bed, a bit bitter at the loss of my cocoon. I needed to get dressed. I looked at Anubis, hoping he'd get the hint, but he just sat there and watched me.

"Um, do you mind? I need to get dressed. Could you step out of the room?" I motioned towards the door.

"Of course." He headed out, shutting the door behind him.

I walked over to my dresser near the door he'd just walked through. I was selecting what to wear that day, when I heard my father.

"Anubis, what are you doing here and why are you outside Jewel's bedroom? Did you just walk out of it?"

"Good morning, Robert. To answer your question, yes and I'm here to collect her for the day."

"I don't think I like you being in her room."

I laughed. My father was trying to defend my honor to the god of death.

"Robert, as grateful as I am that you took on the responsibility of raising her and keeping her safe when I could not, make no mistake, you do not control me where it concerns her."

That was the end of that conversation, and I heard my dad shuffle away angrily. I didn't agree with how he'd handled that situation and made a mental note to remind him of it later. I was fully dressed and ready to go, so I walked out of the room and pretended for now that I hadn't heard them. My dad was sitting in his favorite chair, newspaper in hand and coffee beside him, pretending not to watch us.

"Are you ready to go?" Anubis asked. He went to grasp my hand and do the whole dark portal thing, but I stopped him.

"No, we're going my way or no way." I grabbed my favorite hiking backpack off the hook near the front door and went into our kitchenette. There, I threw waters and snacks into the bag. It was at least an hour hike there and back.

"Hiking today, bunny?" my dad asked as he peered over the paper.

"Yes, we're going to my favorite spot."

He was trying not to seem like he was prying into my business, but I'd heard their conversation, so I walked over to him and kissed him on the cheek. "Don't worry, Dad, I'll be okay."

"I know, sweetie. Have a good day." He seemed reassured, so I left and headed out into the main house.

It occurred to me then that I was walking through the

house with Anubis. Others might see him. "Do you want to portal outside?"

"No, I'll walk with you. We'll go your way." Again he used my own words.

"It's fine by me." There would be questions later that I'd rather avoid. But it seemed I was too late.

The house was mostly quiet. Teddy had started his training downstairs. Andrew was in the foyer, though, apparently waiting for me. He stopped when he saw the mountain of a man standing next to me.

"Jewel, I didn't know you had company. I was going to see if you wanted to spend some of the day hanging out. I heard you mention last night to Teddy you'd be free later." He kept glancing towards Anubis, who stood far above him in height. Andrew barely surpassed my height by a half inch. Anubis was an intimidating view to take in. It didn't help that he was glaring menacingly at Andrew as if, at any moment, he could tear his head off with his bare hands. And I was pretty sure he probably could. I had to give it to Andrew, though; he stood there facing Anubis without wavering.

"She's not free. She'll be busy." Anubis laced his deep voice with just a slight edge of warning. This time Andrew did falter and step back a bit. Despite that, Andrew ignored him.

"I was asking Jewel, not you." The male testosterone was flowing heavily off both of them. It was almost suffocating, so thick that you could cut it with a knife and serve it up as cake.

"Andrew, I'd love to hang out, but I'm not sure what time I'll be back. I'll text you later." Andrew seemed slightly satisfied but still not at all happy with me running off with some danger-oozing stranger. "I'll be fine. I'm just going out for a bit and then I'll be back."

"I'm training today. I'll see you later," I uttered to excuse myself, then waved to Andrew and followed Anubis out the door. He'd already dismissed Andrew and was ready to go.

Outside, the weather was perfect. It was warm, something that rarely happened in the mountains. It snowed in July here, and you didn't even want to get me started on the hailstorms. Anubis was waiting for me to lead the way.

"Follow me. I like to go this way to keep people from following me." I'd take the longer path that included some rock climbing to keep others from following. I liked to be alone on these hikes, yet here I was taking Anubis with me. The path wrapped around a rocky mountain path that edged up to a canyon. Then you had to climb bare-handed up part of the mountain to continue on the path. The climbing always kept people from following me. I'd had a few instances where people in the compound would be curious where I was going and would follow me, but they never made it up the rock. I'd found early on I had the skill to scale a mountain if needed without an issue.

Anubis obviously had the same skill, as I'd known he probably would. He followed me on the rocky climb and then over a cliff. He didn't complain and he didn't seem tired. *This must be child's play to him*, I thought to myself.

"How long have you been coming to this spot?" he asked me as we walked the path, worn down by my feet alone.

"Since I was ten. That was when I occasionally started disappearing for half the day to go hiking. I found this place as if it called to me, and now I come here as often as possible." I looked out across the canyon path we were still walking. The view was breathtaking. The rocks of the conjoining mountains were red, and the pass below was quiet and covered in mountain pines and towering white-trunked aspens. They were beautiful this time of year, a mix of deep green and vibrant orange dotting the landscape. There was also a stream in the distance that rushed through the rocky terrain. Flying high in the sky were hawks, sounding their alarm. We were about to hike down another jagged bluff, then back up. The path would be grueling for the average hiker. I loved it.

"Jewel!" I cupped my hands and shouted into the canyon, and it shouted my name back to me as the echo reverberated.

Anubis's question had reminded me of our deal for this trip, so I formulated my first question. "So what was I like, you know, before?" I tried to play it off as just nonchalant curiosity, but I stopped on the path to look at him and he was smirking again. I hated when he did that. It was like he knew everything.

"You were amazing, as you are now." He spoke with truth and admiration in his voice, but his vague answer rubbed me wrong.

"No, I want details, spill them." I punched his arm, but he didn't even flinch.

"You loved so many things and so many people. You were passionate, stubborn, beautiful, and headstrong. Your laugh was lovely music and you laughed often, unless you were mad, and then the whole world knew about it. Usually you were mad at me, but not for long." He paused as if he were lost in memories with this other Jewel. I was beginning to feel jealous of... well, myself. "You were pretty much the same as you are now, except a different era and generation influences you."

"So you think that Jewel and I are pretty much the same?"

"Without a doubt." His answer was swift and fluid. Which made me think—was I really just like her or did he just see what he wanted to see? He seemed to want me to be her so badly, but what if I disappointed him? That was too much pressure.

"You also always overanalyzed everything, like you're doing now." He regarded me then as if he knew what exactly I was thinking. I was absolutely sure that bastard was reading my mind. Time to test the theory.

I started imagining weird things: balloons invading the canyon and eating people then pooping colored slime on the trees. *Let's see him read that*, I thought. I turned and watched him, but there was no change in facial expression, no laugh or smirk. I decided to kick it up a notch. I thought about some of the dumb one-liners that Teddy loved to tell me.

What's the difference between a dirty bus stop and crustacean crab with implants? One is a crusty bus stop, the other is a busty crustacean.

What kind of a bagel can fly? A plane bagel.

Did you hear about the two antennas that got married? It was a nice wedding, but the reception was amazing.

I looked over at Anubis after I thought each one-liner; it was hard for me not to laugh. He didn't appear to think anything was funny, but he did look over at me.

"I like it when you look happy. You have a beautiful smile."

Geez Louise, this man was Fort Knox. Maybe it was time to try a different tactic. So I thought about last night: the kiss, the way his arms felt around me.

He stopped dead in his tracks.

"You need to stop that." He sounded tortured.

Bingo, I was right. He was reading my mind.

"You *are* a mind reader! I knew it!" I practically jumped in joyful elation at my smarty-brains tactics.

"No, I'm not. You're giving off strong pheromones that specifically call to me, and they can be very *very* overpowering." He sounded like he was in pain again. Why did this hurt him?

"Oh, so you didn't know anything I was thinking?"

"I didn't say that. It doesn't take a mind reader to read your facial expressions. You give everything away in those beautiful eyes."

I closed my mouth and eased my thoughts, just in case. I didn't want anyone to read me right then. We walked on silently the rest of the way.

It wasn't long before we found the small rock quarry. It was located in sort of an odd spot on the mountain, nestled in a private little alcove. A waterfall cascaded into the quarry from a ledge up above it. The best part was that the there was a small cave with another ledge under the waterfall. I loved to dive off it through the waterfall and into the water below. I climbed down with Anubis behind me. I dropped my pack a little ways in the cave to keep it dry and then began to take my clothes off.

"What are you doing?" He looked perplexed. "Why are you undressing?"

"I don't want to get my clothes wet. Relax, I've got a swimsuit underneath." Well it was a bikini but same difference. I had slipped it on quickly as I listened in on Anubis and my father earlier this morning. "Question is, what are you wearing in the water?" I hadn't meant to be a tease, but I realized afterwards that my question could have been interpreted that way.

"Keep your boxers on!" I yelled back at him before leaping through the curtain of water to dive down into the quarry. I didn't want him to come flying down with Anubis Jr. flapping in the wind.

The water was cold at first. I swam to the surface just in time to hear a splash next to me from Anubis. I thought it was from him entering the water, but no, he was surfacing at the same time as me. Odd. He must have jumped directly after me.

I turned to find him floating on the surface a few feet away from—OH MY GOD, this was a bad idea. The man was wearing boxer briefs that hugged his body, and his muscles were lean, sleek, and bulging. His chest was pure olive tones sculpted to perfection. It wasn't fair to the rest of the world for him to be that hot. So I splashed him. Served him right.

He splashed me back, but it felt like half the quarry water smacked me. I even went under a little, only to have him grab me and pull me up.

"I'm sorry, I forget sometimes to tone it down, that you're still changing. And your memories are merging, old and new."

I coughed a little water out and he pulled me closer to him. I realized my arms were around his shoulders again. How did this keep happening?

"What do you mean changing? Please un-vaguely explain." I pulled my arms down and pushed off him to create some distance between us. Being super close to him messed with my senses.

"You'll become stronger and faster, you'll have heightened senses, and there are a few more things you'll discover." He appeared to be searching for the correct terminology.

"You've already started, you just haven't noticed."

"So I'm going to be a badass. Sweet."

"Yes, you will be." There was that smirk again.

"When will this process be complete? Or, more importantly, when will my memories merge?"

"I don't know. Are you remembering anything?" He swam closer to me, hopeful.

I shook my head, not ready to share how I knew he liked it when I ran my hands through his hair or kissed his neck below his ear.

"I'm sorry." I wasn't really. I was scared. I loved adventure and, to a degree, change, but this was far beyond my own sensibilities and it did scare me.

"It's okay. Tell me, why do you love this place so much?" He stretched out so he was floating on his back in a relaxed position. I was grateful he didn't probe. I mimicked him and floated as well.

"I love so many things about it. I love that it's remote and isolated, like my own hidden paradise. I love that it's beautiful and quiet, and I love the water. I don't know why, but I feel peaceful here." I was being truthful—as soon as I touched the water, all my troubles dissipated like magic.

"That makes sense. Your grandmother was Dione. She loved the water. She couldn't live very far from it because it restored her. She preferred the ocean. I first met you near the ocean."

"That's interesting. Tell me more about my other family. What are my mother and father like?" I swam closer; I really did want to know, especially about my mother. I'd grown up without one and always secretly craved the love of a mother.

"You're much like her, your mother. You look very much

alike. You care about others the same way, and she's gentle and kind. But she's not perfect. She can be jealous, petty, and difficult when it suits her. Still, she loves fiercely and to those she loves she's always loyal, even if it tears her apart."

"Well at least she sounds somewhat relatable. And you said she looks like me?" I tried to imagine another me so I could create in my mind the image of my mother.

"Yes, except she has pale blond hair and blue eyes, and her build is not as lean as yours." I constructed what I thought of her as an image to hold onto when I needed to.

"So what about my father or any of the rest of them?" I was trying to pry as much out of him as I could while he was in a sharing mood.

"I'll only tell you about your mother today. The rest will have to wait for another day."

"Okay, then one last question and I won't ask anything else." I paused. What did I want to know most about my mother? "You said she was fiercely loyal, but if she was so loyal and loved me, why would she let me be sent away?"

"She didn't. She and I were both punished, in our own ways. We couldn't save you." His voice was wracked with emotion, deep and never-ending, like he was a tortured soul full of many regrets.

I couldn't comfort him, because I didn't know how. So instead I swam towards him and splashed him, then dipped down to keep from almost getting drowned again. I grabbed his leg under the water and tugged him down with me so that we were face-to-face, with the sun rippling across the water's surface above us. I wasn't even sure why I did it. Perhaps I hoped the water would wash away his pain as it did for me.

We swam up and broke the surface together. Laughing,

I playfully splashed him. This man was a complicated sort of guy, but when he smiled, the sun and the moon danced together in the skies. Or at least that was how it felt to me.

He splashed me and flashed me one of his few-and-far-between smiles. The brooding that seemed to naturally roll off him constantly was gone. I liked this side of him. He was playful, boyish, and almost happy.

The day had gone by quickly. I swam to a rock on the side of the quarry, and Anubis followed me; he swam over, pulling himself swiftly from the water. I thought back to my knowledge of Egyptian mythology. Didn't the myths say the gods had heads like animals? Except, obviously, here stood one self-proclaimed Egyptian myth with a very human-like head.

"Why don't you look like a jackal? I mean, all the hieroglyphics depict you that way."

"As I've said before, the myths aren't entirely accurate." He didn't comment further, just continued to lay there next to me, content to soak up the sun. I sighed; he was closing up shop again. No more answers today—time to head out.

Anubis was apparently thinking the same thing because he jumped back in and swam to the other side of the quarry so he could hike back up to the ledge under the waterfall. I wanted to dive down into the water one last time before leaving, so I leaped in and swam below the surface, opening my eyes under the water. I looked up at the sun glittering off of the surface of the lake. It was beautiful.

Only, as I lay there beneath the water watching as the light danced in ripples, I was suddenly overcome with this overwhelming fear.

And then I was somewhere else again.

A MAN, A rough man. He was dragging me through a crowd. With desperation, I watched as the crowd of people afforded him a wide berth. I knew these people. They knew me. Or they knew what I wanted them to know about me. My friend, someone I had come to see as a brother, was being dragged along with me, but they kept him contained farther behind me as this vile, greedy man pulled me up onto a platform. He was going to hurt me. Worse. He was going to kill me.

Yet, even in my fear, something else took hold of me. Something very painful. Agony washed over me and enveloped me as the man spoke my crimes to the crowd. Through the searing pain in my head, I watched as some of the crowd nodded their sheep-like heads in agreement while others stood back warily, untrusting of this despicable man. They were smart.

The pain in my head intensified, and it began to overtake my whole body. I couldn't concentrate on the things the man accused me of because there was a roaring, rushing sound in my ears. Still, in the very back of the crowd, far away and barely perceptible, I did notice someone through the pain.

Rhea.

She was here watching, waiting for something, and she held my gaze in an act of understanding and support. Had she come to watch me die?

Rhea was the oldest of us all, and her wisdom was to mother us with love. She stood there now with an expression of support and understanding, and through the anguish, I held onto that. The man held a knife now, and I knew then he meant to kill me.

The pain. I knew what it was from. I was activating early. I held myself back as best I could, unsure of what would happen to me, to these people, if I didn't. My friend—my brother—he was here. I didn't want to hurt any of these people, but I would never forgive myself if I hurt Nikon.

I glanced at him, taking my eyes from Rhea. He stood there, terrified for me. When I looked back at Rhea, she was gone.

The man had the knife to my throat then, and I felt a small trickle of blood drip down. He looked me in the eyes. His were full of hate and vengeance. I couldn't fight it anymore. I couldn't hold it back.

I let it go.

A force expelled from me and cascaded out towards the crowd. I watched the man in front of me scream in pain as he crumbled to dust and blew away with the wind. The knife dropped to the ground by my feet with a clink. I looked around me. Everyone, every single one of them, had crumpled to the ground and now lay motionless, even Nikon.

They were all dead.

The pain in my head was then replaced with a new pain— in my heart. I had killed all these people.

I WAS BACK under the water, looking up towards the surface. But I had stayed under so long my lungs were burning, and my head was exploding with a pain fiercer than I could ever remember feeling before. I wondered if what had happened to me in the dream was happening again.

What *had* happened in my dream? What had happened to my friend? Through the pain a name echoed. *Nikon.* His name had been Nikon. I thrashed wildly, trying to swim to the surface, struggling with the pain that had encompassed me. I struggled desperately, tearing my way upward, only to realize I wasn't going to make it. It was odd, the one place that gave me peace would be my final resting place.

That was my last thought before the world went dark and I felt a tug before I felt nothing at all.

I FOUND MYSELF lying on the bank. The pain in my head had ebbed to a less intense agony, but my lungs were burning as much as my head was still pounding. Anubis was towering over me, concern etched into his handsome features. I coughed, retching some water.

"Jewel, are you okay?" Anubis spoke softly, as if he knew my head still hurt.

"Yes, I'm okay, but I think I just want to lay here for a moment." I felt tired. And even more scared about what was happening to me. What was I becoming? Was I going to hurt anyone else?

"*Nikon.*" I whispered his name. I knew he'd been important to me in some way in my previous life, but I didn't know how.

"You remember something," Anubis breathed out as softly as I had spoken. It wasn't a question but more of an acknowledgement. He smoothed the hair back from my face in a tender gesture meant to comfort me.

"Yes. Who was he?" I sat up then, careful of my movements because my head felt like it would burst out of my skull at any moment.

"He was like a brother to you," he softly answered. Then he raised his voice higher in question. "What did you remember?"

"There was a man. And a crowd of people. He dragged

me to a platform. Nikon was there. He—he—he—" I stammered, unable to finish at first. "He was going to kill me, but he died instead."

Anubis nodded in understanding. "The first wave of your activation was very intense for you." He waited, allowing me to process his words and my thoughts.

"Did they...?" I paused, chewing on my lip and looking into his deep brown eyes, searching for confirmation. "Did they die?"

"No," he answered. He didn't explain further, but rather, took my hands and looked deeply into my eyes. They spoke volumes and words were unnecessary. He was letting me know I was safe and he was here with me to help me and protect me if I needed it.

The pressure in my head eased suddenly, like a balloon had been untied and was making a loud, daring escape. The pain disappeared.

I would have sworn that one look from him had taken away the pain. He had that effect on me. He made things *better*.

We hiked back, both quietly immersed in our own deep thoughts. The little special moment we'd had earlier was over and once again our guards were up.

CHAPTER EIGHT

A NUBIS DISAPPEARED BEFORE we even reached the house. To keep from being detected, he bid me farewell and stepped into his portal of darkness before we walked out of the tree line. I knew he'd be back tomorrow. It was time for me to let go of the past and enjoy the now. I wanted to forget the things that I had seen at the waterfall. I now had this unfamiliar heartache that teased me every second of every day and I wanted it gone. Those were *her* feelings, *her* life, and they weren't mine. I ignored them. I took off and raced to the house, feeling the wind in my hair and the past at my back.

I came around the house, passing the pool. There, in a lounge chair, fast asleep, lay Andrew. He was sweating as the sun beat down on him in his full-body suit; he had to have been burning up. I stopped there, observing him. He must have fallen asleep waiting for me. It was later than I expected, and Teddy would be off duty soon. We could all hang out, and Teddy would be a great buffer. I decided to wake

Andrew up before he had a heat stroke—as if he could.

"Andrew." I shook him carefully so as not to startle him.

He opened his eyes, looked up at me, and smiled. He had a nice smile. "Jewel, you're back." As he began to sit up it occurred to me that he might have been waiting here all day.

"Please tell me you just decided to take a nap out here and weren't waiting for me."

"Of course not. I was just tired and needed to be alone." He looked sheepishly at me, which told me he wasn't being wholly honest.

"Sure," I said, letting him know with my tone that I wasn't convinced.

His voice deepened and he sounded irritated when he asked, "So who was that with you earlier?"

Jealous much? I kept my response short, with as little information as possible. "That was my trainer. His name is Anubis."

"I think you should get another trainer. He seems dangerous. I don't feel comfortable with him around you." He paused, thinking for a second. "Is it okay if I ask what you're training for?"

"Andrew, I appreciate your concern, but I assure you that Anubis is not a threat to me." To him was another story. "And I'm training to protect myself."

"You have us, we can protect you." He placed his hand on my shoulder. His answer was so sincere, I bit down the retort I had on the tip of my tongue. He was being chauvinistic and it was annoying.

"Thank you, but I much prefer to take care of myself."

Andrew had never acted this way before. It made me think he was trying desperately to stake a claim on me, but

I brushed his hand away and tried to give him the benefit of the doubt.

"How about we go find the others and we can meet later and all go to the bonfire area?"

Andrew nodded, placated for the moment. I dismissed his earlier attitude and we went to find the others inside the main house of Delphi Glen. We found Teddy in the commons room.

"Hey, Teddy." I smiled at him and he nodded towards Andrew, a gesture I'm sure Andrew caught. I shrugged in our silent exchange.

"Hey, Jewel, where have you been today?" He knew where I liked to slip away to sometimes on my days off. It was one of the best parts of our friendship. He respected my need for alone time and didn't encroach on my hiking.

"You know, the same old same old." I chuckled and playfully punched him in the arm.

Andrew stood quietly watching our exchange before interrupting. "So, hey, Teddy," he started, "Jewel and I wanted to get together with everyone at the bonfire later if you could let everyone know. We'll meet down here right before dusk and head out there." He spoke forcefully and did that Andrew thing where he commanded rather than asked. It was his least favorable quality, but I knew it would come in handy for him later.

"Sure, that sounds like a great plan. Jewel?" Teddy looked at me, dismissing Andrew, in a way.

I chuckled silently. It seemed there was plenty of testosterone to go around today.

"Yeah, that sounds fun, but I do have some work to get done for school first and then I'll catch up with you guys later." I turned towards Andrew, smiling sweetly and waving as he stood there with a slightly annoyed look on his face. It occurred to me that he'd wanted to spend the rest of the day with me, but I wasn't in the mood for more company at the moment. At least not his.

"Hey, that project we have in world history together, do you want to go over some of it real quick?" Teddy asked as he followed me towards the door. He knew me so well.

"Yeah, sure that'd be great!" I needed some best friend time, and Teddy seemed to understand that. Without another glance back at Andrew, we walked together upstairs towards my place.

Once we were upstairs in the apartment suite that I shared with my dad, Teddy began to laugh hysterically.

"Hey!" I exclaimed. "What's so funny?" I threw one of the couch pillows at him, but he dodged it and continued to laugh.

"It's just you and Andrew." He stopped, trying to catch his breath as I threw another pillow his way, this time catching him square in the face. I joined in with his laughter

"What about us?" I sat abruptly on the couch and exhaled a long breath. "We're just friends."

"Has anyone told him that?" he teased.

"Yes, we talked about it. I'm not into going out with anyone right now," I explained, my shoulders slumping as I recalled our awkward conversation.

"I don't think he fully understands that. Girl, you're going to have to give him some tough love," Teddy insisted as he sat next to me. "What's up with the giant dude that stole you this morning?"

"Geez, did everyone see us leave this morning?" I asked,

my voice raising in exasperation. My life was on display for all to see.

"No, but enough people saw you leave with him and they didn't see him arrive." Teddy paused, looking off to the right before continuing. "I mean, you know how it is with new people coming to our place. It gets people talking." Teddy shrugged, letting me know he didn't share their thoughts. I had an inkling of what they might be saying. I didn't care. No one could guess he'd spent the night in my room. Well, some might know, like the empaths and telepaths, but we didn't do anything, so I wasn't concerned.

"He's the guy I told you about, who's training me." I gave Teddy the same basic answer that I gave everyone else. Despite our closeness I couldn't explain everything that was happening to me. At least not yet.

"Training you for what?" Teddy looked at me imploringly as he asked.

"To fight. To protect myself." I sighed, tired of the this and ready to move on to something else, but Teddy wouldn't let it go yet.

"He seems...." Teddy trailed off, thinking. "He seems like he knows you well. And exactly what are you needing protection from?"

"Wait, I thought you didn't see him when he was in the house?" I asked, confused.

"I didn't. I saw him the night he met your father in his study, and I saw him look at you. A man doesn't look at someone he doesn't know like that." Teddy expressed this with concern, but he looked at me as if he were wondering if I'd explain further. But I didn't have answers for him.

"I mean, he kind of knows me, but I'm not sure if it's in

the way you're implying. Hell, what am I saying? I'm not sure of anything these days." I blurted the last part out and then looked sheepishly at Teddy.

"So, you didn't answer my question," Teddy stated as he stood up.

"What's that?" I asked, but I knew what he was going to ask me again.

"Why do you need protection?"

"Hell if I know. Probably because I'm a pain in the ass and one day someone is going to get pissed at me." I said this jokingly, but in a way it was the truth. One day I would be in a fight, maybe even a war. I hoped it didn't hurt the people I loved in this life, like it had in the other. My thoughts trailed back to Nikon and sadness overwhelmed me. I sighed, pushing the emotion back down. "Hey, Teddy, I'm feeling a bit tired. Do you mind if I just spend some time alone?"

"Of course." Teddy smiled and hugged me. The hug was warm and affectionate, and it seemed to ease the sadness away. I walked him to the door and told him I'd see him later at the bonfire.

After he left I took a nice, long, dreamless nap. It was pure bliss.

IT WAS DARK outside when I woke, and I realized it was time to go meet everyone downstairs. I stretched and rubbed my eyes before combing quickly through my hair and braiding it to the side. I threw on a blue hoodie over my shirt and rushed out my door. Andrew was waiting for me in the foyer. He looked relieved to see me. I wondered then how late I was.

"Hey, you made it." He sighed with obvious relief as he moved towards me.

"Yeah, sorry I fell asleep." I noticed he was dressed far nicer than was needed for a bonfire. He had on a collared shirt and his hair was gelled back. And as I leaned in closer I realized he had on cologne.

"It's okay. Are you ready to go?" He looked me over as he said this, stopping on the disheveled clothes that I'd slept in. I hadn't been out to impress anyone when I'd thrown on this hoodie.

"Yes, let's go. But where's everyone else?" I looked around for Teddy. He wasn't here.

"They left already, but it wasn't that long ago. We can catch up." He gestured towards the door and I followed, careful to keep a comfortable distance between us.

The bonfire area was just a circle of rocks about a half-mile from the house. It was surrounded by an enclosure of trees, so it was a private area for us to hang out at without the constant watch of the adults of the compound. We often got together here, telling stories or playing and listening to music. During the colder months, we couldn't meet here, though. It snowed a good deal of the year so high in the mountains, and then we were stuck indoors.

I was grateful that, when we rounded the corner to go inside, I saw Teddy coming out the front door. Gale, Jeff, and Monica followed behind him.

"Hey, Jewel, we were just coming to find you guys." He looked relieved. I wasn't sure why.

"Hey, are you guys going to the bonfire site?" I knew they were but still asked. They all nodded their heads.

Gale, Jeff, and Monica were the only kids on the

compound that tolerated me enough to hang around me, other than Andrew and Teddy. Teddy had a huge crush on Monica, but she was super obvious about her affections for Andrew. I hated to be in the middle of the drama, which was another point to add to the list of why I was hesitant to date Andrew. Gale and Jeff, on the other hand, were happily together. They barely paid anyone else attention. It was sweet and gag-worthy all at once.

"Great, we are too." Andrew looped his hand in mine and pulled me along before I could even protest. I knew what he was doing. Monica sent me a death glare as we all walked towards the trees that housed our small bonfire area. I tried to ignore her and, slowly and as inconspicuously as I could, I pulled my hand out of his. I pretended to be interested in a group of constellations as I pointed to them with the offended hand.

Once we reached the bonfire site, I sat down next to Teddy, hoping Andrew would sit a little away. I still wasn't ready to "process" anything yet. And I wasn't digging the whole forced relationship. I think after that he realized what he'd been doing, because his demeanor changed. Which was good because he was about to be voted off the island.

"Hey, Andrew, light the fire." We were told to never use our powers outside the basement, but I knew we were safe and that I could control his abilities. Plus, I had three other people to pull various abilities from as well.

"Okay, but if I set the place on fire…." He stood and I could tell he was really scared, so I stood with him. I pulled the energy from him as I stood close. It enveloped me like flames licking firewood. I felt his powers flow through me and I knew that if he lost control, I could control them.

"Just focus," I whispered in his ear. Then I sat down, watching. I gave the reins over to him. I wasn't controlling the situation anymore. And I really freaking hoped I'd made the right decision and we didn't all burn alive.

Fire shot in a precise stream straight into the stacked wood, lighting it. I could see the look of triumph on Andrew's face—this was a small way of showing him he had control, even in an uncontrolled environment. He beamed with happiness, and I was thrilled for him. I could tell that everyone else was proud of him too, which gave me even more reason to smile.

"I did it!" Andrew exclaimed as everyone cheered him on. He stood there with awe on his features, as if he couldn't believe he hadn't burned the whole place down. I released the breath I'd been holding and smiled at him.

Gale came to give him a congratulative hug. Gale was a sweet person and I liked her. She was tall and slender with latte-colored skin and dark hair, both making her Native American heritage obvious; she was pretty. She could create forcefields, and she could also push energy out from the forcefields as a defense. We were sure there was more she could do with her powers, but she had yet to discover what that might be. My job was to help the Evols learn control; the rest was up to them as they discovered more about themselves. Gale was always nice to me. At one point, we'd even been relatively good friends.

Her parents had lived on the complex for a long time. Her mother had grown up on an Indian reservation in Arizona, but she'd sought us out when her powers presented themselves. She was beautiful, just like Gale, and she had an impressive ability. She spoke to animals and influenced them.

Gale was lucky to have a mother, and I had to admit there were times I envied her.

Gale's father worked closely with my own. He was like Gale, also able to create types of forcefields and shields and even manifest certain types of energy around his body. He was a large and gruff man, but I'd seen his eyes soften when he looked at Gale.

Gale's power level was greater than both her parents', and I knew soon she would begin to discover this.

Gale, like me, also loved the land and the mountains. I had accidently discovered her many times on my hikes, trying to stay hidden. I either pretended not to notice her at all or smiled at her and continued on my way. We both understood the need for solitude in nature—I wouldn't be the one to disturb her, nor would she intrude on me.

Jeff was the same height as Gale, which was short by male standards. He was very lean, almost too skinny, and his face was long with a straight, slightly upturned nose. His hair was a blond spiky mass that shot up on top of his head in every direction, while his skin was tanned from the sun. And he was fast. He had the potential to be faster than light.

He'd come to our compound at the young age of eight after supposedly being abandoned by his parents. When my father searched, though, he discovered that Jeff's parents had died in a horrific accident, so he was adopted by a couple of childless members of our community. He always seemed sad when others weren't looking but then would quickly put on a cheery smile that never quite reached his eyes. He wasn't one to allow others to feel sorry for him, and he seemed private about his emotions, so he put on a brave face and hid behind jokes and laughter so they didn't see through him—but I saw him. I saw them all.

It made sense that Jeff and Andrew had become friends. They, in some small way, had something in common, even though it was a commonality of tragedy.

Monica was not as attractive as Gale, but I still thought she was pretty. She had light brown hair that hung straight down her back, large doe-shaped brown eyes the color of milk chocolate, perfect porcelain skin, thin lips, and a short nose. She also had the ability to persuade. She could tell someone to do something and they had to obey. Thankfully, her power didn't work on me.

Her family left her here just a few years back in hopes that my father could help her. They were Evols that had decided to live with the norms. Only, Monica made it very difficult for them once she'd activated three years back. She'd activated earlier than most and decided to use her abilities to start getting her way. Since she'd come to the compound she'd been trying to change her ways, but she struggled daily with it. She'd tried several times to persuade me when she first arrived, only to become angry and frustrated when it didn't work. Soon she began avoiding me, and I was pretty sure she hated me. I'd never really cared. I hated to think of anyone as evil, but I worried that if she let herself, she could easily become just that.

The night went by quickly as we joked and Jeff pulled out his guitar. Sometimes we had to remind him to slow down, but he was a pretty good player. The air became cooler. We had already missed dinner, but Teddy had grabbed some snacks for everyone as he walked out the door so we weren't too hungry, except Jeff. He was always hungry.

We stood up to walk back together as a group when

Andrew stopped me.

"Jewel, can we talk?" He was still standing in the bonfire area, while the others were walking into the distance. Except Monica. She stopped to look back for Andrew, only to see him talking to me, so she rushed off, probably upset.

"Sure." My answer was hesitant. I knew he wanted to talk about me going out with him, but I wasn't any closer to figuring out my feelings.

"Will you sit with me a few?"

I sat, letting the dying fire illuminate my face. "What's up?"

Andrew sat next to me. He didn't say anything at first, and there was an awkward silence.

"Andrew?" I was tired and I kind of wanted to just go to sleep.

"I'm sorry." His words rushed out. "I'm sorry for being an ass today, and I'm sorry for being pushy. The thing is, I really like you. I've never really liked anyone like this."

At first I didn't say anything, wrestling with my thoughts and feelings. What could I say? *Sorry, dude, for stringing you along for my own selfish reasons?*

"No, you're not an ass. I am. Listen, I can't commit to anything right now and I'm sorry. I'm just trying to work out who I am." I paused. I wanted to tell him—to share this with someone, to get a different perspective—but I didn't. We sat there in silence instead. I felt like a grade-A douche. I needed to talk to Anubis. I needed more answers. I couldn't take being in the dark anymore. I wanted all this uncertainty over.

"I understand. Take all the time you need. I'll still be here waiting." He sounded sad, but he managed a resigned smile as he stood. "Here, let's walk back together." He pulled me to my feet, and we slowly walked in contemplative silence back to the house.

All I could think was that I didn't deserve his affection. I was, indeed, a selfish ass because I kept that thought to myself.

CHAPTER NINE

THAT NIGHT I tossed and turned, as had been the ritual recently. My brain was full of the myriad of questions I still had. The small respite of peace Anubis and I had at the rock quarry was over. My brain was in overload. I wanted to know more about my parents. I wanted to know more about where I came from and who I was. I wanted to know about my past, who I'd hurt, and if this Nikon had survived. And why I felt such pain when I thought back to that vision and what happened to him.

After two hours of trying desperately to sleep, I finally gave up. I threw my feet out from under the covers and onto the cold wood floor and padded quietly towards the desk and my laptop. Who was my mother? Anubis said that mythology held a trace of truth in it.

I pulled up a search engine and looked for her stories. Then I looked up Ares, Zeus, and the rest of the Greek gods. There wasn't much here I didn't already know. They were selfish, self-serving, and petty. After reading the many myths that surrounded my supposed family, I wondered why there weren't any myths about me. I was a goddess as well, right? Why was my legendary tale not told? You'd think that the tale of two different royals from adversarial planets becoming involved would be an interesting tale for the books.

I typed Anubis's name into the search bar. An Egyptian-style drawing of a man with the head of a dog popped up in my images. He was listed as the god of the afterlife and mummification. Gross. What was his role in mummification? I continued reading, but found that most of the information was vague and just touched on his duties as a god.

Then I ran across a story that said he was married to someone named Anput and had a child. And to think I was starting to believe this man and I had a thing. He was a cheating, married liar!

I closed the laptop, padded back to bed, and tossed and turned some more until, out of pure exhaustion, I fell into a restless slumber.

My hands were in his as we stood in the sun. He beckoned to his Ra for our blessing. There were but a select few surrounding us. We knew the dangers of our union but knew the pain of separation was greater. I gazed into his eyes, bonded as we were.

"I am yours, and you are mine. Together we are one." I recited his people's passage for eternal bonding. I meant every word.

In return, he recited my own people's passage as he cupped my face with his strong hands. "One heart, one soul, one love, forever and always."

Power surged through us as our bond was finalized. Our

souls had chosen each other. Our love was true. Our love was unique.

Our love was deadly.

Anubis

SPENDING TIME WITH Jewel in her element, the place she loved most, had reenergized me and brought me back to life in ways I hadn't felt in thousands of years. Yet, I also almost lost her before she even remembered who I was. It had terrified me. Her activation was turning out to be very dangerous for her. This time she'd almost drowned. What would happen next time? It was all I could do not to snatch her up and lock her away to keep her safe. Yet, I knew that wouldn't be a good idea. It would push her away and I'd lose her, possibly forever. It had been a sad, lonely existence without her.

I'd returned to my residence, wishing I'd taken Jewel back with me. Knowing I couldn't.

I'd known that it would be a slow process, bringing her back, but I hadn't anticipated how different she would be—yet still so much the same. I'd watched her for a while swimming in the water, in her element and there was peaceful contentment on her beautiful face. I'd seen that same expression so many times before, a long time ago. I'd almost forgotten the way she laughed and the way she smelled. Simple things that one takes for granted were slowly fading from my memories. Yet here she was once again, in front of me, and I couldn't touch her or hold her. It was almost akin to torture.

I sighed. With one victory, so many more were needed.

Yet, there wasn't anything in life worth a damn that came easy. Jewel was worth everything to me, and I would fight to the death to win her back and to keep her safe.

I walked aimlessly through the house until I reached the bedroom I had once shared with Jewel. I hadn't changed much over the years. Her clothes were locked away in a stasis closet. Every once in a while I would open it and there would be her smell. It brought me back. The images I kept and the paintings also helped. Even love that was so passionate it burned the heart and mind with its force couldn't stop the memory of another from slowly eroding.

I lay on the bed, going over the day spent with her. I longed for the day we didn't have to part ways. It hurt to be away from her. Our bond was so strong even now; I wondered how she didn't feel it as well. It was like a magnet—it didn't matter how far the distance had been between us, the need and the desire, the pull to be near one another was always so great. Now that she was actually here, it was overpowering. I needed her. I wanted her. Still, in the years since she'd been brought to this time, I'd managed to give her space. I stayed away to allow her to grow, but now that I'd been near her again it literally took all the strength I had to keep my distance. I didn't know how much longer I could do this.

Jewel

WAKING UP THE next morning wasn't as rough as it had been recently or as tough as I'd anticipated it would be. I didn't feel exhausted; I felt energized. I was ready to take on a Saturday with Anubis and push him to give me more answers. I sprinted out of bed and rushed through my shower then changed into my favorite pair of workout pants and a tank. It was always unbearably hot at his place. Not that I'd seen more than one room.

I knew as soon as he arrived. I was brushing my long strawberry blond hair in the mirror and throwing it in a high ponytail when I felt the change in the air, and the hair on the back of my neck stood up straight. It was almost like an electrical charge had shot through the room. And then in stepped the tall, muscular, hot-as-hell god. It occurred to me he was so sinfully good-looking that he could be the devil. Which was actually accurate, in a way.

"When you look at me like that, it drives me crazy." His voice was strained.

"Does your wife drive you crazy when she looks at you as well?" I was back on operation shakedown. Who knew? The gods seemed like they had several lovers on the side, so maybe that was what the first Jewel was, a distraction.

"Indeed." He was trying to hide a smile. I saw it anyways.

"So this Anput, who was she?" I moved away from him, pretending to be indifferent.

"Is this your question for the day?" He sounded amused.

"Maybe…." I trailed off then turned around. He was silently laughing. "What is so funny?"

"You're jealous." His laugh vanished and his demeanor changed. He looked at me with intensity. The same look he'd given me the other night after our kiss.

"I'm not jealous of anyone." I noticed that my hands were on my hips as if I were throwing a childish fit. His eyebrow went up, suggesting that my reaction implied exactly that.

Damn him.

"I'll tell you all about her after our session today." He left it there, his tone short and blunt. Then he took my hand, opened a pitch-black hole in the room, and pulled me through before I could say another word. We stepped into the training room.

"Are you ever going to give me a tour of the place?" Being back here reminded me of the last time we'd trained, when someone almost walked in on us. Was that his wife?

"If you wish to see more, I'll be happy to show you. After our session." I hadn't been expecting that answer. I also didn't expect him to lunge at me.

He knocked me on my ass, so I attempted to kick his legs out from under him. They didn't budge. Hey, it worked in the movies. I pulled myself up and prepared to fight. He didn't take it easy on me.

Before I knew it, we were both drenched in sweat and breathing heavily. Apparently gods did get tired. I stumbled over to the water bottles sitting on the wooden benches. I felt like I was dying of thirst.

"Jewel, it's time we discuss a few things. You've started changing, and you need to be aware of the repercussions." He sat down next to me on the bench.

"What do you mean I'm changing?" Was I about to turn into a dragon or mythical monster?

"You're gaining strength and endurance fairly fast. Faster than I thought you would." He paused. It was in that moment I realized, I'd never seen him tired. It had never seemed as if he actually had to try before in our sessions.

"How do you mean?"

"You're as fast and strong as I am now. You've not noticed

because I've been matching you." He took one of the water bottles and drank it down quickly and eagerly.

"So I thought we... er... you were above tiredness and sweat." I had to admit I was enjoying the glisten of his skin.

"In some ways, we're the same as the people here, except evolution has enhanced our abilities."

"So we're like Superman?" I was imagining myself in spandex flying across the sky. I wasn't so sure I would want to be a hero. It seemed a tedious position.

Anubis smiled but didn't answer. Instead he looked over to one of the areas of the room that was masked in darkness. I peered in that direction and I began to see definition in that area. There was something in one of the corners. It was some sort of device, almost like a video camera. Someone was watching us.

"So who's watching us?" I crossed my arms, feeling betrayed and spied on. He didn't appear surprised by my question.

"Your eyesight is improving as well. I believe it's time you meet our friend." So someone else had been spying on us and Anubis had hidden it from me. He may have been one delicious-looking man, but this made me question if I should trust him. But I decided to wait and see before passing judgment. My gut, for whatever reason, told me I could trust him with anything.

I watched as he walked towards the door I had noticed last time, near the back of the room. It was strategically located just under the camera. I hadn't noticed the camera before, but Anubis had quickly shoved me through a portal. I wondered if it was his wife we were going to meet. That would be just my luck.

Through the door was a long corridor. It was bare and looked to be made of some type of steel or other metal. I confirmed this when it was cool to my touch.

"Is this a bunker?" It reminded me of areas of the basement at our compound.

"No, it's merely a place I stay." I noticed he didn't call it a home, nor did he have any emotion in his tone when he referred to it. Most people have some type of pride or love for their things, especially when it came to their living spaces. He seemed disconnected and indifferent.

Down the corridor there was a set of doors. The hallway continued to the right, but he pushed a button and the doors slid open, just like they did in the pantry at home. The area beyond the doors appeared to be set up as a lounge of sorts, but the chairs were strange. They were a scooped shape and they appeared to be floating. They were black trimmed with white and appeared to be made of some sort of synthetic leather. I pushed one of them, and it moved slightly. Odd. Why would anyone have floating chairs?

"Why not have floating chairs?" A voice I hadn't heard before broke through my thoughts. I looked up quickly at the man standing on the other side of the odd lounge. He was dressed in what appeared to be a black smock. He was tall, as tall as Anubis, but his skin was darker; it was the color of coffee with a splash creamer in it. His eyes were glowing a bright iridescent green. Anubis's brown eyes glowed like this on occasion, but his glowed blue. The man's hair was long and braided down his back. His long nose flared wide at the base. He was leaner than Anubis, yet still imposing. For some reason, I knew this man marveled over everything and laughed often.

"I agree. Can I have one? Can I ride it to and from school? It'll be like a Segway but way better." He chuckled, exactly as I knew he would. I would kill for an opportunity to take one of these chairs apart to see how it worked then put it back together. My father, when I was younger, was always shaking his head to see that I'd disassembled some new toy. Once I started on the electronics he stopped me and put me to work downstairs.

"You could, but it actually doesn't do anything other than float." He moved closer and took my hand. "You have yet to remember me, but I am Thoth and we were once friends."

Something about him reminded me of a phrase. I couldn't remember ever hearing it before, but it was present in my mind at that moment as I looked down at the hand that clasped mine. "Wisdom is the key to happiness and true power lies within."

"Indeed it is." He appeared to be impressed, and his previously stoic face was now animated with pride and something else I couldn't place.

I knew this man—or, no, she knew him… or I did. It was very confusing. It was similar to when I met Anubis, but the emotions were different. This man felt like a friend, a confidante, someone who cared about me and I about him. Was this what Anubis had meant, that I was… merging. Is this what it felt like?

"Yes, I believe what you're feeling is what we would call the merge." He smiled faintly, only for a microsecond, but I caught it. His thick eyebrows bunched up as he contemplated.

I glanced over at Anubis. Had Thoth just read my mind? Anubis was standing quietly to the side, observing us. He had thick eyebrows as well. They framed his eyes perfectly. My perusal of him made him give me a lopsided smirk. Those lopsided smirks made him look irresistible, and my thoughts turned in that naughty direction.

"I had forgotten how hard it is to work around you two." Thoth's voice pulled me out of my distraction. I turned towards him, ready to pull him into operation shakedown.

"So you're a telepath?" There was no doubt in my mind that he'd read my mind. I decided to borrow his ability and see if I could use his own power on him.

Nothing, just static.

"We all have our special talents. Mine is that I use all of my brain. I was given the title of god of wisdom for a reason." He paused, rubbing his chin. There was a bit of rough stubble on it. "However, you cannot harness my powers as you have with the humans."

"Why not?"

"I'm not sure." He was still rubbing his chin, deep in thought.

It was indeed interesting. I turned towards Anubis, wondering if he too had been reading my thoughts as I'd previously suspected. Even more interesting, I wondered what my special talents would be once this merge had occurred.

I stood in the odd-shaped room, watching Thoth and being watched by Anubis. The room was obviously a lab. It also held an observatory feeling, with its dome shape. The windows were covered, as if Thoth and Anubis were in hiding. The room was larger than the usual lab; there were several stations set up with different equipment. Each station seemed random but methodical, all in one.

"You like my lab?" Thoth's inquiry broke through my perusal of the room.

"Is this the part where I get to help in some top-secret mission to annihilate mankind?" My voice was playful, but I was a little worried. What were they doing here? I guess I shouldn't have been worried since I lived on a secret compound with its own small labs, but this was far more vast and intricate than anything I'd previously seen.

"Annihilate? Why, I much enjoy most parts of humanity. The food, the slow progression of science..."

"The women." Anubis's voice was playful from behind me.

Thoth took no offense to Anubis's comment. "Indeed, and the women."

"What are the windows for?" I looked around at the dome-shaped windows, wondering what I would behold if I were able to look outside. It was hard to tell where Anubis had been taking me when we went through the portal, and until today we'd never left the training room.

"Shall I show her?" Thoth looked past me at Anubis, awaiting his permission. Anubis remained silent, and as I turned towards him, I didn't see any indication of an answer, yet Thoth walked across the room to pull up a touchscreen and started tapping on it, much like he would an iPad. It was then that I felt the floor below me move and I had the distinct impression that the room was rising. It was a shock at first.

"What the hell?" My balance took a few moments to right itself. I looked up at the windows, which were slowly opening, as we quickly rose higher. At first I could see nothing at all, but eventually the barriers fell completely away from the windows and light shone through. I walked closer to the windows. We were in a tower above a vast desert terrain that stretched far and wide, as far as the eye could see.

"Welcome to Egypt." Thoth paused, glancing at Anubis briefly before continuing, "Or I should say, welcome back since you've been here many times before. The training room is down the hall and around the corner."

I knew my mouth was hanging open. I'd felt us move, but I never imagined we would end up in a completely different, faraway country. I thought, okay, maybe another compound in the mountains or something. I did not, however, expect to find myself all the way across the world in Egypt. Yet here I was.

"Welcome *back* to my home." Anubis spoke the words and they caressed me as if they were an invitation to make Egypt *our* home. He moved forward, taking my hand, which seemed to further confirm this. This man was trouble.

"It's..." I paused, trying to think of the perfect word to describe the beauty in front of me. There was indeed a beauty to the desolation and a hidden liveliness depicted in the barren terrain before me. "It's amazing." I breathed the words out with awe and conviction, turning towards Anubis to look deep in his eyes. I smiled at him. The desert around him fit him in so many ways. It was complicated, misunderstood, beautiful, and lonely, yet upon closer inspection it was lively and full of so much promise.

"Indeed, it is." As if we were part of some corny love story where the guy pines after the girl, Anubis was looking at me as he agreed; only I had the feeling he wasn't speaking about the landscape. I quickly looked away, trying to hide the crimson I knew was spreading across my face. Damn, my life was so complicated.

"So you can transport your home anywhere in the world?" I thought to myself how convenient this would be if he were an Evolved and I could borrow his power to vacation anywhere I wanted. Of course, I'd already found out that, for whatever reason, I couldn't borrow their powers.

"I can. Why, did you have someplace in mind?" He was smirking now. He did that often. It was a knowing smirk. I found it incredibly sexy.

Stop it. You are not helping matters here. I had so many conflicting emotions, and the situation seemed painfully complicated. I felt a pull towards this man. One I could not deny. It was intoxicating to be around him. Even now, I wanted to be closer to him, as if he were the oxygen that my lungs needed. But I felt like this need for him, this desire, had been decided for me long ago by the other me. And I still didn't feel like *her*. Part of me felt rebellious and wanted to run screaming so I could try to have a normal life. Maybe even give Andrew a chance.

I realized that Thoth was watching me carefully. Was he reading my thoughts?

"I feel it is time we continue with our purpose here." If Thoth had been listening to my thoughts he gave no indication.

"What exactly is our purpose here?" As much as my soul was telling me to trust them, a part of me was fighting to the surface, yelling, "Run!"

It was Anubis who answered. "We're trying to help you. We've had years to prepare for this, and Thoth believes he's discovered a way to make the transition easier on you." Anubis walked over to me and gently held my face in his hands. I looked into his beautiful brown eyes and found I couldn't look away. "I want you to understand that we aren't trying to replace who you are now or change you in any way. I love both Jewels equally and only wish to see you happy."

I knew he said this to comfort me, but I still wasn't convinced. I needed to know more about this other Jewel. As much as I felt deep down I could trust both of them, I couldn't bring myself to give in to this feeling.

"I understand you *feel* that you're helping me, but I'll be the judge of what's good for me, hot stuff." I turned away from him, intent on getting the answers I needed from Thoth. I resolved to demand to go home if I didn't get them.

My inner voice gave me a quick pep talk. *I can do this.* I only hoped it helped.

"Thoth, tell me what I'm doing here." My voice was a bit demanding, which was my intent. I crossed my arms over my chest, ready to battle if needed.

"There is a machine towards the rear end of the lab; if you will follow me, I will explain its use and how it will benefit you." Thoth's tone was matter-of-fact and gave no indication as to whether or not I should be concerned.

"Lead the way." I wasn't sure if I was going to regret this—curiosity did kill the cat—but I wanted answers, so I hoped the risk was worth it. He led the way towards the back of the lab, weaving around several workstations. The lab at first seemed endless, but finally we reached the back. There sat a machine that looked similar to a CAT scan machine.

"I know the machine does indeed look very primitive, but we are limited on resources here. I assure you that, undeniably, it is far more than what it seems." He spoke in the same matter-of-fact tone he had earlier. I began to realize this was pretty much how he sounded most of the time.

"So you want me to get in that contraption? No way, not happening, buddy." Again I crossed my arms and may have even thrown in a childish jut of my chin. I wasn't budging till they talked.

Thoth turned towards me. "You may ask your questions and I shall answer to ease your mind. First allow me to explain the machine to you." He paused, assessing whether or not I was listening. "The machine is meant to access your hidden memories slowly. We are afraid that any day now you will be bombarded with everything at once, and the repercussions could be detrimental to your psyche. Even as a goddess there are limitations to sanity."

"I was told they would start to come back slowly as it was." I was now even more confused and a new state of fear gripped me. I could wake up tomorrow a completely different person? This was bullshit. *Hey guess what?* Bam! *You aren't who you thought you were and now you're fully not you anymore.* "What if I don't want to transition into this other me?"

"Believe it or not, you already are her. How it will change you I cannot be fully sure, but you will still be the same person." He motioned towards the machine again. "I promise at any point in time we can stop, but here lie the answers you are looking for."

Anubis turned me towards him. "My love, please trust us. This is for the best. Your activation and the merge have already shown signs of becoming dangerous. The pain you've been experiencing—it's not normal. You could have died yesterday." The problem was, hunk or not, and even with my gut telling that they were really trying to help, it wasn't enough to ease my apprehension.

It was then that Thoth spoke up again. "You may not understand why there is a war waging inside you right now, but I do." He stopped, put the pad he was holding that appeared to be the control to the machine down, and gave me his full attention. This time the matter-of-fact tone he'd used earlier was gone; there was emotion in its depths. "You were betrayed. And as much as you feel you can trust us, there is a battle inside you because of this betrayal. Only, you are confused because you can't remember it." He stopped there, leaving me with this bombshell.

Wait, who betrayed me? Did Anubis and Thoth betray me? More questions. With my inner voice screaming for answers, I had a hard decision to make then and there. Did I want to put all my trust in these two men...? Not even men, but self-proclaimed gods. I looked at the machine, my mind racing. Could I do this? I wanted the answers to all my questions and I wanted to know about this past... or this other person that was me.

Breathe. Just breathe deeply and stop thinking. There went that voice that had been present lately in my head. Was this my voice? What if this was just her trying to break through? What if I was already changing... merging... whatever they were calling it? I didn't breathe deeply as I had instructed myself. Instead I felt this overwhelming sense of fear and dread. It was overpowering, gripping my mind and soul as the intense anxiety overcame me.

I can't. I can't do this.

I began to quickly back away, and just as I turned to run away screaming, Anubis grabbed me gently in his arms and pressed my body to his. He leaned in towards my ear and whispered, "Calm yourself, love." His gentle command seeped into me just as easily as the fear and anxiety had enveloped me. I no longer felt the need to run. I felt loved, secure, protected. This man—for whatever reason, I knew he would never hurt me. It was as if even just his nearness kept all my worries at bay. I began to listen to the inner voice that had tried to help me previously. I took deep breaths, inhaling the intoxicating scent of the man holding me. It felt good to be in his arms. I didn't want to leave.

"I'm okay." I pulled back, despite my desire to stay, and reassured him that I would be fine. "This is just all very overwhelming."

"I fear that unfortunately, my dear, we are very short on time, and as much as I would like to ease you into this process, I am unable to do so," Thoth said from behind me. He had attempted to seem more empathetic, but it sounded awkward, as if empathy were a foreign concept to him.

"So this will give me answers and keep me from going crazy? And it's safe?" I felt I had to trust them, and I knew that sometimes you had to take a risk in order to get what you wanted. I was still scared, but at least I could say no to a second time around with this hulking machine if I was still me—and coherent. "Is this going to affect me in any other way? Such as put me under, make me stupid, turn me into a zombie, or give someone control over my mind?"

"No!" both Anubis and Thoth answered in unison.

"Okay, but if anything happens to me, I'll kill you both!" I still wasn't entirely convinced this was a good idea, but sometimes you had to weigh the good and the bad. I walked over to the machine, hoping that this wasn't my death march. I could just hear that quote from *The Green Mile* playing in my head, only tweaking the gender: *Dead girl walking.* When did I become so doom and gloom?

"So lie down onto the mat, and I'm going to place these pads onto your head. The machine is going to start here in a moment. Don't worry, it is not loud like the machines that you use today, but it does emit a soft hum. It is not painful. Close your eyes once it starts."

I followed Thoth's instructions. Once I was on the bed-shaped mat, the sticky pads were placed on my head, then the soft hum he'd mentioned began. Before I closed my eyes, I looked at Anubis. He winked and gave me one of his sexy lopsided smiles to reassure me. It made me feel hot and I imagined my skin was flushed. Leave it to him to turn me on even in my state of unease.

I closed my eyes and focused on the hum of the machine. Before I knew it, I wasn't in the lab anymore.

CHAPTER TEN

*T*HE SUN WAS *bright, and I could taste and smell salt in the air. I could hear waves crashing softly on the shore. The air was warm and sticky. There was sand beneath my fingers, I could feel it. The ocean stretched out before me. It took me a moment to orient myself, but I finally realized I was on a beach. Around me was sparse foliage, and a few trees were littered behind me on the landscape. I watched the waves crash ashore as I stuck my feet deep into the cool, wet sand beneath me. The water was getting closer to my toes. I thought about walking out into the surf; I loved the water. It washed away my worries. My grandmother Dione once told me it was because I was her descendant and therefore craved it. As if that explained everything.*

The sun was beating down upon my head. I should be scared, as I was on the very edge of the Egyptonian border. Although I was hiding from my family, as it was, so either way I was in trouble. I came here contemplating the consequences of crossing the border. My family would never find me here, but the Egyptonians very well could. Sometimes you have to weigh the good against the bad. Anything was better than the alternative.

Except death. *My inner voice, the one that had plagued me all my life, poked its ugly little head out. It was a gloomy voice. One that, at times, filled me with doubt, even though my soul wished to be free and fearless. The water pooled around my feet now. Would Poseidon know if I took a dip in the sea? Would he have his minions searching this far out? Best not to tempt it. It had been a risk as it was to travel across the sea to this new landmass.*

There was a lone man in the distance. Did I know him?

THE THOUGHT SENT *me cascading into a new memory, as if I were being pulled backward through time....*

MY MOTHER WALKED, *in full goddess mode, into my quaint home on Earth, where I had lived with a lovely human family for the past seven years. She was dressed in a bright red dress that flowed out around her. Her pale blond hair was long and cascaded down her shoulders, her bright blue eyes full of motherly concern. I shared so many of my features with her, yet did not feel half as beautiful. "Jewel, my dear. You need to leave these people and this place," she said. "I fear that you are in danger."*

"Mother, Earth is my home now." I had moved away from the Olympus many years back, not by choice. What began as curiosity ended in a new life. Yet, as I grew older and looked back at my years growing up on the Olympus, I realized that I had easily grown tired of the rules, mundane duties, and

expectations that ruled me there. I had also gotten tired of the pettiness, the greed, and the constant backstabbing I witnessed at such a young age. I didn't want to live as a goddess, but as a simple person.

"You must come back. Your transition is almost complete, and your father and grandfather have something they wish to discuss with you." I hadn't told my mother that I had started my transition, but she knew anyway. She looked so sad. I loved my mother, and despite her moments of vanity and greed, I knew she loved me as well. My father, on the other hand, wasn't as warm and welcoming. He was a warrior and had little need for me.

My mother had been coined the goddess of love and beauty for a reason. She loved my father, but had been forced to wed another due to our one archaic tradition: arranged marriage. This was another reason I disliked the confines of my family. I knew what my father and grandfather wanted to discuss with me.

Before I left the Olympus my aunts, the fates, had shared with me the prophecy that was attached to me.

ONCE AGAIN, THAT thought sent me tumbling through time towards another memory. The memory of the day I'd learned that something awaited me in the future, though I didn't yet know what....

I WAS FIVE years old and standing in my aunts' wing of the family home on the Olympus. I would sometimes sneak into this wing and pester my aunts with a gazillion questions and tales from my silly imagination. Everyone else in our lovely family steered clear of Clotho, Lachesis and Atropos due to their *abilities to see beyond, but I loved them. They were strange, but I felt a connection to them. And I knew, despite their separation from the rest of the Olympians and their sometimes frightening and frustrating abilities, that they loved me too. Of course, they never said it, but every once in a while they would ruffle my hair, hug me tight, and even sneak a kiss before telling me I was bothering them and scampering off.*

My aunts found me standing in the hallway and Aunt Clotho looked at me strangely. Before I could ask what was wrong, she reached out and touched my hand. Her eyes clouded over, telling me she was in a trance. Then, almost simultaneously, my other seer aunts followed suit. Afterwards they all gave me pitiful, sad looks. I knew their vision had been about me.

I WAS HURTLING through time again, wondering where I would land this time....

I WAS BACK in the same hallway in my aunts' wing, but I was older this time, about eight. For the last few years I'd begged my aunts to tell me about the prophecy they'd seen, but each time they told me that knowing one's future was a burden in itself.

Then one day Aunt Clotho finally told me. She warned me that I was in danger on the Olympus. She told me that soon my soul would feel the pull of the place I truly belonged: Earth.

We were walking past one of the many mirrors when she turned towards it. I watched as her eyes glazed over. She gripped my arm tightly. Mumbling things I couldn't understand. Then she cried out, reaching out towards the mirror. There were tears streaming down her face and her grip tightened uncomfortably. I tried to pull my arm out of her grasp, but she held me tight, still muttering incoherently. Her eyes were completely white and she looked possessed.

"Aunt Clotho," I cried out to her, hoping to break the vision's hold on her. I'd seen my aunts in the throes of visions before. They were lost to everything around them until they passed. But this seemed different—my aunt seemed distressed, and the vision seemed to violently encompass her. I pulled at my arm again, jerking her roughly. She remained fastened to my arm.

"Aunt Clotho, please!" Her grip was beginning to hurt; her nails were digging into my skin. Blood started to trickle down as I jerked my arm harder. Then the white cloudiness passed from her eyes like a cloudy day meeting the sunshine.

She looked at me then, running her fingers along my cheek and my chin. "You, my child, have a very dangerous and troubled future." Tears streamed down her face as she realized the damage she had done to my arm. Then as if it was all too overwhelming to bear, she collapsed in front of me in the sea of fluffy tangerine organza that was her dress.

I waited there for her to regain consciousness. My aunt Atropos found us and brought water to her, waiting for her to share what she had seen. Aunt Lachesis was gone but would be back later.

When my aunt Clotho regained consciousness she looked at my damaged arm. I had cleaned it up, but the claw marks remained angry and red.

"Oh, Jewel!" she exclaimed, stricken with guilt as tears began to well up in her eyes. "I'm so sorry. I didn't mean to hurt you."

"I know." I smiled, hoping to reassure her. "It was an accident. Don't worry." My arm was stinging as I said it, but I knew the pain would soon ebb away.

"Clotho." My aunt Atropos spoke calmly as she awkwardly took her sister's hand and stroked her hair. Out of my aunts, she was the most reserved and the least used to showing affection. "What did you see, dear?"

Aunt Clotho looked at me then her sister before responding. "I saw Jewel's future."

"And?" I heard myself ask as I leaned closer in interest.

"It's all possibilities," she exclaimed with exasperation. "It's not set in stone." There was a desperate shrillness to her voice.

I looked at Aunt Atropos and saw that her eyes were sad and knowing, as if she had shared in her sister's vision or knew something I didn't.

"Please tell me." I knew the risks of knowing one's future, but I didn't care. I may have been young, but I would meet my fate with bravery and as much knowledge as possible so that I could change my path. Aunt Clotho must have seen my resolve because she and Aunt Atropos exchanged looks before Aunt Clotho nodded.

"Very well." She sighed the words out. We helped her stand as we walked over to sit together on the stark white couches. I watched once again as she and my aunt Atropos exchanged looks in some silent conversation. I waited patiently as they did this and tried to discern what I could from their facial expressions.

Aunt Clotho exhaled heavily as if she carried a heavy burden. "You, my dear child...." She paused, straightening her back and facing me squarely before continuing. Her voice before had been full of anguish, but now it took on an edge of finality. "Jewel, you will bring down the house of Zeus and herald in a new dawn for mankind."

I sat there, my mouth hanging open, shaking my head.

"You must be wrong!" I exclaimed. "I would never hurt my family!"

Aunt Atropos shook her head before speaking. "You never know how the future will change a person. The choices you make will determine your road, but once certain paths are chosen, there are things that cannot be changed."

"But you just said that it wasn't set in stone!" I demanded of Aunt Clotho, my voice rising in frustration.

"I did," she softly responded. "And it's true. But all your paths are leading in a single direction, at least in one area of your life." Her eyes glazed over again, but there was a smile on her face, so my future couldn't be that bad. "You will know great love. One that will span the hands of time."

Aunt Atropos took Aunt Clotho's hand, her eyes glazing over as well, as if she was viewing something unseen with her, yet Aunt Atropos did not share Aunt Clotho's smile. She snatched her hand out of Aunt Clotho's as their eyes cleared.

"It's not possible. It can't be." Aunt Atropos whispered the words, so I was barely able to hear them, but I leaned closer. She again looked at Aunt Clotho in an emotional silent exchange before they turned their sad eyes towards me.

"Why are you sad?" I asked.

"Because we are going to lose you," Aunt Atropos exclaimed, the tears flowing down her beautiful, perfect face.

"I'm going to die." I didn't ask but rather stated this observation.

"No," Aunt Clotho answered me. "I will tell you what I can about your future, but I can't tell you all. The rest you must discover on your own. Do you want to know?"

I had made my decision earlier but uncertainty took root in my mind. What if my future was so bad I really didn't want to know? I sat there contemplating, chewing on my lip before sighing loudly. "Yes, tell me."

"You will know a great love. One you cannot deny." She paused, moving to sit next to me, a flow of tangerine following behind her. Taking my hand, she continued, "You will first meet him in your dreams. Trust him, even when it seems you can't."

"Even when it feels you've been betrayed," Aunt Atropos added, glancing at me briefly before turning her eyes back to Aunt Clotho.

Aunt Clotho shushed her before continuing, "He is a great warrior, and he will protect you and teach you to protect yourself."

I made a face of disgust. Love was the furthest thing from my young mind. "Why?" I asked.

"The love you will have is a gift. One from our own ancient gods that was lost to us when we fell from their grace." She said this as she looked off into the distance, as if recalling something. She continued, "Before we found our own godly powers and immortality."

I glanced at Aunt Atropos, who nodded her head.

Aunt Clotho continued, more urgency in her voice. "You will both fight the gift at different times. You must not. Gru té mor is a truly unique gift," she added but then stopped, as if realizing she'd said too much.

"What is Gru té mor?" I asked, confused by a term I'd never heard before.

"It is the truest of true bonds between two people. It was lost to us before we came here, and very few among us experienced it before it was lost," Aunt Atropos explained, but she cast annoyed looks at her sister for putting her in this position.

"While many Olympians and Egyptonians are bonded with their spouses, the Gru té mor is a deeper, more intense bond. Only one person still alive has experienced it," Aunt Clotho explained despite the warning from Aunt Atropos. "It didn't end well."

"Why?" I asked.

"His beloved died. Now he is forced to live with the pain and grief of the loss forever, never to love another," Aunt Clotho sadly answered, tears springing to her eyes.

"So why then would I want this?" I asked again, not understanding how it was a gift.

"You will not be able to resist, and this man you meet will help shape your destiny. By the time you begin to dream of him, you will want the destiny that awaits you." Aunt Clotho wiped the tears away as she spoke, her voice breaking at the end.

"I suppose you must tell her the prophecy, Clotho," Aunt Atropos said with resignation.

Aunt Clotho looked me straight in the eyes and spoke, her voice clear and determined. "The first and only. An Olympian born to Earth shall usher in the beginning of the end of the reign of those deemed gods over humans. She will find love with a warrior of death, one who is forbidden to her. A love that is Gru té mor. Together they shall break down the barriers between the races and take down the ruling houses, heralding a new age—the age of mankind."

Aunt Clotho looked away then and spoke with less determination and more compassion in her voice. "You will suffer, Jewel. And the man who is your destiny will suffer more, but your sacrifices will, through the span of time, bless you in so many ways. Still, you will each deny the other—"

"Enough, Clotho, you say too much." Aunt Atropos rose,

looking pointedly at her.

She shrugged. "She will forget most of it."

I will not, *I said to myself.*

AND JUST LIKE *that, I was moving again, being pulled forward in time. This time the conversation I'd had with my mother flashed through my mind as I hurtled forward. "...your father and grandfather have something they wish to discuss with you," she said....*

"MOTHER, YOU KNOW *I cannot come back." I was standing before her again, firm in my resolve to stay with the humans. Most of the Olympians abhorred humanity, but for whatever reason, I found solace in their company. I felt more kinship with them than I did with my own family. My mother said it was because I was the only one among them born on this planet. I was, in all technicality, an Earthling. "This is necessary. I will not be a pawn in their game to try to control me." I jutted out my chin and crossed my arms to strengthen my resolve. I would not go back to that place, and I would not marry whoever they saw fit to match me with. Whether or not the imaginary man from the prophecy existed remained to be seen, but for now I was happy right where I was.*

"I knew you would say that. You get that stubbornness from your father." My mother sighed deeply and furrowed her brow. "I knew you would choose this route, so I've come to help you as far as I can. You must leave here. I found you easily. They will as well. You must go into hiding or they will try to harm you."

"Who will try to harm me?"

"Your aunts' foretelling has been discovered, and now my

father feels threatened. Grandfather or not, Zeus will destroy you in order to remain on the throne." My mother walked over to me and caressed my hair lovingly. Then with more conviction and urgency than I'd ever heard in her sweet voice, she said, "You need to leave as soon as possible."

And I did. I packed up what I could carry and took the little gold I had saved, and I took off. The family who I had grown to love over the last seven years begged me to stay, but I gifted them everything I had and tearfully walked away. As I began to plan my journey, I knew I needed to get as far away from my family as possible. I had to cross out of Olympian territory, something that was very much against the rules. I had to either go north or go west. So I threw a feather into the air and it floated to the west.

West it was, across the sea.

THE YANKING SENSATION *overtook me again, as I was pulled further through time, hurtling back towards the beach....*

AND THERE *I was, sitting on the edge of the Egyptonian border, contemplating. Yet, as I sat there in the sun with the foaming, salty waves moving ever closer to me, my mind calmed and I was able to pull myself up, preparing to cross into uncharted territory.*

Only, before I could take that monumental step, the lone man who had been in the distance appeared on the beach beside me. We spoke....

WAIT, I'D HAD *this vision before... I knew this man. Death. My destined love. But this vision was clearer somehow, every sense heightened, every emotion amplified....*

"ARE YOU GOING *to kill me?" Perhaps I had made a mistake. He was one of them. Was I going to die?*

But I could feel a pull towards him, like he had fastened an invisible rope to me.

I knew I should run, but I couldn't. My eyes were locked to his, and I couldn't pull myself out of their depths. There was something in his eyes that I'd seen before, having grown up with Eros and Aphrodite. It was passion, need, and pure lust.

"No, I think I'll do something better." Before I could mutter another word, he grabbed me and his mouth was on mine.

I WOKE UP then to find Anubis and Thoth looking at me quizzically. I felt a little dizzy, but other than that I felt whole. I seemed to still be myself rather than the mindless zombie I feared I would turn into. I turned towards Anubis after slowly pulling myself up. The dizziness was still there, but it was slowly subsiding.

As I looked over Anubis, I realized I couldn't stay quiet about what I'd seen anymore. I didn't want to.

"Why did you kiss me? We didn't even know each other. Not that I'm complaining—that was one hell of a kiss." I scooted my legs over the side of the machine, preparing to step down. I heard Anubis's deep chuckle as I debated whether I could manage to stand.

Anubis leaned in closer to me as I tried to compose my thoughts. The familiar, annoying pain sprang forth in my head, only this time it was only a small annoyance and it quickly disappeared, almost as if had never occurred. Thoth had been right. This was better.

I watched as something rose in Anubis's eyes; a blue fire

seemed to make his eyes glow with iridescence, something I'd seen a few times before.

"It might have been our first real kiss, but we'd met in our dreams many times before." He paused, his eyes moving over my face with hunger. "I kissed you because no matter how hard I tried to resist it, no matter how many times I told myself I could, it was impossible. When I saw you sitting there, looking longingly out at the sea and hiding your fear of stepping into my realm, I meant to comfort you. But instead my hunger for you took over."

I sat there in awe. I couldn't respond. What did this mean? He and I were... what? Lovers? My aunts had called it Gru té mor. I filed that away to think about later.

Thoth interrupted our moment and instructed in his straightforward tone, "I would wait a few moments before you try to stand. You need to regain your equilibrium." There was Thoth again, trying to tell me what to do, as always. This thought struck me as odd since I hadn't known him before today, at least not in this life.

"What else did you see?" Anubis spoke, breaking through my thoughts. He had moved to stand in front of me. He was so close I could smell him. He smelled so damn good—like sunshine and pure masculinity. I sighed and closed my eyes, thinking of what I'd just experienced in the visions.

"My mother is Aphrodite and my father is Ares—which I already knew, but now I kind of know my mother firsthand. She loved me, but it seems like my father was sort of indifferent to me. My grandfather is Zeus and he wanted me either wed to someone of his choosing or dead. He was fearful of my aunts' prophecy—the one that was linked to me." I paused then, running through the newly acquired memories. "I had to hide. I decided to cross a border into some other territory. I'm not entirely sure why it was such a big deal. And then I met someone on the beach. A man." I stopped again, looking into Anubis's deep, warm chocolate eyes. "I saw you." I touched my lips then, thinking back to the kiss.

"And what did I do?" Anubis peered closely at me, waiting for something.

"You kissed me."

He ignored that, much to my frustration. I wanted more of an explanation. "Anything else?" I couldn't think of anything else, but it appeared that Anubis was waiting for me to say something important. I thought hard, pulling out as much information as I could muster. Maybe there was something hidden in my subconscious.

I closed my eyes, breathed deeply and searched. There was something there. Something that was poking at the outer edges of my mind. Before I knew it, the memory invaded me. I knew what he was looking for.

"You… you pulled me over the borderline as you kissed me. I was contemplating turning around and leaving, but you showed up. And the prophecy began. Didn't it?" This was all unreal. No matter how many times they explained it to me, I still didn't understand how this was all possible. I didn't understand how I could be this person, this alien goddess from an ancient world. Which brought a question to my attention: How old were Thoth and Anubis? They looked amazing. Would I stop aging as well?

"Indeed you will, little bird." Thoth smiled, but his smile was sad, as if it pained him to admit this.

Stay out of my head! I yelled inside my mind to make sure he truly heard it.

"I apologize. Sometimes I forget, and you are a very loud broadcaster." He then switched back to his matter-of-fact tone and mannerisms as he put away the equipment from the machine I'd just been on.

"What happens now?" I looked at Anubis and was not reassured by the expression on his face. It was sad, yet hopeful. His warm brown eyes were full of kindness. I also knew for some reason that his eyes could easily look like death was coming for you. A shiver ran up my spine and I shook it off. If Thoth heard my thoughts he didn't comment.

Anubis said, "Now you will begin to remember in a safer manner. Every day, something will come back to you. With maybe a mild twinge of a headache, but nothing so intense it will overwhelm you again. At least it shouldn't in theory." He stopped, glancing briefly at Thoth, who was still preoccupied with his duties. "The alternative would be, we believe, that your memories will all come crashing down upon you once you've almost fully transitioned. This would be too much for you."

I like how he decided for me, I thought sarcastically. Everyone in my whole existence had decided things for me. I needed to speak to my father... the one in this time, Robert.

"I'm ready to go home." It wasn't a question. It was more a demand. I was done with this for the day. I wanted to go home and process what had happened.

Thoth finished busying himself and turned back towards us. "That is fine, but we will need to continue these treatments once a week." He was still in monotone, matter-of-fact Thoth mode.

I nodded my head, ready to leave. I needed to be alone. I wanted to just go home. Anubis grabbed my hand, creating his portal of darkness in a corner and pulling us through the black depths once again. I noticed this time that the ride was much easier than in previous trips.

We ended up in my bedroom and he bid me farewell, kissing my hand before jumping back through his portal.

CHAPTER ELEVEN

Anubis

I STEPPED BACK THROUGH the portal, my mind on Jewel. She was beginning to piece things together, but it was difficult to stand back and wait for her to fully remember and for her to find her way back to me. I had all confidence that she would. We were meant for each other, but there was now a small part of me that knew it was possible she could choose another path. Even those mistakenly pegged as gods were capable of free will. I walked through the underground house I shared with Thoth, back to his lab, where I knew he would be going through the data he'd retrieved from Jewel today. He didn't respond when I entered, but I knew he was aware of my presence.

"Anything to help us?" I pulled Thoth from his deep thoughts, hoping he could find some answer to a mystery we were walking into blind.

"Yes, yes. Many new developments." He was responding

absently, still perusing the data.

"Care to share?"

It was then that Thoth stopped and addressed me directly; he did so begrudgingly, as he hated to be interrupted while studying something. "She is transitioning quickly. Faster than anyone ever has before." He seemed to think this would satisfy me and turned to continue his work.

"We already knew this. What else?" I insisted. Refusing to be brushed off, I walked over to study the data with him. "Show me everything."

"Since she was almost fully complete in her activation when they sent her here, her cells are moving rapidly through the transition process. It could potentially be very damaging for her, as we suspected. She will need to continue coming here, or in a month's time she will have come into the full spectrum of the transition. It will be too much for her mind and her body to handle." Thoth pulled up the data as he spoke, pointing to different lines on the graphs, expecting it to make sense to me.

"What can we do to prevent it, other than slowing her down and exposing her to small bits and pieces of her memories at a time?"

"We cannot do anything besides what we are doing now." Thoth sighed, rubbing his hands over his face. Jewel had once meant almost as much to Thoth as she did to me, only in a different context. Jewel had understood Thoth on a level that no one else could.

"She's different now." I paused, looking for any signs of affirmation from Thoth. "She's still adventurous, but she seems…"

"She seems happy, even carefree, had we not been forcing

her into a machine. I'd also suspect she is even fiercer than she was before," Thoth finished for me, smiling to himself as he thought back to our Jewel.

"I was worried about how her new life would change her, if she would be the same person. If she would still be the same Jewel we know." I stopped abruptly, realizing my fears were spilling out. I wasn't sure I wanted to voice them all.

"She is different." Thoth walked over and placed his tan hand on my shoulder. "Yet, she is very much still the same. Once she begins to transition fully, she will be two halves made whole. She will still have her experiences from this life, but she'll also remember who she was before." He patted me reassuringly, and I could tell he was doing it just as much for himself as for me. All these years of waiting, planning, preparing for the day she would return. Then once she did, we'd had to wait even longer. Now the day was near, and the fear of what might or might not happen scared me even more than the fear of never seeing her again that would take hold of me every few hundred years. Thoth always brought me out of it. I owed him so much.

"I pray, indeed, that you're correct." I was ready for the pain and suffering to end. Jewel was my love, my wife, my soul, but even more importantly we were bonded together. Being bonded was not something to be taken lightly; being away from each other for too long caused great pain, and our souls needed one another as if we were what sustained each other's lives. As a man dying of dehydration needing water, I had suffered through the years without her. Now I felt deprived and desperate to be near her. Suddenly I had the urge to go back and check on her again.

"Leave her be, friend. Give her time to adjust. She will

dream tonight, and every day she will be one day closer to re-membering. Just a little more time now." Thoth usually tried not to read my thoughts, and I was capable of blocking him, but in that moment I didn't mind the intrusion because he was right; I needed to continue to wait or I might ruin every-thing I had worked so hard towards. "Go get some rest. Even we proclaimed gods need sleep."

"You're right. I'll leave her alone tonight and try to rest." With that, I lumbered off to my lair to try to rest some before pursuing Jewel again tomorrow.

Jewel

I WANTED TO be mad at Anubis, my father, my real parents, but I wasn't. Instead I squeezed my hands tight over this new knowledge and then I let it all go. There wasn't anything I could do about my past. It made me happy that I finally knew something of my mother. I'd never had a mother in this life. I wondered if she missed me. Obviously Anubis missed me and we had some sort of relationship. Thinking of Anubis made me realize I missed him as well, and not in a way that was simple to explain. It was like I physically missed him. My body was a traitor!

I glanced at the clock, realizing it was still pretty early, so I decided to go downstairs and see my friends. When I left the apartment in our wing of the house and headed down, I could hear laughter from the living area. In most houses you'd call it a living room, but this was much larger. It was made to feel homey, with a large fireplace and several smaller, more intimate areas for people to lounge.

In the far-right corner of the room was a small couch and loveseat arrangement with end tables and a coffee table and bookshelf not far off. The couch was maroon and made of microfiber with gold lined pillows that were soft to the touch, like fur. The coffee and end tables were made of black and white marble with cast iron legs and a shelf. This corner of the room was Teddy's favorite spot near the warm fire. Yet, today Teddy wasn't there, Andrew and his group of friends were.

Gale and Jeff were snuggled together on the loveseat. I was surprised no one had told them to separate, but then they had their powers now. Evols were treated like adults as soon as they went through the process of acquiring their abilities. That rule just didn't apply to me, because I'd had my abilities since I was a child and I was basically only borrowing them.

On the couch sat Monica and Andrew. She was rather close to him, staring daggers up at me because of my intrusion. Andrew tried to move away from her as soon as he saw me.

"Jewel, come sit with us!" He stood and motioned for me to sit.

No thanks, buddy. Three's a crowd, I thought to myself.

"No, thank you. I'm looking for Teddy. Have you seen him?" I looked around the room, trying to see if I could spot him, but I didn't see him anywhere.

I noticed Andrew's face fall. I knew it was unfair to do this to him—to keep stringing him along. I wanted a normal life and Andrew could be that normal; well, normal by my terms. I wanted to just jump in and do it. Tell Anubis I wasn't ready for all this and just be Andrew's girlfriend, have a semi-normal experience. But I was far from normal, even by Evolved standards.

"I haven't seen him all day." Andrew sat back down on the couch, still putting distance between him and Monica. It occurred to me then that Andrew's control lately had been phenomenal. It seemed odd to me, since not but a few days ago he'd been confined downstairs. Usually people took longer to gain control. Thinking of the downstairs reminded me that Teddy had been working there. Maybe he was still there. I decided to go check on him and a few of the Evols.

"Okay, well thanks, guys. I'm going to go find him."

Monica had a victory smile on her face, and I felt the urge to stay just to drive her crazy. Instead I walked to the hidden elevator and waited patiently to reach the basement. The corridors were long and had UVA lights across the top. We'd put them in years ago to improve the productivity of the staff, who were low on Vitamin D levels due to low exposure to sunlight from working deep in a mountain. It helped somewhat.

While searching the many different basement rooms for Teddy, I thought back to Thoth and his lab. It was similar in nature to the labs here, but his lab was one massive room. Here we had individual areas for different things.

Thoth seemed so familiar to me. He reminded me of someone. *Probably him,* I thought.

At the end of the long, bright corridor I turned right. I always felt the Evols' abilities when I was on the complex, but the power here coursed through me unchecked. Normally by the time they were allowed to go to the surface, Evols were able to rein in their abilities. I continued down the hall to a massive room that held a large tank; it was almost like an oversized pool. A few of our inhabitants had manifested water abilities. They were my favorite to borrow from, only I couldn't venture far from them when borrowing their powers. My abilities had a close-proximity flaw.

I loved water abilities because the water called to me. I loved being near it. Although my father never took us anywhere, I had dreams of the sea. The sound, the salt, the feel of the warm frothy water around my feet as it crashed into the shore, and the sand under my toes. I always suspected this was why I loved the waterfall and quarry so much. It was as close a connection to the sea as I could get. When I was in the water it soothed me. All the cars in the world couldn't compare to diving down deep and gliding through the water.

I could hear the water lapping against the side of the tank. Someone with water abilities must have traveled to the compound or one of the younger students must have manifested an ability I didn't yet know about. I was curious. As I walked into the room, I saw that there was someone in the tank, swimming very fast. I moved closer, trying to make out who it was, but they were so fast it was hard to catch a glimpse through the thick aquarium glass. Then, all of a sudden, the whirlwind stopped right in front of me.

And there, in swim trunks, was Teddy.

He was so shocked to see me, he just stayed in place, staring. I think he even mouthed my name since little bubbles floated up to the surface from his mouth. As he swam up to the top of the tank, I noticed the gills on his side near his ribs.

This reminded me of a conversation we'd had a few years ago when Teddy was patiently waiting to go through the transition. He'd asked me, not knowing that I already had a gift, what power I wanted. I remember sitting there contemplating what I loved and what I longed for. I loved my little secret hidden lake. I longed to swim in the ocean and bask on the beach as the sun beat down on me. So I told Teddy that I wanted to be a mermaid. He'd laughed and said it was perfect for me.

And here, sputtering to the surface of the tank, was my best friend, a bona fide mermaid without fins… or did he have fins? I looked, and his feet were indeed webbed.

"Jewel, what are you doing here?" He seemed shocked and a bit embarrassed. It occurred to me that he might have lied to me about working down here to hide that he'd evolved before me. It was sweet that he was sparing my feelings. I couldn't be mad at him, since I'd done the same thing. It seemed I was hiding so much from people. I couldn't judge.

"Teddy! You evolved. That is so amazing! I'm excited for you." I really was happy for him. I'd felt awful keeping him in the dark for so long. In our community everyone was used to keeping things to themselves and treading carefully. Still, I was always worried that one day someone would let it slip to Teddy how I'd helped them learn to control their abilities. I wanted him to find out from me first. Since he'd started working down here, I knew I'd have to tell him soon, but I'd never imagined it playing out this way.

"Yeah, I did," he admitted, looking up over the top of the tank at me sheepishly. "Give me a sec to come out and I'll explain everything." He swam quickly over to the far side of the room where the tank was set up like a swimming pool that had a staircase leading down to the glass observational part of the tank. I stood there waiting for him. I couldn't believe I hadn't realized he was transitioning earlier. Usually it was a longer process, and I'd notice the signs of the transition early on. This made me realize that, with everything going on in my life, I'd lost sight of the people who had always been there for me.

"Let me look at you!" As he approached, I felt it. The power cascaded off him. I was also able to determine the strength of his powers. He was easily a level six. We measured the strength of our powers on a scale from one to ten, ten being highest. Normally when someone first transitioned the level was inaccurate, though. Some would transition and their strength level would be highest in the first week, only to gradually lower. Others would grow stronger as they learned control. Most Evols remained at a level that was almost always under five.

"What do you think?" He was excited, still breathing heavily from his swim.

"I think it's amazing. I'm truly happy for you." I meant it.

"You aren't mad? It just happened. I swear I didn't keep it from you. I'm a little shocked I ended up manifesting an underwater ability, but it's pretty cool." His excitement was evident as he stood there dripping in his orange and yellow swim trunks.

I sighed; it was time to tell him. "Teddy, I've something to confess to you."

"What's wrong? You are mad, aren't you?" I watched as his gills slowly disappeared as he dried.

"No, I'm not mad. I already have an ability. I've had it for a very long time. I'm sorry for keeping the secret from you." It felt as if a weight was lifting from my shoulders, but I didn't want him to be mad at me either. "You aren't mad at me, are you?"

"I know."

"What do you mean, you know?"

"I suspected when you started spending every day helping in the basement. You were just sparing my feelings." I'd thought he was in the dark this whole time, but he knew me better than I thought. He walked over and placed his arm around my shoulder. "But I am curious, what are you? It's obvious I'm an aquatic. So how about you?"

I contemplated my answer for a few long seconds. How should I respond? Should I casually mention that I was an alien? A goddess? A semi-reincarnation who'd been sent through time and had my life rewound?

"I'm complicated." It was all I could muster in that moment. But then I added, "I'm a borrower who has the ability to pull other Evols' powers into myself and use them." I left out all the other stuff.

"That settles it, then. You need to come swim with me." He grabbed my hand and pulled me towards the tank.

I glanced around as if I were expecting someone to come barging into the room at any moment, but we were completely alone. Aquatics normally didn't need a babysitter; after their first few tests they were left to their own devices. It was apparent that Teddy had reached that stage of his evolution.

"I don't have anything to wear."

"Don't play with me, Jewel. You know as well as I do they have extra suits in the locker room. Throw one on and hop in." He was right. As a matter of fact, I had my own suit waiting for me. It was purple and lined with silver; the sides were cut out so that the material covered only my stomach. I thought it was pretty, and I'd snuck it past my dad. It made me feel like a fish, odd as that was—free to swim in the sea. And it also made me feel just a little bit daring.

"Okay you're on, but don't cry like a baby when I beat you in the tank."

We spent the rest of the evening laughing and swimming. I drew on his power and showed him the extent of his abilities. Which had him asking me more about mine. I explained as best I could, but I knew I was still holding back. And then, when we decided to take a break and sit on the side of the far end of the tank near the locker room, he asked about one of those complications.

"That guy... the one who walked through the house with you the other day. Who is he? I mean, who is he really?" He was trying to seem like he didn't care, but the fact that he was trying so hard was evident. He leaned closer to me as he dangled his newly webbed feet next to mine in the water. I focused on the webs between his toes. They reminded me of something. Something that was nagging at the back of my mind. I shook it off and remembered Teddy's question.

"His name is Anubis. He's training me." I was trying to avoid any further questions. I had a pretty good idea of who he really was—and not just that he was an ancient god from an even more ancient alien race. I was starting to realize who he was to me, or had been to me at one point. I couldn't deny the pull I felt towards him, the longing that swept over me in his presence, but I still wasn't sure that was what I wanted.

"What's he training you in? And he is huge. He has to be almost seven feet tall." I realized then that Teddy must feel threatened because of the amount of time I'd spent with Anubis. He needed reassurance of our friendship.

"He is pretty tall, but so am I. He's only training me for right now; beyond that, I'm not sure." I leaned into his shoulder and bumped him playfully. His brown hair was slicked back from the water. I'd noticed he was letting it grow out, but it had grown exponentially recently. It was curling around the back of his ears. There was even a five o'clock shadow starting on his chin. My best friend had turned into a very powerful man overnight.

"He looks dangerous, Jewel. I don't trust him." He turned towards me to emphasize his point. "He'd better not hurt you. If he does, you tell me, okay?"

"He isn't going to hurt me, Teddy." I wasn't sure if I was telling the truth, but I suspected that if either of us were going to hurt the other it would be me hurting him.

Teddy looked at me with his big brown eyes and I realized his eyes were changing too. It wasn't unheard of. The transition could change people in many different ways to suit their needs. His eyes now had flecks of green and blue in them, as if they were turning the color of the sea.

THE SEA. *It's constantly moving and changing. It is the most beautiful and dangerous of places. It's full of life, it's deep, and it's constantly changing. Just like me, it's full of adventure. I love the sea more than life. I need it like I need to live. It is I and I am the sea.*

THE THOUGHTS HUMMED through my mind like a monologue. Where had I heard that? I'd never been to the ocean. I'd begged my father many times to take me, but he always had an excuse as to why we couldn't go. I sighed, realizing then that my stomach was growling dangerously loudly, and as if in response, Teddy's also growled. We laughed, pulling our legs out of the water to head over to the towel cabinet.

"What time is it?" I asked Teddy. I'd given up on trying to

keep track of the days of the week, and now the time seemed to evade me as well.

"It's about dinnertime. Let's get dressed and we'll go upstairs," Teddy quickly responded as he toweled off, throwing the towel into the laundry pile afterward. I did the same, heading towards the locker room to change. Teddy just threw on a shirt that lay on the side of the patio as I disappeared to put my clothes back on.

A few minutes later we were headed towards the elevator to go upstairs. The rooms and corridors were empty; the staff had gone home for the day. The skeleton night crew was probably just coming in. I thought this moment would be the best time to make Teddy understand why I'd kept my secret from him.

"Teddy, listen, I'm truly sorry I didn't tell you about my ability. I know you said you forgive me, but my life is complicated beyond anything I can explain." I grabbed his arm, stopping him in front of the elevator.

"I get it. It's okay. I understand why you did it. Also, I know there's something more to you than there is to the rest of us. I heard them talking about you. I didn't believe it at first, but then I thought about everything and realized it made sense somewhat. I'm still trying to comprehend some of the conversation." Teddy had an odd look in his eyes. Almost like admiration beyond anything I deserved in that moment.

"What do you mean?" It seemed that everyone knew more about me than I did.

"Okay, don't let it go to your head, but I heard you're some sort of messiah or something." Teddy smiled, but I wasn't sure if he was serious or teasing.

"Messiah?" I snorted. Me, a messiah. Yeah, right. "I am

not a messiah. Who did you hear this from?" I couldn't even figure out my life, and I could be a pretty big asshole at times. Messiahs walked on water and stuff like that.

"Hey, don't kill the messenger. Anyway, honestly I didn't understand all of it." He paused, looking up towards the ceiling as if he was trying to remember everything he'd heard. "Your dad was with some people in a meeting room. I couldn't see them, but I was hiding behind the door listening. He said you were close to the end of your transition. A lady asked if you knew who you were yet and then asked something about death meeting you." He stopped then, looking at me inquisitively, as if he was waiting for me to answer that question. I didn't and I wasn't going to. So he continued, "He told her yes, you knew some of your history but not all of it. But he didn't comment on the death thingy. Are you dying?"

"No, I'm not dying. I don't know what he was talking about," I lied again, feeling guilty. We stepped into the elevator.

"She said something about you being the humans' salvation and that with you everything would change. After that, he closed the door—I think he might have known I was there." He watched me carefully, trying to gauge my reaction.

I wasn't surprised. I'd learned that they had high expectations of me, but I knew I was just going to let them down. No use in buying into the other crap, then.

The elevator opened and we headed towards the dining area. We sat at the back of the room since the rest of the tables were full. I quickly ate and Teddy scarfed his food down as well. I felt famished all the time lately. As I finished the simple meal of pot roast, vegetables and French bread, I bid Teddy good night. I looked around for my father, but he wasn't in the dining hall tonight, so I quickly left before I had to watch Teddy lay into the dessert.

I climbed the stairs, keeping an eye out for anyone that might stop me—meaning Andrew. I didn't want to deal with that mess right now, but luckily I was clear to go. I sprinted to our apartment and had almost jetted into my room when my father's voice stopped me.

"Jewel."

I stopped and turned. "Yes, Father."

He was standing there in one of his suits. He wore those when he had business to attend to, which reminded me of what Teddy had told me earlier. "How was your day?"

"It was fun. I spent a lot of it with Anubis, and then I hung out with Teddy in the tank downstairs. I found out he evolved. It's amazing—he's a level six at least!" My words came out fast. Although I was dead tired, I felt newly energized by the memory of Teddy and his newfound abilities.

"Okay. What did you learn about yourself today? I mean, learn about your past?"

I had, for a moment, forgotten about the events from earlier. The memories that had bounced around in the recesses of my mind now came to the surface, but I wasn't sure if I was ready to share with him yet. Something told me to wait. I needed to know more about this other me and to figure out who I could trust. Well, I trusted my father, but after what Teddy told me, I wasn't sure how much he needed to know yet.

"Nothing new, just how to fight dirty." I winked as I moved closer to him. I gave him a hug, hoping he would drop the subject, and turned to go towards my room. I heard him sigh deeply behind me.

"Goodnight, bunny. Sleep well." I turned towards him, noting that he looked worn down. I smiled, hoping to reassure him.

"Good night, Dad." He'd never asked me to call him dad. In fact, when I was very young I would call him Robert. But as I grew I started to use this term of endearment with him. It made sense—he was the only father I knew, and he'd been a good one.

I walked towards my room, wondering what Anubis was doing right now. No matter how hard I tried, that sexy hunk of a man wasn't far from my thoughts.

I quickly changed into my nightclothes. It was cool outside, but the room felt like a furnace to me, so I put on shorts and a tank and slid under the covers, only to throw them off realizing I was hot. I tossed and turned, trying hard to sleep, but my mind was on everything that had happened today. I had a mother. One who, at one point in time, cared about me.

I thought about Anubis and the times his hands had brushed against my body while we were training. It felt like the heat was increasing even more in the room as I flushed at the memory. It felt right to be touched by him. I tried desperately to forget about the memory of meeting him and what his kisses felt like. My traitorous body wanted him here with me. I felt so connected to him. It was as if I'd always had this feeling of something missing, and now that I'd been around him I'd found the puzzle piece that finally fit.

I knew I needed to let fate take control and to stop fighting the emotions that kept nagging at me, but I just couldn't let go of the desire to be free to choose my own path. I thought back to the new color of Teddy's eyes; they reminded me of the ocean, not that I'd ever seen it in this life. Yet, I imagined it to be amazing in so many ways and, best of all, free and ever changing. I longed for that in my life now.

It was with that thought that I finally fell asleep.

I WAS RACING around a corner as fast I could go. The hallway I was in was bright. I needed to see my aunts. I had been on the observatory deck and there, far below in the distance, was the vast sea. I wanted to know what it was like, the ocean. It seemed so big and blue. It was beautiful, and I wanted so badly to go see it in person. Every once in a while as we hovered, there would be a ship with tall sails that would slowly trudge across the crashing waves or a whale that would pop up and splash down onto the surface as ocean water sprayed out around it. I wanted to go feel the water and see the creatures that lived there. I knew from my lessons it was full of many different species, each one more unique than the last. I wanted to know about the way it smelled, the salt it held and how these creatures could live in such salty waters. I wanted to know what it felt like to swim in its depths. My aunts usually told me anything I wanted to know, unlike the other people on the Olympus.

My aunt Lachesis was in the apartment, sitting there reading. I ran up to her, excited. "Aunt Lachesis, I saw it again. It was in the distance, but it was there." I'd waited patiently to meet my uncle and ask him about the sea, but I never had. He never came to the Olympus.

"You saw what, dear?" But before I even answered, she continued, "Ah, yes. You saw the ocean." She leaned over and ruffled my hair affectionately. "It's something, isn't it?"

"It looks AMAZING! I want to go!" I sat there next to her, contemplating whom I could get to take me. I was still only

eight in human years, and we weren't allowed—or at least, I wasn't allowed—to go to the surface until I was older. Everyone else on the ship was far older than me. There had been no other children for me to play with growing up. Once my mother had taken me to play with a group of human children. It was the best time of my life. I'd since driven her crazy, asking to go back. That was a few years ago.

"Do you think I'll get to go?" I was sure she knew the answer, since she was able to predict possibilities in the future.

"You'll go." She didn't look up from the tablet in her hand that she'd gone back to focusing on.

"When?" I spoke with exasperation and some whininess. I hated when my aunts spoke in riddles. It drove the other Olympians even crazier, to the point where they stayed away from my aunts, but I loved them. Right next to my mom, they were the best. Everyone else treated me like a pariah, even some of my more than a dozen siblings, many of whom I hadn't even met but maybe once.

"You will go when you decide to go," she said absentmindedly, still concentrating on what was in front of her.

I looked around the apartment she shared with her sisters. They kept it bright and airy. There were lots of windows and the space was large. Each of my aunts had her own separate compartment that was conjoined with a shared living space. The apartment was decorated with white furnishings and some gold accents. Wildflowers sat in a white vase, and they were full of color against the stark whiteness of the furniture. My aunts, although not vain, liked mirrors, and there were various sizes, styles, and shapes of gold-framed mirrors hung all around the room. To the right of the room was a large gold bowl. I'd seen them huddled around it, staring into it and whispering to each other many times. The gold and the colorful bouquet were really the only splashes of color in the living space.

Even my beautiful Aunt Lachesis, who looked exactly like her two sisters, was dressed in a white flowing gown. Her porcelain skin was devoid of any imperfections, and the long dark hair flowing down her slender neck was pulled to the side so as not to get in her way. Her nose was long and straight with a slight upturn, and her eyes were big and blue framed in dark eyelashes. All three of my aunts were beautiful. It was hard to tell them apart. Only one who knew them well or spent time with them could find the differences. It was their mannerisms that gave them away. Aunt Lachesis, who sat in front of me, was quiet and sweet. She was graceful in her movements, poised, and thoughtful in her actions. Aunt Clotho was energetic and full of life and all about action. She was adventurous. She walked into a room and commanded its attention. She was the most liked out of the three because she was the most approachable. Aunt Atropos, on the other hand, was the complete opposite—she was slow in her reactions, melancholy, and very careful, almost predictable. She was never in a hurry for anything. Because my aunts were so different, they would have fights all the time. When they were in an epic battle, the whole of the Olympus knew about it.

"I want to go to the ocean now." I kind of wished that Aunt Clotho were here. She would tell me to just go and take her with me, even though she wouldn't really mean it. The fate sisters weren't allowed anywhere, it seemed. They were crucial to the mission. Blah, blah, blah. Or something like that. It was grown up talk, and I didn't care much about it.

"You're right. You should go."

Was I talking to Aunt Lachesis? Maybe I'd missed

something. Maybe this was Aunt Clotho and she was playing a trick on me. Yet, she continued to sit there poised and perfect. Aunt Clotho would be flying around the room like a whirlwind, and Aunt Atropos would be off complaining about some serious offense to her person.

"Really?" I sat there rubbing my hands together, thinking about how I would do it, when Aunt Clotho and Aunt Atropos did indeed join us. They had simultaneously left their separate bedrooms, as if pulled towards us at the same time.

"What is it she wants to do?" asked Aunt Clotho.

"She wants to go to the surface to see the ocean." It was Aunt Atropos who answered. She hadn't even been part of our conversation, but she did things like that from time to time. She knew what was going to happen or what you were going to say before you did.

Finally Aunt Lachesis looked up from her tablet and spoke to her sisters. "Yes, she wants to leave the Olympus. It's that time." They shared some cryptic look between them. I hated when they did that. I never knew what it was about.

"Do you think someone will take me?" I asked, but I knew it wouldn't happen, no matter how much I begged.

"No." They said it in unison. Well, there went that hope.

"You will go on your own," Aunt Atropos said. I turned, giving her an incredulous look. Going to the surface by myself would more than likely get me in a ton of trouble.

My aunts all stood together then and walked hand-in-hand towards the gold bowl they tended to stare into. Some more color had been added to the room with my Aunt Clotho's flowing red dress, but that seemed to be counterbalanced by Aunt Atropos's black pants outfit. They stood together around the bowl, holding hands and staring. Soon they looked at me with the creepy white eyes thing they did and repeated in mono-toned unison:

"She will go to the surface. She will find the sea king. She will fall in love with the World. She will fall in love with its creatures. She will long to stay with the humans. She will find death, and she will love it. It is time."

I felt shivers run up my back. Aunt Lachesis must have realized how unsettled I felt because she broke away from her sisters.

"My child, my beautiful Jewel, as foreboding as that sound-ed, I promise you it isn't as it seems. You will have a happy end-ing, only it will take a very long time for you to get there. I know we've spoken to you of suffering in the past, but you mustn't fear what is to come but embrace it." She walked over to me and knelt down a bit. She then took my face in her hands and kissed me gently. "If I'd ever had a child, I would have wanted her to be you." Tears fell from her eyes as she hugged me.

"That goes for me as well." My aunt Clotho had walked over and wrapped me in another tearful hug. "Always remem-ber to listen to your heart and be adventurous; love your life, and love with everything you have. Don't give in to your fear," she whispered in my ear as she held me tight.

I wasn't expecting yet another slightly more awkward hug from Aunt Atropos. She'd always been more reserved in her af-fections. Yet, here she was, holding me tightly to her. She pulled back from the hug and said to me, "You will remember this one day, and I want you to know that it's okay to choose your own path. You do not have to be tied to fate. You are special. But the future you needs to know that what you desire most will be always in your thoughts and in your heart. So listen."

My aunts acted as if they would never see me again. Like

I would leave the Olympus and never return. I just planned to go down and take a quick dip in the water and head back. I'd borrow Hermes' pilot pod and head down to the surface, and then enjoy the beautiful beach and the sea and be back in no time at all.

That was indeed the last time I ever saw my aunts.

CHAPTER TWELVE

Jewel

THE SOUND OF the alarm woke me. I felt more rested than I had in a long time. I stretched and rushed through my morning, ready to go back to school. I realized as I walked downstairs that I would be attending school on my own. Teddy would finish his schooling online with a private tutor with the rest of the Evols, and I would be the last man standing, so to speak. The students would whisper behind my back about yet another one of us seamlessly disappearing. It was ridiculous because, from time to time, my friends still went out in public. There had even been times when they'd attended school functions with me and Teddy. As a matter of fact, the back-to-school dance was coming up soon and Jeff and Gale had requested I buy them tickets. Andrew would also attend, as I'd accepted his invitation previously. I hated dances, though—all the shuffling and pretending to dance. It seemed like a stupid activity, but I couldn't pass up an opportunity to rub the fact that I had a super-hot date in the bitchy girls' faces—and Andrew was indeed that. I could just imagine if I showed up with Anubis; they would shit themselves with envy. Anubis was drool-worthy sexy, to the zillionth degree of sexiness. Thinking about Anubis made me want him here. I fought that urge and pushed it down. I wasn't sure what I wanted anymore.

Downstairs I found Andrew sitting in the living area, obviously waiting on me. I realized I wasn't really happy to see him as I should have been. He was hot, sweet, and he wanted me to be his. What more could a girl want? *I just need to get to know him better,* I told myself.

"Hey." He stood there in distressed jeans and a blue plaid shirt that conformed to his body perfectly, showing off sculpted muscles. He had a strong jawline and jet-black hair that was cut short on the sides but longer on top. It was messy but still made him look like the heartthrob he was.

"Good morning, beautiful." Andrew walked slowly over to me, trying to gauge my emotions this morning. I watched as his eyes swept over me and he gave me an appreciative look. I should have felt special and cherished with such a look. Instead I felt a bit annoyed.

"Thank you. Why are you waiting by the front door?" I stood there an arms-reach from him, waiting on his answer. I knew I sounded a bit bitchy, but I was upset with the reality that Teddy wouldn't be joining me on my way to school. I was on my own.

Andrew tried to hide the hurt my words caused. I felt guilty for my callous words and tried to soften my expression, realizing how I sounded in that moment. Still, I stood there waiting on his answer, my stance more relaxed than before.

"I was waiting to escort you to the bus. I didn't want you to go on your own. You know, with Teddy gone." He looked suddenly nervous. Like one of the boys at school who'd just asked the girl of his dreams out on a date and was afraid that she would reject him. And here I was rejecting him. Asshole Jewel had made an appearance, and I felt like a piece of crap.

"I'm sorry, Andrew. I seem to be apologizing a bunch lately. You can walk with me." I almost added, *not because I need you to,* but realized that would just be another jerk comment and I should keep it to myself. Andrew's stance relaxed and he moved closer to me. I noticed the suit that contained his powers poking out from under the plaid he wore. Yet, I still felt the heat emanating off him. It was as if he had a bad fever, but he didn't look a bit flushed. I reached out, worried, and touched him. He was hot to the touch. He quickly realized what I was doing and pulled his arm back out of my reach.

"I'm fine, just a little heat is all," he said, trying to brush it off.

I stood there concerned, debating if this was something I needed to pursue. If he was losing control again, he would need to go back downstairs. Andrew wasn't extremely powerful. He was maybe a three on the scale, but his type of power made him dangerous. He was a walking volcano.

"Andrew." My voice had softened. I was concerned and I wanted him to know it. "If you need help, you need to tell me. I'll stay home today and I can help you if you need it." I meant it. I put his feelings for me and my confusion aside in that moment. I would drop everything to see that he was okay.

"No, I'm fine, and I'm here to save you for once, not the other way around." I realized Andrew was embarrassed, and he was trying to win me over as a normal teenage boy would. I forgot how young he was sometimes lately. He looked like a full-grown man standing in front of me, but in reality he was just a boy.

"You know, I'm sorry. I had a rough night of sleep and may have woken up on the wrong side of the bed. I would very much appreciate it if you would accompany me to the bus stop." I wondered if the heat was tied into his emotions because I reached out and tested his power and realized he was reining it in now that I'd agreed to have him come along. This could be bad. What if he was really rejected? Would he lose control? I pushed that thought away to think on later.

"Great, the van is outside waiting." He grabbed my hand but quickly let go.

I busied myself by braiding my hair to the side as we waited for the driver to pull up and motion for us to hop in. The trip was five miles through the property, around twists and turns through the wooded aspens and the mountains, and it ended at a gate. A bench next to the road marked our stop. The trees had begun to change colors already, marking the turn of seasons. The chill was getting a bit nippy, a fact that was much more pronounced at such a high altitude. Golden yellows and orange splashes of leaves clung to the trees before fluttering to the ground. Scattered among the deciduous trees were evergreens that stayed a deep hunter green among all the bright, lovely fall colors. I loved fall almost as much as I loved the warm ocean on a summer's day.

I walked over to the bench, Andrew by my side, as I wondered where that last thought had come from. I'd never been to the ocean. At least not in this life. Still, I could almost smell the salty air and hear the crashing of waves upon the beach. And when I closed my eyes sometimes, the feel of the waves washing over my feet and the warm water on my skin as I swam through the water was clearly defined in my mind. I could smell the frothy, salty water, and I knew what it felt like when a cool breeze swept out from it and enveloped my senses.

Now that I knew more about myself, I knew those feelings and memories were from the other Jewel, but I couldn't help at times being envious of her life—or my life, depending on how you looked at it.

Andrew didn't seem to mind the silence, nor did he comment on my distant thoughts. I didn't really know what to say to him. I pulled my thoughts back to the present, and I realized that the van had left and Andrew sat next to me, without a ride back.

"How are you getting back?" I looked at him inquiringly. Unlike Anubis, who could create a portal to anywhere in the darkness he created, Andrew had to walk or ride like the rest of us.

He pulled out a smartphone, waving it slightly for emphasis. "I'll call for a pick-up when I'm ready." He turned towards me, giving me all his attention. We sat there a breath longer, him staring at me as if he wanted to say something, but he kept his words to himself. I was grateful because I didn't want to have another of those conversations. This guy never gave up. I had to admit I admired that about him.

"So, I heard the theme for the fall dance is a night on the town." I laughed softly. The town was a very small one, consisting of only a few thousand people, not counting Glen Delphi—we were only a part of the town by default since it was the closest in proximity to our hidden valley surrounded by mountains. It was mostly a mining town. There were even still remnants of an old western building that had first sprung up hundreds of years ago.

"That sounds…" Andrew trailed off, probably thinking the same thing I was. "It sounds like fun." He left it there, knowing that it wasn't important what the dance was called. Even if we didn't have much of a town to speak of, it was nothing more than a theme. "Are you going dress shopping? I think Gale is going this weekend. You should go with her."

I nodded my head yes, but I knew, more than likely, I wouldn't have time, what with my training and the new treatments with Thoth. Thinking of Thoth reminded me I had this whole hidden life I couldn't share with Andrew, and as if he'd read my thoughts, he asked me a question I couldn't answer.

"So, this guy you train with, exactly what type of training are you doing?" It wasn't the first time I'd been asked. Everyone was interested in my life-changing situation, only they didn't realize how life-changing it really was.

"He just teaches me different fighting moves in case I can't defend myself using other methods." In a way, that wasn't the truth, but it seemed to appease him. "Listen, I really can't talk about it any further than that." I could feel annoyance once again bubble up to the surface. I wasn't sure if it was from the fact I couldn't share yet another thing in my life with others or because he was questioning me. "Either way, to be honest, it's just something my dad has me doing. He thinks I need to prepare and learn how to defend myself. As a woman, he feels it's important and I agree. As much as you guys are great and you do look out for me, I need to learn to look out for myself as well. I mean, what happens if one of you guys aren't around for me to borrow powers from? My abilities are very limited."

I felt bad for not sharing more with him, but I needed distance between us. I didn't want him reading more into our relationship than there was. Right as he was about to comment, the bus appeared around the bend. I hopped up quickly and he closed his mouth, deciding against whatever comment he was about to make.

"Listen, Andrew, I appreciate you sitting with me, I do, but you need to get back home and go to the basement. I sense your suit needs an adjustment. I'll check on you later." My voice was more commanding than I'd meant for it to be, and I didn't leave him room to respond as I turned my back to him.

"I'll see you later, then?" There was hope in the question, and I found I couldn't deny him. I turned back and nodded silently to him and smiled.

As much as I knew there wasn't a future for us, even if I wanted one, I didn't want to be mean. And who knew, maybe there was some glimmer of a hope we could be together. Quite frankly, I wasn't even sure what I wanted. Everything had been such a crazy whirlwind lately that I hadn't had time to think. I waved to Andrew, realizing a little too late I might have been too harsh with him as I climbed onto the bus and into my seat. My life was a mess.

The rest of the day wasn't as tedious as I would have thought. Lots of people asked about Teddy, but I told them he'd decided to cash in his extra credits and graduate early. The whispers started again, and I knew everyone was talking about the "cult" that kids disappeared into. They were wondering when it would be my turn. I didn't really give a shit what they thought. They could remain nice and safe in the normal, boring world, free from all knowledge of the real story. And in a way, I was envious of them and it pissed me off. I wanted to be just as blissfully ignorant as their dumb snickering assess.

That pretty much set the tone for the rest of my day. I was a big grumpy mess. Then as the day continued my head once again began to pound like a drum. At first the headache was minor, just a big fat addition to my list of annoyances for the day, but as the day went on, it began to worsen. Since I hadn't gotten any headaches since Thoth had put me into the machine, I'd thought I'd gotten lucky and they'd be gone for good. The difference between this headache and the others, though, was that no vision preceded this one. Which I found odd at first until I was in too much pain to think about it.

"Hey, are you okay?" Allison sat next to me in her usual spot in chemistry.

"I'm fine. My head just hurts." I lay my head back down on the cool desk, trying to avoid moving. The noise in the room was intensifying the headache, and the lights seemed harsh every time I opened my eyes. I barely noticed Allison looking at me closely.

"I don't think you are fine. I think we need to get you out of here." She was already looking around the room assessing the situation and forming our escape plan. I tried to form some sort of protest, but my words fell flat as a sharp pain stabbed through my skull. I grabbed my head with a suppressed moan. It wasn't until the room started to spin that I looked at Allison with a plea in my eyes. The spinning and the pain knocked me off my stool, but she quickly reacted and caught me before I fell. I didn't think normal people moved that fast. She picked me up, practically without even struggling, and supported my weight with her shoulder.

"Mr. Joiner." She raised her free hand to get his attention. "Jewel is sick. I'm going to take her to the nurse." The look on my face must have convinced him that there was a legitimate reason for me to go to the nurse because there wasn't any protest as he nodded and we left the classroom.

Allison veered away from the direction of the nurse's office and pulled me into a deserted bathroom. I didn't protest, other than in groans, as my head continued to pound. It felt as though the stabbing pain was getting worse. I barely registered where we were, and I certainly was in no state to ask her what she was doing. I felt the cool wood bench in the girls' bathroom under me, and she easily propped me up against the concrete wall near the window. If my head hadn't hurt so bad I would have sworn my friend was glowing brightly for just a second before I shielded my eyes.

"Jewel, can you hear me? Look at me, Jewel." Allison was facing me and I felt her hands on my face.

"No, it hurts. You're so bright. It makes it worse." I tried to open my eyes. Allison was standing in front of me, not glowing at all. I must have hallucinated it after all, but that still didn't explain how she was so strong.

"Jewel, I need you to drink this." She pulled out what looked like a flask of some sort. She tried to place it on my lips, but I pushed it away.

"I don't drink alcohol, and I don't see how it will help here." The words were forced and strained as another stabbing pain shot through my head. It felt like it was splitting in two. I doubled over and grabbed it, holding it tightly in my trembling hands.

"Jewel, please listen to me." Allison was on her knees in front of me. Through the haze of pain I realized something.

Allison had the same strange blue-green shade of eyes that I had. They were even similar in shape. "It's not alcohol. It's just special water. It will stop the pain."

I giggled. Even with the stabbing pain I couldn't resist. "I've heard that before."

Allison smirked at my pained laughter. Then she raised the flask once again to my lips. I decided in that instant I didn't have anything else to lose. If a shot of something helped take away the pain, I'd try it. I tipped the flask back and drank. Some of the liquid splashed down my face. I always did have a hole in my mouth. The water was sweet and cool, and as it went through my body it warmed me. My head slowly began to ease. "How...?" I didn't know what else to say past that.

"I guess you have a bunch of questions now." She smiled and tapped me on the nose like I was a child, then stood. I sat there gaping at her. She was shining brightly again, but only for a moment and then she dimmed.

"Yeah, what happened to me? What are you?" I decided to start with the basics and, rather than demand answers, I sat there in awe of her, waiting. I wasn't used to not being in control or having to rely on someone else for answers. It felt similar to when I was with Anubis, and that rubbed me a little wrong.

"You and I are the same." She almost sang it. Her voice was higher and more melodious than it had been before. "As for what happened to you, well, you're going through something quite difficult right now." She didn't comment any further, but rather sat next to me. She placed her head on my shoulder in a familiar way I wasn't used to.

"You're an Evolved." It was more a statement than a question. I had no doubt she was something more than human, but I didn't want to voice my real questions, such as, *Oh, hey, so you're like me, a former goddess sent through time?* Yeah, how much nuttier could I sound?

She smiled and looked off into the distance, tapping her chin as if wondering how to respond. "No, not exactly, although good guess. Try again." She smiled gleefully as if she were enjoying my struggle to understand the situation. I was starting to like Allison less, even if she had saved my head from exploding.

I sighed, tired of the game. It was either put myself out there or not. She hadn't been surprised by my reference to the Evolved, so I decided to gamble. "You're an Olympian goddess of the royal family who was sent to the future as punishment for some crime or other. And you're possibly in danger from the very people who are supposed to be your family. Oh, and you have no memory of any of this previous life, other than a few flashes here and there that just started because, through the process of being sent to the future, your life was rewound to that of a toddler." I watched her for a moment after my swift declaration. She wasn't in the least bit surprised. She knew. "Who the hell are you?" I crossed my arms, waiting for a response.

"I'm someone who has missed you." She smiled brightly then, wrapping me in her arms. I was so perplexed and taken off guard I didn't fight or pull back. I just sat there awkwardly, trying to decide what to do. As I did, I breathed in deeply, trying to relax myself. The smell of the ocean's salty air briefly invaded my senses. Since I had never even been to the ocean, yet I knew she smelled like it, this didn't seem right; something was nagging in the back of my mind. Something very familiar that I had felt when I first met her, but quickly discarded. It was starting to now make sense.

"Who are you?" I pulled back, my voice more demanding now. If she was an Olympian I could be in danger. Anubis told me to be careful of them—that they were not to be trusted unless he said they could be. This war seemed so complicated. I wasn't even sure if I should trust Anubis, even though trusting him was somehow ingrained in me, as if it were a part of my essence.

"I'm your friend. And I'll be here if you need me, when you're ready."

Damn it, more cryptic crap. Just like Anubis: *All will be revealed, blah blah blah.* Screw these people. I turned my back to Allison, shaking my head. I was done with this. I'd thought I'd actually made a friend, one that was separate from my crazy world.

Just as I was about to leave, I turned to glance back at Allison. She was gone. When it came to crazy days, this one had to top them, though I'd had quite a few of them lately.

I decided in that moment I was done with the day. I didn't want to be here anymore. I didn't want to deal with snickering behind my back or eating lunch by myself now that Teddy was gone. I felt tired. I turned towards the nurse's office. After what happened in chemistry class, no one would second-guess I was sick with a little dramatic performance.

Forty-five minutes later my dad pulled up in his black sedan. I slid into the passenger's side, avoiding his eyes. It didn't matter to him if I skipped school; he'd been trying to talk me into joining the tutors at the compound for a while now. I'd always used the excuse that I wanted to stay for Teddy, but now I didn't have an excuse. The only reason to stay now was because I wanted something I couldn't have.

"I'll graduate early. I have enough credits." There was defeat in my voice as I continued to look out the window, avoiding his eyes. I knew he wouldn't be surprised. My dad knew what could be and sometimes what would be.

I thought back to the first time I'd learned about why my father was able to see fragments of the future. I'd asked what made him different from the other Evols. He sat me down and told me another one of his stories. He said he'd once lived in a beautiful place called Delphi, which was why he named our home after it. His mother was a gifted oracle and his father was one of the most powerful men in Greece. (I hadn't realized it at the time, but I'd recently figured out that he was telling me, in his own way, that his father was one of the gods of ancient Greece.) He never told me his father's name, and I suspected as I bugged him through the years it was because he didn't have a fondness for his father. Yet, he'd still been the best one in the world to me. He told me that day that he'd made a promise to someone and he'd gladly spent his long life fulfilling this promise. I remember saying that this person must have been really special to him. He got a really funny and faraway look in his eyes as he smiled and agreed. He had hugged me and said, "More special than you could ever imagine."

"Bunny, what happened today? I received a concerned call from your teacher on the way here. You fell off your chair?" There was real concern in his voice, and in my moody bout of melancholy I wondered how long it had taken him to think of me as his daughter. I knew he had been thrust into the role. I was about to ask, but he did that thing where he sometimes knew what a person was going to say before they said it. "You've been one of the greatest, most wonderful parts of my long life, and I'm grateful I was fortunate enough to be your dad for what little time I have with you."

Damn, what a way to hit me in the feels. I turned towards him, the tears welling in my eyes. With all the crazy uncertainties and whirlwind of changes in my life, he'd always been my constant for as long as I could remember and I was grateful for it. He was everything a father should be to me.

"Thank you, Dad." The tears were now pouring down my face unchecked. I didn't care. I was tired of being strong. My life was one big overwhelming mess and this man loved me completely. For this one moment, my world was perfect once again.

"No, bunny, thank you." He left it there. The silence that pressed in around us was a good silence. His words had healed some part of me that I didn't truly understand yet.

Before I knew it, we were at the main house, and I'd just started towards our apartment when my father stopped me. Without saying a word, he walked to me and hugged me tightly to him. I snuggled into his black cashmere sweater. Tears threatened to leak out once again as he kissed the top of my head. Even if my life was falling apart I had my dad. I sniffled, hoping he didn't notice as I once again went towards the sanctuary of my room. Luckily the rest of the house was relatively empty and no one paid me much attention.

I finally made it to my room and turned to close the door before walking over to my dresser to change—only to look directly into Allison's eyes in the mirror. She was sitting on my bed, looking like she comfortably belonged. I whirled around, facing her.

"How did you get in here? Why are you in my room?" At this point, she was just being plain intrusive and I was done with her. We were about ready to fight, and I was going to fight dirty if I had to. I glanced at one of the daggers that I'd taken from Anubis's, which was lying on my dresser. As I was going to grab it, it flew to the other side of the room and stuck in the wall. I shot a look towards Allison; she still sat there calmly.

"You always were funny about your personal space." She sat there, allowing a pause as she continued to watch me. This person I had liked instantly and called a friend. She had me at a stand-off. I didn't know if we were indeed still friends or if I should count her as a foe. I studied her for a moment; her hair was different and she wasn't as short as she'd been before. But otherwise her appearance remained the same.

"I'm going to ask this again, and if you don't answer me, you need to leave and never come back."

She'd been lounging on my bed, but now she rose up and stood before me. We were the same height. "I'm not here to cause you problems or to scare you, Jewel. I'm truly here to help and I need you to remember. I need you to remember everything." She faced me. Her eyes were full of what looked to be hope. But hope for what? Because, as far as I was concerned, being all cryptic and invading my space wasn't helpful at all. It made me want to knock her out.

"I'll ask you again. Who are you?" I gritted my teeth as I said it. My fist was balling up. Whoever she was, it was about to go down.

"I'm your sister and you are in danger. I'm here to help you."

My fist relaxed and my clenched teeth loosened, my mouth hanging open in what could only be astonishment. Shit, I had a sister? Rather than give me more details, she sauntered over to the wall where the dagger was stuck into it. She pulled it out and studied the intricate design of a jackal on the hilt. I tensed up again at the sight of the dagger in her hand, ready if she flung it my way. Instead she looked up after studying it.

"When did Anubis start coming to see you?" That put me on edge again. Why was she asking about Anubis? Weren't they working together?

"Why do you want to know?" When he'd first started presenting me with information about my past, it had occurred to me that Anubis could have been be leading me wrong. Now, even though I wasn't sure of our future together, I was sure that I could trust him further than this person claiming to be my sister.

"Listen to me closely, little sister. Anubis was your downfall before. He'll be your downfall again if you're not careful. You cannot live with death." If she was trying to convince me that she was on my side, she was failing miserably.

"What was in the drink you gave me?" Had she been trying to poison me? At the very least she'd been deceiving me, masquerading as a human girl named Allison. That right there didn't exactly encourage me to trust her. "And who are you, as in your name?"

"I am Beroe, daughter of Aphrodite and wife of Poseidon." That explained the smell of the sea on her hair and skin. She paused, allowing me to process this information. "I am also your sister, one of very few left." I looked her over then, peering closely at her. Yeah, it would be great to have a sister, and as I looked at her now I could see the similarities that I hadn't seen before. Her features were very feminine and we shared the same eyes and shape to our mouth and the same pale, milky skin, but her nose was more aquiline than mine and her hair was much darker. She was stunningly beautiful, far prettier than me. I'd liked her as Allison, and I yearned for the closeness of a sister, but I didn't trust her at all. Usually my instincts were pretty much spot-on. She was lying about something.

"Okay, and the water you gave me? Did you poison me?" I felt it was best to be blunt and gauge her reaction. She didn't look shocked but rather smiled at me.

"I was starting to think my memory of you had faded, but obviously you're still, in so many ways, my little Jewel." She walked over and took my hands in hers. Was this some alien god/goddess thing? They did this a lot. I'd more than once had someone take my hand and try to talk to me soothingly. I didn't like it. I pulled my hands out of hers, preferring the absence of her touch.

"First, the water, then explain the rest." I was tired of her deflecting. I knew my tone was harsh and commanding, but I didn't care. I knew Anubis would show up at any minute to take me to train, and I didn't want her here. I wanted answers and then I wanted her gone.

"The water just postponed the inevitable. It was just water with healing properties that keep you from being overwhelmed by your memories. Thoth can only help you so far. You need me too." She looked at me as if that explanation were sufficient. It rubbed me wrong. I wondered how we could have ever gotten along as sisters before.

"And the rest?" I crossed my arms then, waiting.

"I helped raise you. My husband and I kept you safe for years." With those words, I remembered my dream from the night before. How I left the Olympus in a pod to go see the ocean. Did I ever go back? Obviously I didn't, but why?

"Why did you help raise me?" I wasn't fully buying this crap. Just when I thought I had a friend, one who accepted me as normal, she ends up being just another person from this past I don't even really remember. It was like a slap in the face to my dream of being normal. I couldn't even deal with it right now.

"You came to us. Wanting to see the ocean. Our aunts, in their own way, sent you because they knew what was to come. Mother couldn't keep you safe any longer. So you came to stay with us for a time."

"For a time?" Was she for real? I thought hard on how old I'd been in my dream last night. I'd been young. How long was a time? I seriously didn't trust this Beroe person, no matter how close she said we were in the past.

"What do you want from me now?" I looked over at the clock on my nightstand. I was surprised Anubis hadn't knocked on my door or appeared in my room yet.

"You're waiting for something? What is it?" She watched me. Watched my every move. It occurred to me then that she'd been doing that the whole time, and my trust for her dissipated even more.

"Why are you here now? Why decide *now* to come back into my life?" I asked, even though I knew she wouldn't give me the answers I was looking for. She was hiding things too.

"Little sister, the years have been so long. Things have changed. I would have been here sooner, but they've been hiding you." She lay back on my bed, glancing up at the stars I'd painted years ago on my ceiling. Orion was one of the constellations over my bed. I'd painted one of the stars brighter than the rest, and I noticed she smiled up at it.

"Why would they hide me?" I decided to keep the edge and distrust from my voice, but rather allowed pure curiosity to envelop my words.

"I should be going. Stop going to school; there's no reason for you to live in the realm of man. You're chasing something that's not possible. You know this, Jewel." There was no malice in her words, but what sounded like real concern. "We'll see each other soon." And before my eyes, she disappeared.

I fell onto the bed she had previously occupied and looked up at the constellations on my ceiling. I felt like my world was spiraling out of control, and I didn't know who to trust. I lay there for about an hour letting these thoughts run through my head. Why was all this happening now?

It was then that Anubis appeared before me. The darkness opened up in the corner of the room, and I could feel the cold emanating from it. I found it interesting that the portal he moved through was freezing cold, but he was so warm to the touch. Once Anubis stepped into my room, his looming height and lean muscular body took up much of the corner of my room. Before I could speak, I watched as his body went into high alert.

"Who was here?" There was a menacing edge to his voice, laced with danger and making it apparent he was ready for battle. I pitied anyone on the receiving end of the murderous look on his face as he checked the room for intruders. He was ready to mess someone up. Once he realized I was safe he relaxed. This worried me. Why had he been so tense?

"What's going on? Why are you worried?" I stood from the bed and crossed my arms in front of me. My irritation level was high, and no matter how deadly of a look he threw my way, I was going to take him on. Foolish indeed, but I didn't care.

"Someone was here, someone who shouldn't be. Who was it?" His expression changed from ready to battle to concern, but rather than change my stance, I became angry. How dare he ask questions without giving me an answer! I dropped my arms and rushed over to the other side of the room to stand directly in front of him. I re-crossed my arms and tilted my head, glaring into his eyes. I could battle too. *Bring it.*

"Why should I tell you?" I didn't care if he knew Beroe had been here. I mean, why should I? But this was about more than that. This was about everything. It was about my mess of a life. It was about all the secrets and it was about my fears.

"Because I'm trying to protect you?" He glared right back at me.

"Why do I need to be protected? What if you're lying to me, and it's you that I need to be protected from?" I stepped closer to him. I could smell him. He smelled like sweat and something sweetly musky and definitely manly. He smelled amazing. With my words his expression changed; the battle left his eyes completely, replaced by something else that almost looked like yearning.

"I'd never lie to you, and I'd sooner die than see you harmed, ever," he whispered, his voice low and husky and filled with so much emotion. There was pain and regret in those words—and truth. I knew it in the depths of my soul. This man loved me... or, well, the other me. It was then that jealousy surged. It was silly, but I was jealous of this other version of me.

"Which me?" I was so close to him. As if I couldn't help it. It would have been too easy to lean in and kiss him. Yet, instead I stepped back and sighed, deciding to change the subject. "Shall we go?"

Anubis refused to allow me to run away. He stepped back up to me and grabbed my chin, pulling it up towards him. I saw the raw need in his eyes and tried to pull my face away but couldn't. He leaned in closely and said in his deep baritone voice, "You. Only you. All of you."

Everything that was me melted in that moment, and I didn't protest when his lips brushed mine, but before it could turn into anything more, I came to my senses and turned my face away. I knew that in just one kiss, I would lose everything. I would lose me. It was his turn to sigh then.

"We will speak about this later. This conversation is not over. You need to tell me who was here." Before I could protest, I found he had pulled me through another deep, dark, cold portal. We landed on the other side, directly outside Thoth's lab.

CHAPTER THIRTEEN

I was happy when I didn't embarrass myself and fall on my rump again. I did, however, find myself clinging to Anubis, which was equally embarrassing. Thoth was standing with his back to us peering into a microscope. I watched for a few minutes, trying to assess my surroundings. The lab smelled like a hospital and was just as clean. Everything was sparkling and appeared to be new. The smell of bleach and sterile objects permeated the air. Thoth continued to focus on what he was working on as we moved closer. It occurred to me he did this often. He became lost in a subject, forgetting the world around him. He was always alone.

"It is better at times to be alone, when you have a mind such as mine." I had forgotten about that interesting ability of his. He looked up from the microscope and then gave me his inquisitive stare. It was as if he was always constantly analyzing everything around him. "Indeed, I am," he answered my thoughts once again, causing me to cringe. He shrugged, peering back into the microscope. "You need to teach her to guard her mind, Anubis."

"I do, but I'm more concerned with her safety than I am with you not being able to keep your mind to yourself." There wasn't any anger in Anubis's voice, but rather the ease that comes with dialogue between old friends.

Thoth smiled at his friend. "Indeed." He then turned to me. "Look here, in the microscope." He moved out of the way and I stepped over to peer into the microscope. I was looking at blood cells. Except, from what I remembered from biology class, these were not normal cells. They looked similar but some were colored strangely, tinged purple on the outside, and despite being crushed between glass, they were moving quickly around the other cells, bouncing off them and causing chaos. I looked up at Thoth, who was analyzing me still.

"What am I looking at?" I thought I knew the answer to that, but I wasn't sure what was wrong with these cells and why it was important.

"It's your blood, as of yesterday." He turned then, going across the room and leaving me to contemplate what he'd said. He grabbed another vial of blood then a syringe and supplies. Anubis and I patiently watched him. When he walked back over to us, he laid the supplies down on the pristine counter next to the microscope. He then pulled out two more glass slides, dropping a small drop of blood from the vial he'd collected onto the glass and placing it under the microscope. "Look again." He once again moved out of the way, allowing me the chance to look once more. This slide contained blood cells that were fully purple, and they moved together rapidly on the dish, bouncing on one another wildly. They were thicker and more textured than the cells from the other dish. He pulled the slide out once I looked up at him. I wasn't sure what he was trying to tell me with this, except that my blood was different than the average human's.

"Why are you showing me this?"

"Because sometimes we believe better when we can see. Hand me your arm." He grabbed my extended arm and cleaned it with an alcohol wipe. I glanced over at Anubis, who was silently watching us. I felt a prick in my arm and almost pulled it away, but Thoth held it tight.

"Ouch, a little warning next time." It wasn't painful, and Thoth gave me a look of *Oh please, I know you're faking.* Instead of being upset, I laughed as he extracted a sample of my blood. He left my arm to fend for itself as he transferred the blood to another empty vial and placed the last drop on yet another slide.

"Look again," he said as he placed the new slide under the microscope and motioned for me to look. The cells were even more purple, as if, like a virus, they were consuming the red blood cells. The purple ones were larger, more textured, and faster, bouncing around the slide. Then one bounced into a normal red cell and the red cell began to slowly change. My blood was, without a doubt, changing to match the slide I'd seen a moment ago. I looked up from the microscope.

"What does this mean?"

"It means we are quickly running out of time. It means you need to put away your fears and we need to move forward. It means you need to trust us."

I wondered then if he was reading my mind. "It means you need to answer all my questions, and now." I put my hands on my hips, glaring at them both. If they wanted my trust they needed to earn it.

"Indeed, it means we do."

I hadn't been prepared for his compliance. It threw me off at first, but I quickly regained my composure. "Tell me everything I want to know," I demanded, my tone leaving little room to argue.

Anubis, however, interrupted before I could demand anything else. "First tell us who was in your room earlier today."

I knew we wouldn't go any further unless I told them, so I decided to do as Thoth asked and trust them. "Beroe. Apparently she's my older sister." I paused, watching their expressions and noticing they weren't surprised. "Will Cupid be visiting me as well soon?" I joked with a smirk.

"Eros went home quite a while ago to govern a new colony on the mother planet, Olympia." Thoth's words were expressed as mere facts. He was indeed serious. "He was always full of such hope for our worlds and in humanity as a whole. No one has heard from him in years, as we cannot communicate that far, so no one knows if he was successful."

I'm sure my mouth had fallen open, although with all I'd learned of myself and my supposed family thus far, this shouldn't have surprised me. "Good to know. Anyone else waiting to ambush me?"

They paused then, their silence deafening as it sat there between us. It was Anubis who finally answered. "There is a war brewing once again for power, one that has been building for some time. You are at the center of this war, and we're trying to keep you out of it." He paused again, opening his mouth briefly, only to close it, as if thinking on his next words and whether or not he should tell me.

"Spit it out. You said you would tell me."

But it was Thoth who continued, "You know a little about

the prophecy. No one knows who it is about, specifically, but it has always been suspected that it was you."

"My aunts seemed to think so in the vision I had. But it's not like it said my name or anything. They could be wrong, couldn't they?" I knew I was grasping at straws here, but I still didn't want to believe all of this. It was too much.

"It says that someone powerful, born to a new world but of another, will herald in a new dawn for mankind. One where man will inherit the gifts of the gods and push them from their thrones." Thoth stopped and looked down at the vial in his hand before he continued. "Some of the Olympian and Egyptonian rulers wanted to kill you, but they couldn't because of the support you received from those of importance, so instead they delayed the inevitable and left you and Anubis to suffer in different ways. Now you must make a choice, and they are counting on you to choose as they want this time. Due to our strict rules we cannot force you to make one decision or the other."

His words overwhelmed me and my head began to throb again, as it had at school. "I've heard all this, but what do you mean, I—or whoever it is—will herald a new dawn for mankind?"

Anubis interrupted Thoth before he was able to answer. "Make no mistake, it is indeed you that the prophecy speaks of, and those in power know it as well." He didn't further explain this, though. Instead, he turned his attention back to Thoth for him to continue.

"Indeed, mankind is beginning to grow to be more and more like our own people. The Evolved have abilities, but not immortality."

"But the people in my father's community have always

had these powers. They've had them for generations." I paused, thinking this proved that everyone obviously had to be wrong. "Their abilities are the product of a mutated gene many, many centuries ago."

"It was you." Thoth interrupted my thoughts, and his words struck me like lightning.

It was me?

He answered my thoughts and repeated himself, this time with more humanity than was normally in his analytical, factual tone. "It was you."

"How?" I looked at Anubis. For some reason I wanted him to answer this question. I felt pain like a knife through my chest. I now lived with the ancestors of the people I had supposedly infected with these curses. I'd witnessed the struggle and pain the Evols had endured, and here these two were telling me that their suffering was my fault.

"You began your activation among humans and your gifts manifested themselves. We Egyptonians and Olympians all have standard abilities, like strength and speed, but we also each have an ability unique to us. Yours was the ability to open up humanity to their own gifted possibilities." He called it a gift, but it felt like I had cursed them. I thought about Andrew and how his parents had died due to his gifts—and the pain of so many before me as they hid and tried to desperately control the abilities they'd developed.

"One question: What role does Beroe have in this fight?" I looked at Anubis, still insisting he answer me.

"She wants you to activate humanity, because she's the daughter of Adonis, a human granted immortality, and your mother, Aphrodite. She is both of this world and of ours. She wants to use you to hurt the royal families and allow all of humanity to gain abilities. She and Poseidon will do anything and call it an act of love in order to see this happen."

"I'm confused on a few points." I paused, looking expectantly at him. "Immortality. When was it granted and how was I born if two gods can't procreate?"

Thoth spoke softly and his voice broke with obvious emotion, which was unlike him; I had to lean closer to catch his words. "I can answer these questions for you. I created immortality inside my lab. I gave the formula to my people thinking I had saved them." He paused, closing his eyes only to continue with deep sadness laced in his next words. "Instead of saving us it led to the destruction of both my people and yours. Including the love of my life."

Anubis walked over to his friend and placed his hand on his shoulder in understanding and comfort, but then he turned to me, still holding his longtime friend's shoulder. "The formula was taken by the elite of our planet. They were greedy and refused to share with everyone. Thoth gave it to his own Gru té mor. She felt everyone deserved it and took it to the Olympians, who were originally her people. The truce between the two planets was broken and this act caused the war to reignite." He paused, taking his hand down from Thoth's shoulder and turning fully towards me. His words were echoing the pain in his own heart. "Many, many people died on both sides. Yet, those who were innocent and those that were of a lower class standing are the ones that truly suffered and lost."

I felt their pain, their losses, and they reverberated through me as if they were my own burden to bear. I knew this was a sensitive topic, but I wanted to know more. I needed to know more. They hadn't answered why I was born on this planet or why the other gods couldn't have babies together but could have half-human children. "I'm sorry for your pain, your loss, and the struggles you've endured." I spoke with compassion and paused to give them time to adjust to their memories. "I still need to know, how was I born?"

Thoth spoke again, his voice shifting back to his bland, monotone tone. "We do not know. One of the costs of immortality was the inability to reproduce children. It only affected the elite, of course, since they were the only ones who were granted immortality, but they were also the only ones sent to Earth. Life among the rest of the citizens of Olympia and Egyptonia—those who were not gifted the *serum*—carried on." He spoke the last sentence with distaste before continuing, "You, my child, are a fluke, a phenomenon of—well you, dear, are indeed a truly remarkable miracle. You are the only child born after the immortality phase to the immortal. All your siblings were born before your mother took the serum. You are the youngest of your people."

I watched as Anubis nodded in agreement. "You changed things for humanity on this planet when your first wave of activation took place. We think, had you reached the final stage, you would have changed the whole planet."

"So once I'm fully activated, I could change the whole world so that everyone will be like the Evols at Delphi Glen?"

Thoth answered, his tone eerily dark in contrast to his usual monotone indifference, "Yes, but not on such a large scale. And do you feel that even now, thousands of years later, humanity can handle such a large amount of power?"

"No." My answer was immediate. I knew from my observations over the years that the powers that consumed the Evols often became unbearable. They could not learn to control them fully. Many accidents happened, especially when emotions were involved. Then there was the fact that at least some portion of Earth's people were always at war over some small difference or other. If you threw in mass planetwide abilities, it would be pure chaos. I sighed. "I don't want them to be like your people. Like my people." When I said this, the words caught in my throat. And I felt like I was lying to myself, not about my decision, but because they didn't *feel* like my people.

Thoth spoke again, his words distracting me from my dark thoughts. "You think because you can 'borrow,' as you put it, the powers of the those on the compound and show them how to use them, that you have activated your own abilities, but that's not true. You have yet to activate anything. The reason you can borrow from them is because they came from you many, many years ago."

I stood there for a few moments as he allowed me to absorb his words. "What happened? Why did I infect the Evols' ancestors? How many people did I infect?" Glen Delphi held a good number of people, so I determined after a quick assessment that it had to have been quite a few, as many family lines tended to become genetically diluted or die out over time.

"There are many secret compounds like yours around the world. They each house hundreds of people. You manifested powers in four individuals before your sentencing." My sentencing, as in a punishment.

"So four people became hundreds. How is this possible?"

"It was more in the fifteen hundred range last time we counted, but that's with us keeping it contained," Anubis answered. At the sound of his voice, I snapped my head in his direction, and I directed my next question to him.

"Why was I sentenced?" My eyes narrowed. I knew it had something to do with him, but I didn't have all the details. I was scared it might have had something to do with what happened to the four people who'd manifested powers, and guilt enveloped me. It pained me to think about the ramifications of my ability, the suffering I'd caused for these people through the many, many generations.

"You were punished because you crossed into forbidden territory—and because you married me." Well damn. I hadn't been expecting that. I guess dating Andrew was definitely off the table now. I was already married.

Wait, hadn't I read that Anubis was married to someone named Anput? Was this another case where mythology got it wrong?

"What do you mean, married?" My voice was laced with irritation. Irritation at the fact that my life wasn't my own. That even though, yes, I couldn't deny being attracted to this sexy man, I'd never had a choice to begin with. Once again, other me had something that I wanted. And although I knew it was just plain dumb, I was jealous—of myself. I glared at Anubis as if angry at him, but I was really angry at the fact that I didn't have any control over my life. Anubis stood there sheepishly, as if he'd slipped up big time by giving me that information and knew he'd screwed up majorly. I watched him silently wage war with himself, deciding whether or not to speak again, only to open his mouth and close it, choosing silence instead.

Good idea, I thought to myself, ready to make him a martyr when in reality I was upset at my situation.

"And what is your part in all this? Beroe wants me to

activate humanity, and you told me before that Zeus and Set are working to control humanity once again. What about you two?" I asked instead. This was the golden question; I needed to know where they stood and what they wanted from me.

"We stand with you as always," they both answered in unison without hesitation. What had this other Jewel been like to garner such devotion? She must have been... impressive.

It was then that I realized the fear that had gripped me before was gone. As if, like a revelation, I was finally ready to accept her, to get to know her better.

"I'm ready for the machine, but this time give me more. Stop playing it safe." I was already headed towards the back of the lab where the CAT-scan-like machine was located. I was resolved—I needed to understand my past better in order to be prepared for what was to come. Thoth and Anubis followed me quietly.

At the machine, I turned, allowing Thoth to prepare me with the headpiece. I looked into Anubis's eyes, unable to read him. My fear was gone with this new sense of resolve, but there was a nagging bit of uncertainty that still wrestled to the surface of my emotions.

Was this what I wanted? It didn't matter anymore, I told myself. It was time to see.

The headache that had started earlier and mostly gone away after the drink Allison—or, I guess, Beroe—had given me was intensifying, and I had forgotten to tell them about it. But I was afraid they'd stop me from moving forward if they knew. I knew it was risky, but I climbed into the machine, hiding the fact that my brain was on fire. I was ready to see it all, and a headache wasn't going to stop me.

Before I even had a chance to sit fully back, the memories enveloped me. I was the other me once again. Only this time it was even more intense. The memories began to come hard and fast. I couldn't even shuffle through them. They were too much. My head began to pound even more. I was being flooded.

I remembered everything. I felt everything. I knew everything.

I became her and me, all in one moment, in one large burst of intensity. It was too much to handle. The memories were overwhelming as they cascaded into my consciousness. I felt as if my nerves were exploding and my mind was being pressed, squeezed, forced to take it all in. The intensity of the pain that shot through me was beyond anything I could have ever imagined.

I could hear the shouting and the shuffling of both Anubis and Thoth in the background as they rushed to help me, but I couldn't respond. The whole universe had exploded inside me and it was too much.

Finally, I succumbed to the darkness that was taking over—and there was nothing. It felt good.

I COULDN'T BELIEVE I was here. My grandfather would find out soon. My mother would come looking for me and my aunts would pretend they didn't know anything. But I was tired of playing by their rules. I had lived my whole life cooped up on the Olympus. It was time to have some fun, consequences be damned!

I was inside the pod, exploring while using the invisible shield feature that Hermes created to keep the primitive humans unaware of our technology. I'd reached the surface and was traveling along the shoreline, my emotions a tangle of excitement and fear. I was sure to be in big trouble with this new escapade.

I'd never actually been to Atlantis. Poseidon lived on the island, which was hidden in the Mediterranean Sea. After his first wife died I heard that he'd mourned her for years, preferring to no longer live under the sea with the creatures that inhabited it but on an island, hidden from everyone. There he met my sister Beroe; she was hiding from Dionysus, who wanted to force her to marry him. Instead she married Poseidon, and together they turned the island into a paradise called Atlantis. Getting to the island was tricky because there was a forcefield around it that deflected most travelers. You couldn't actually see the island unless you were inside the forcefield. The navigation system on the pod took me to the general area of the island, but it could only locate a broad spectrum, a circumference that spanned several dozen miles. It was only by luck that I found it.

I'd been traveling just above the surface of the ocean, marveling at the sea creatures that broke the surface every once in a while, and then I spied the shadow of a large fish-like creature. It rose and sent a spray of water up towards my pod; I veered to the right just in time to miss it. I decided to watch the creature from a distance as it jumped up out of the water in a graceful arc, creating a large splash on its way back in. It dipped down and then came back up at an angle that made it apparent it was getting ready for another jump, but before the fish came back up from the water it vanished. I waited, wondering if maybe I'd missed it and it had gone deeper under the surface, but I'd clearly seen it attempting another jump. I moved the pod closer to where I'd last seen it. I couldn't go any further. It was as if there were a wall here. I pushed the controls forward, but *the pod wouldn't budge, and I heard a crunching noise, as if the pod were hitting something. I quickly pulled back.*

I sat there for a moment, studying the navigation system. Then I looked out at the vast, crystal-blue water as it gently swayed before me. Then it occurred to me. The barrier must have been above the water, but not below. I knew these pod vessels had the ability to submerge in water; I thought back to the time Hermes had given me a quick ride around the Olympus and let me play with the controls a bit. He'd mentioned there was a button that did that. I looked across the dashboard, at first missing it, only to glance back and see the button I was looking for. I clicked it, hearing the pod make some sort of adjustments, but I was unsure if this would work.

"Here goes nothing." I grabbed the controls and plunged them downwards, sending the pod into the water. It quickly became submerged and I found myself gasping. It was beautiful down here—absolutely amazing.

There was a whole city under the water! Sea creatures of all different types—ones I'd only heard of or read about—swam about the city. I realized then that I had to be careful where I steered the pod because the underground city had large coral-like structures that rose up from the seabed. They were bright and colorful and almost seemed to sparkle in the water. Just to the right of the city, the floor of the ocean gradually sloped upward. I followed the slope until I realized that the water was much shallower here and that I was headed towards a shoreline. It was a quick incline as the shore began to ascend higher towards the surface and the underwater city was left not far behind. After I allowed my gaping mouth to close, I pulled the pod out of the water and turned off the submerge function as I broke the surface. I rose up and there was a beach, a normal beach like any other, with sand and waves lapping at its sur-face. I hadn't been able to see it from outside the forcefield. A slight distance from the beach was yet another city, except this one was above water. The shock didn't end there. The city also had large structures that rose to the sky, much like in the pic-tures and video that had been archived from our home planet. They were tall, so tall they tickled the clouds and the birds flew among them. The sun glittered off their shiny surfaces and there were windows so clear you could see everything inside them. And I was amazed to see that there were flying contraptions that zipped through the city. This was Atlantis.

Before I knew it, something took hold of my pod and pulled me into the city. I had lost the ability to control my course, so I decided to take a look at the small city as I was pulled through it. It was almost a perfect smaller replica of so many cities that had appeared in our history books from Olympia. Before I knew it, I had reached a landing dock. There stood a tall man; he was not young but not old either. His sandy blond hair was longer than I'd expected it to be and wavy, much like the sea he controlled. He didn't have a beard as many pictures depict-ed him with, but rather had the shadow of a beard just start-ing to grow. His jawline was strong and his chin was round-ed. What was most noticeable was how muscular he was as he stood there grasping his triton. I knew this to be his weapon of choice because it harnessed his powers. The people of this planet who'd created stories to understand us had spread a tale that Zeus, Poseidon, and Hades were brothers, but it wasn't true. They belonged to three different royal houses from our home planet. The line had once been one, but that was so long ago in history that no one remembered exactly how. The idea that they were brothers came from the fact that they'd teamed together in an effort to fight our enemies. They were brothers in war. Of course, the humans didn't know that the war had gone on long before the Olympians had even come to Earth. That, when there was no hope for the sustainability of our planet, Zeus, Poseidon, and Hades were the ones that saved who they could and left.

Poseidon possessed the ability to manipulate the sea and other bodies of water, as well as many other skills that I'd yet to discover. He, like Hades, hadn't stayed on the Olympus, though he had his own reasons.

Once the hatch opened to the pod, I cautiously got out. When faced with the actuality of the situation, I began to lose some of the gumption I'd had before. Here stood Poseidon, a king in his own right, and a very powerful one. What if I wasn't welcome?

I squared my shoulders and straightened my back, deciding to face what was before me with as much confidence as I could muster. As I neared him, I could tell there wasn't a smile on his face. He looked annoyed. Crap, I was in trouble indeed.

"Poseidon?" I asked tentatively, all my pretend bravado dissipating. I watched his scowl disappear quickly and a smile light up his face.

"Jewel, welcome to my home." He bowed to me, which I found to be odd. I was in his kingdom, his home. I shrugged it off.

"Atlantis... is... is... amazing," I said in breathless wonder. I spun slowly, taking in the marvel that was this small city on an island. The city as indeed amazing, with its flying machines and buildings that reached up into the sky, made of the same material as the pod I'd come in. As I looked into the streets, I saw that there were people here. And I knew without a doubt *they were not our people, but rather humans from this planet. Something spectacular was happening here. Yet, also something very dangerous. Before I could ponder that thought any further, a beautiful woman walked up behind Poseidon.*

"It is indeed beautiful, isn't it, Jewel?" Her voice was musical and she looked so familiar. Her smile was large and turned towards me. Her hair was dark and her features feminine and delicate. Then I realized as she wrapped her arm in Poseidon's— this was Beroe. This was my sister. I'd only met her once and I'd been very young. She didn't visit the Olympus, as she was part mortal and there wasn't an open invitation for her kind.

"Yes, it is marvelous." The excitement was clearly evident in my voice. I couldn't help it. I had always wished we could live around the humans of this planet in harmony, but that was a forbidden concept.

Beroe said, "I'm so happy you're here with us, Jewel." She paused, moving gracefully away from Poseidon to come closer to me. She then wrapped her arm around my smaller one. "We'll explain everything to you shortly, but we've actually been expecting you. We—"

"Eros is here, my love. We should go meet with him," Poseidon interrupted my sister, as she was about to say something more. I was interested in what she had to say, but the fact that my brother Eros, whom I had a very close relationship with, was here stopped me.

"Eros is here? Why?" I looked at both Poseidon and Beroe, trying to figure out what was going on here that I didn't understand.

"Yes. We will explain. Let us go meet with him and all with be revealed." She again tugged me along with her as we disappeared into one of the shiny structures that rose into the sky. We

walked into a moving box room that had glass on two sides, allowing me to see as we moved downwards into the building. Each floor was for a different use. One seemed to be a gathering place of sorts, containing strategically placed sitting chairs, another looked to be a place of eating. This was a home, but there were many people here. We continued downwards until the box stopped, and in front of us was another glass door. It opened and Beroe pulled me forward.

"Come along, Jewel, my dear. I want you to see something." My sister was smiling and so happy. I'd wondered about her for so many years, but very few of my siblings and I had a relationship. And now here I was with one I knew so little about. Was she a good person? Could I trust her? I decided I had no choice and followed her into the room. She let my arm go as Poseidon placed his hand on a pad and the door opened. This place was, in many ways, much like the Olympus, yet so unlike the primitive world it was on. Once we stepped through the doorway, we were encased in another glass box. Through the glass I could see a man with his back turned towards us. As Poseidon opened the next sliding glass door, the man turned. It was Eros, my brother.

"Welcome, little bunny." His handsome face was lit up with the warm smile he always reserved for me. He'd always been my favorite sibling, mostly because we spent the most time together. "It seems you have discovered my secret." He winked at me and I winked back.

"No worries, I won't tell. If you give me that bow I wanted." He wasn't getting away with this without me getting something in return.

"Very clever, bunny. I suppose that would only be fair. Although, you can only use regular arrows." With that he bent

to his knees so he was closer to my height and I hugged him tightly. Something made me realize that this was both the start and end to something important, so I hugged him tighter than usual. Even at such a young age I knew to trust my intuition. After we released each other I looked around the room. It looked to be a workstation of some sort.

I turned to Eros. "Why are you here? What is all this?"

"This is the start of our future." My brother had stood up and was dusting off his legs. I realized then that he was wearing pants. When Olympians went to the surface, from what I'd gathered from listening to others, we dressed as they did. But he dressed as though he were home. He must have seen the speculation in my eyes because his bright blue eyes twinkled and he laughed, making the curly blond hair around his face bounce. Someone once told me that my brother's beauty started wars among women. He looked like a dolt to me and always would.

"Here we can be free from the restraints of the outside world." He paused, looking at Poseidon and Beroe. "Jewel, it wasn't a coincidence you came here."

"He is right." Poseidon spoke from behind me. His voice was deep like my grandfather Zeus's, but it held more compassion. My grandfather was a hard man; I was sure he held no love for me or for many others. Both Zeus and Poseidon looked young, but not as young as the next generation. They were the original Olympians, the first to gain immortality, and it was obvious they'd aged more than the Olympians of the next generation.

They waited silently for a minute, as if allowing me time to think. To be honest, I didn't know what to think. This was so much to process. Finally I was able to have that adventure I'd always wanted, not worrying in the moment about the consequences that would befall me later. Of course, It was obvious that they'd orchestrated everything to get me here.

"Why?" I looked pointedly at each one of them. My hands went to my hips. I was upset that, rather than just tell me that they wanted me to come, they'd strategically, with my aunts and who knew whom else, managed to direct me here.

Beroe stepped from Poseidon's side. "Because, my dear, you were not safe. And you have a big destiny to fulfill. One we wish to see to fruition." My sister smiled sweetly at me, but I felt some of this was a little staged for my benefit.

"Bunny." Eros, my favorite brother who I'd followed through the halls till he became sick of me, addressed me with the nickname he'd coined when I was very young. "Look at me, please." There was a pleading tone to his voice and I felt my anger dissipate slowly.

I sighed. There was no reason to stay mad. It was never helpful. So I turned my green eyes to his bright blue ones and waited.

"We all have our parts to play in the coming years. You are too young to fully understand, but one day you will." My brother didn't have the gift of foresight like my aunts did, but he was able to see a person's future love life and potential, and he could gift them in some ways when it came to love. He was a diplomat who consistently pushed for peace between the races.

That was the day that I learned about his other desires for our people. That was the day I gained more of him, but lost him all at the same time.

"Why am I here?" I thought asking simple questions at first would be the best plan of action.

"This place will keep you safe. Mother knows where you are. She will visit when she can and is very sad that you have to come here, but things are not good on the Olympus, and your life is at stake." He spoke calmly and steadily, but there was emotion hidden in his words. He didn't fool me. "There is something I want to show you."

What more did they have to show me? They'd already blown my whole world to pieces. Rather than speak my thoughts, I remained quiet, following them through yet another door into a brightly lit corridor. At the end of the corridor was another door made with a reflective mirror rather than glass and another pad to open it. Eros placed his palm on the pad and the door slid open. Beyond it, there were sounds of birds chirping, or what sounded like birds. We walked into the vast room, which was crowded with many different species of plants; there were even bugs of different shapes and sizes among the plants. And swooping down above our heads were a few flying creatures, but they weren't exactly birds. Towards the back of the room, slightly masked by the foliage, was a man hunched over what appeared to be what was left of a table. It too was covered in various types of plants and interesting forms of life, and it looked like he was using a device of some sort to study them. He looked up and turned towards us. We walked towards him, stepping over roots and spiky plants. There appeared to be a newly worn-down path through the mess of pulsating life emanating around us.

"Hello. You must be Jewel." He paused as if listening to something.

I wondered to myself if he was the reason so many new species of plants and creatures were bursting from the seams in here, and I studied him. As he appeared otherwise focused, it didn't occur to me that this tall, curly-haired, brown-skinned man was actually listening to my thoughts.

"Indeed, my child, I am the reason for this mess of a lab. And to be honest, I am not particularly fond of messes. I much prefer meticulous cleanliness. Allow me to introduce myself. I am Thoth."

My mouth gaped once again as I rudely stared. I'd never met one of them before. Yet, here stood the most famous of them all: the Egyptonian that had once betrayed his people.

"If you must know, I didn't actually betray them. I shared my knowledge with people they perceived as their enemies. I did it to save someone I loved." His words were direct, and on occasion his monotone voice broke with the emotion he obviously held so tightly back.

"What happened to her?" I didn't want to reopen old wounds for this man, but I felt it was important for me to fully understand what was happening around me. Especially since they said I had some part to play in all of it.

"She died a very long time ago." He spoke it with a complete lack of emotion in what felt to me like an attempt to hide the raw pain he held deep inside.

Eros interrupted our exchange. "Thoth shared his knowledge of immortality with our race, and that's what caused the war that destroyed both our planets and took many lives with it." Eros's usual smiling and carefree tone had turned serious, which pulled my attention fully to him.

"I know the story, or at least some of it." I looked at Thoth thoughtfully then, seeing the pain that he tried so hard to hide, even so many years later. Our races were similar in so many ways; we'd begun as the same people, and then the Olympians had decided to form our own colony on a nearby planet. Through the years of separation, the ties to the other race and our home planet became strained, then completely severed.

Politics between the two planets became deadly. Both sides became greedy and corrupt.

Thoth was a great scientist, one who'd made numerous amazing discoveries for his people. But while on a diplomatic mission, he was said to have shared their most guarded secret with their enemy, resulting in an all-out war between two planets. The war continued until both planets were nearly destroyed and many of both races had died. They were forced to call a truce, and those who'd survived left the galaxy, seeking out a habitable planet close by. That planet ended up being the primitive Earth. The two races selected dominions of Earth to call their own, and old habits set in as they once again became scorned enemies.

"She was originally from your planet. She died as a result of our love, as a punishment to me." This time his emotions were unfiltered. As the daughter of Aphrodite, I felt his pain as my own, and without even really knowing this man I felt a need to comfort him. I walked over to him and put my hand in his. I willed myself to take his pain away, knowing that I could not. He seemed shocked by this at first and tensed up, only to relax after a moment and accept my comfort.

"I am sorry for your loss, great sir. I hope that you will find her when she is once again born into the universe, as it is told. Everyone deserves to enjoy the happiness that comes with finding his or her true mate."

"Indeed, thank you. I appreciate the sentiment, my dear child. I look forward to the day." He smiled, and I released his hand.

I decided I needed to change the subject and distract us from the sad direction our conversation had taken, so I inquired, "May I please ask, why there are so many plants and odd things flying about in this room?" It was as if we were standing in a jungle encased in a large room.

It was my brother that answered, "We've been working together to find the best way to terraform a planet. We intend to terraform our home." My brother became excited as he explained the complexities of terraforming. I didn't clearly understand them, but I did get that they intended to terraform our home planet so we could eventually return.

"Why do you want to return?" I was confused; we had been here so long it seemed unnecessary to go back.

"Because that's where we belong. I'll be leaving tonight to start the long journey back and start the terraforming process on both planets. By the time I return you will be much older and far wiser than any of us." He teasingly nudged my shoulder, but he quickly became serious as he leaned in. I tried to hold back the tears that were forming in my eyes, but I couldn't. He was leaving me. Leaving me to fight my destiny alone. He reached out and gently wiped my tears away. "Listen to me closely, Jewel. You must stay here for a good long time. You cannot go back. And I have a gift for you."

"Why can't I go home? And what's my gift?" There was a slight whininess to my voice, which caused me to receive a raised eyebrow. I ignored it. The tears were still forming and I let them cascade down my cheeks because now I was beginning to become upset. Upset because I felt he was running away. Upset that he was getting away from all of this. And upset at myself, for the fact that I was going to miss my home and him every single day for forever. I looked up at him through the tears, and with a quivering voice that I tried desperately to steady I asked, "Well?"

"It's time for dinner," Beroe interrupted our conversation.

I had forgotten Beroe and Poseidon were even here since they were merely quietly observing.

I turned to Thoth. "You will join us?"

"I wouldn't miss it for the world."

We left Thoth standing there as Eros walked me back through the long corridor. He motioned for Beroe and Poseidon to continue on as he stopped to talk to me.

"Jewel, I won't be back for a very long time, but what I'm doing is important." He looked towards the door to the square elevator as Beroe and Poseidon disappeared behind it, and then he continued. "Your future is also very important, and I'm not sure you can always trust in them." He motioned towards the door. "But trust your instincts. And you can always trust Thoth."

"And my gift?" I felt my lip begin to quiver once again, and to keep myself from breaking down, I bit my lip and nervously chewed on it instead as a distraction. Afterward I felt composed enough to be sure I wouldn't melt into the snotty, tearful child that I was desperately fighting against. I smiled up at him, confused by his words but trying not to ponder the ramifications of them quite yet.

"Your gift is this. He pulled a small bag out of his pocket, dropping a necklace from its opening into his palm. On a chain was a bow and arrow with what looked to be a ruby fastened to the center of the bow. The ruby, however, pulsated when he ran his finger across it. "This gift was made for you, my bunny. No one else can get it to work. It is my parting gift and will help you find love, and it will also allow you to know the true intentions that lie in the hearts of others as you await your own day of transformation. This pendant will bring your true love to you when it is time. You'll need each other when the days become

ACCEPTANCE

dark. *I pray they are not too dark for you." He then placed the
pendant around my neck and kissed my head. I looked at it,
admiring its beauty.*

*"Thank you." There were tears in his eyes, and my own I
let stream down my face. I realized then he wouldn't be back
for a very long time and I hugged him tightly to me. "I love you,
Eros."*

*"I know, bunny. I love you too. Now let us go eat before
Beroe gets upset with us."*

*"Wait for me." Thoth quickly caught up with us as we held
the door open for him.*

*"You are always welcome." My brother motioned for him to
enter, and they clasped hands and gave each other a long knowing look as we waited to ascend in the box.*

*"No worries, my friend. I will watch over her." And he did.
He became like a father to me.*

CHAPTER FOURTEEN

*B*EEP.

Beep.

My head hurt, and as I slowly opened my eyes the soft light seemed harsh and made the pain pulsate deeper. Where was I? The room seemed familiar, but I was pretty sure I'd never been here, at least not in this life. The walls were a dark shade of purple. The bed was large and covered in soft velvet covers. Next to the bed was a machine that had an IV drip, which was inserted into my arm. In a chair not too far from me was Anubis, who was quietly watching me. I realized then that I was insanely thirsty and I wondered exactly how long I'd been out. Before I even opened my mouth to croak the request for water, Anubis began to pour me a cup. The water was cold and it soothed my throat as I drank it down. Once the cup was empty I looked up at Anubis. Concern was etched on his face.

Memories began to invade my thoughts. I remembered meeting Beroe—and Thoth. Where was Thoth?

"Where is he?"

"Who? Thoth?" He sat the empty cup down on the side table and regarded me thoughtfully. Ever since I'd met him, on occasion I would catch him studying me, as if he were trying to burn my image into his brain forever.

"Who else would be here?"

"No one, but are you not more concerned with what happened?" He looked at the IV bag that dangled next to me. It was almost empty.

"You guys stuck me in the machine again. It hurt. I passed out. I remembered a bunch of stuff and now I'm awake. Did I miss anything?"

His expression wasn't surprised but intrigued. He smiled that sexy, crooked smile that always made me blush. Only this time I felt more annoyed.

"What do you remember?" He leaned in, waiting for my reply.

"No, I still don't really remember much of you. I remember..." I paused. I was about to say that I remembered my brother, but was he really my brother? He would be the other Jewel's brother, but to me he was just a distant relative. Or was he? That thought made my heart ache wondering where he was, if he'd made it, if he'd been successful. These were *her* feelings. "I remember Eros leaving, meeting Beroe and Thoth... and Atlantis." My last words were encased in the wonder of the child I had just been when she arrived at the amazing city. Atlantis was real. Shut the front door! It was then that Thoth walked in.

"Did you find her?" I wasn't sure why I needed to ask him that, but the pain I had witnessed still felt so real.

"I beg your pardon." Thoth walked to the side of my bed,

peering down at me as I struggled to sit up. Damn, how long had I been here?

It was Anubis who answered. "It appears she remembers going to Atlantis and meeting you."

"Indeed. I can see." He meant he could see my thoughts. I thought up a clear way to tell him to stop. I imagined a middle finger. "Clever as always, my dear child."

"How long was I out?"

"Almost a week." Anubis moved closer to my side, checking my IV. "We were a bit concerned."

"What happened?" I looked to Thoth this time, realizing he hadn't answered my previous question but deflected it. It occurred to me that I now instinctively knew things about him, even if I couldn't remember everything.

"It was too much for you. Apparently you became overloaded. We aren't exactly sure how it happened, except there was a foreign substance in your bloodstream?" He phrased it as a question and then they waited, expecting me to answer it for them.

I sat there, thinking back to that day. What had happened that day?

"Beroe." My feelings for her were not the same as they were for Eros and Thoth. They were more... guarded. Thoth shared a look with Anubis.

"That explains it," Anubis answered bending down to take my hand. "Jewel please tell us what happened that day."

"She's been at my school pretending to be a student. She was trying to get close to me. That day my head hurt. I barely made it out. She gave me something to help and then later she was in my room." I looked first at Anubis then at Thoth, noting the disappointment on both their faces.

210

"You should have told us, Jewel," Thoth insisted. The monotone was gone from his voice. I didn't understand why but it made me feel guilty, knowing that I'd somehow disappointed him.

"Yeah, I'm sorry. I just… I needed to learn the truth and I was afraid you might stop me from using the machine if you knew about the headache. It happened without a vision." Thoth's eyebrows raised at that. I paused, adjusting myself in the bed. The covers were amazingly comfortable. "Wait, if I've been here almost a week, what does everyone think happened to me?" It occurred to me I might have missed the dance, my last chance at teenage normalcy. Damn it!

"We had Robert spin the story that you had to visit family suddenly, and in your community it isn't abnormal for people to disappear for a bit." Anubis stood then, walking across the room to where a tray of food sat. He brought it to me and set it in my lap. The fragrant smell made my stomach growl like a ravenous bear. There was a seasoned baked chicken breast, some steamed vegetables, and bread. I began shoveling food in my mouth in a very rude and desperate manner. Oh. My. God. It tasted amazing. I imagined, when the time came, it would be equal to sex. I hadn't even realized how hungry I was.

With food still in my mouth, I mumbled, "The dance. Did I miss it?"

"No, it's tomorrow night. You can still attend." Anubis looked unconcerned. If he was upset with the fact I was attending the dance with another person, he didn't show it.

"I still need to get a dress. I might as well cancel." I sighed, realizing it was a lost cause. "Damn it, I'll just go in jeans. Why not?"

"Faced with a weeklong coma and new memories and all she is worried about is a dance." Thoth shook his head at me, so I turned my nose up at him.

"You bet your sweet ass I'm going. I'm graduating early, so there won't be any other chances."

Anubis laughed quietly at me. "That's my girl. No, worries, I can help you in the dress department." He smiled coyly at me.

"What, do you just have dresses lying around?" I asked, between mouthfuls of chicken. "Are you a cross-dresser and just haven't told me? I mean, hey, no judgments from me."

"Not exactly. When you're done I'll show you."

I shoved the last bite of chicken into my mouth, clearing the plate. I thought about licking the juices but realized that would be going a little far.

"Alright, boss, lead the way." I put the tray aside and swung my legs over the bed, standing before anyone could stop me—and immediately crumpled to the floor. *Damn, that was meant to be way cooler.*

It wasn't until a few minutes later, after they pulled the IV out and helped me up and slowly walked with me around the room until my legs felt less wobbly, that I found myself standing with Anubis in front of a door just to the left of the bed.

"Press the red button on the pad to take it out of stasis, then place your palm on it."

It reminded me of the pads in Atlantis. Rather than bring that up, I followed his instructions and the door slid to the side. I walked in and noticed that the air felt stale.

"What do you mean stasis?" As I finished the question the lights flickered on and I stood there in awe. It was a closet. Full of clothes.

"Stasis means the contents of the room are in suspended animation until you open the door." He looked at me then with an expression I didn't understand. "Choose anything you like."

I walked along the line of clothes. Some of them were from a different time period, almost in a classical sense. Yet, others were similar enough to the clothing of this time that I could wear them to the dance. I stopped at a gold dress that was in an Olympian style that resembled modern clothing. It was a ballgown with a sweetheart neckline and corset waist. The skirt flowed out in cascading layers from the waist, along with a long train. The back of the dress came down to a point, exposing the wearer's back, and it looked like it would be open almost all the way down to my tailbone. It was gorgeous.

"There are shoes and jewelry as well," Anubis said, breaking me out of the stupor I was in over the beautiful dress.

I checked for the size but there was no tag. I turned towards him with dress in hand. "I'm not sure if it will fit. I'm taller than most people and have to shop carefully."

"Everything will fit." Anubis motioned over to the other side of the closet where there was a display of shoes and jewelry. There was a perfect pair of matching gold flat sandals. I hated heels. They were cumbersome and I was already too tall. These were perfect.

I walked over to the beautiful shoes, marveling in the intricate gold braiding, when something from the corner caught my eye. In a display case was the necklace Eros had given me. That he had given *her*. I dropped everything and stood there staring at it. I could almost feel it pulsating through the glass at my closeness. I pulled open the case and reached for the gold bow and arrow pendant necklace. The red stone was warm at my touch.

It occurred to me then that everything would fit because it was hers. I grabbed the necklace, leaving everything else on the floor, and marched out of the room. Anubis followed, carrying what I had previously picked out.

"Jewel, wait," Anubis called.

I didn't wait. I stormed out and searched out Thoth. Luckily he still stood in the room taking the IV bag off to throw away.

"What is this?" I held up the necklace. The red stone became increasingly warm as I held it but not burning hot. It felt alive.

"You ask a question to which you already know the answer." He barely turned towards me, unconcerned with my mental distress.

I realized he was right. I knew what it was. It didn't know exactly what it did, but I knew where it had come from and who gave it to me.

"Eros, where is he?" I wasn't sure if I really wanted to know, but it felt important to me.

It was Anubis who answered, "He came back, but by then you were gone. He returned to our old world to try to continue to replenish it and create a colony. He took many others with him." Anubis paused as he carefully placed the dress on a hanger and looped the sandals through the top. I watched him, mesmerized by the care he took with such a simple thing as a dress. Did she really mean that much to him that he'd preserved her clothes? Apparently. Oddly, I felt a sting of jealousy. Which seemed funny since it was me that

I was jealous of.

"I remember him giving this to me, or I mean her, but I don't remember exactly what it did. He said it would show me what lay in the hearts of others. Their true intentions." I said this as I studied the gold pendant, remembering that he owed me a bow—or had he left me one? I turned then to Anubis. "Thank you for allowing me to borrow the dress and shoes. And may I keep the pendant as well?" I wanted to study it further in hopes of remembering what its purpose was, but I didn't want to wear it quite yet.

"You cannot borrow what is already yours. Take whatever you like." He was doing that thing again where he expected me to accept that this other person was me, but even after gaining more memories I still didn't feel like her. And I still wasn't sure I wanted to. "As for the pendant, that is something you must discover for yourself when you're ready. It was made specifically for you by Eros."

I nodded and, looking down, realized that I was wearing pajamas. I couldn't wear pj's home. "My clothes?" It suddenly occurred to me that someone would have had to undress me to change my clothes. I instantly became mortified, and I looked accusingly at both of them.

"We didn't undress you, although should the need ever arise...." Anubis playfully winked at me. "Your mother came to divulge information and helped us with that part."

"My mother, she was here?" There was awe in my voice and a deep-seated need. She came to visit Anubis but couldn't visit me. She had undressed me! I didn't know how to feel in that moment. Instead I decided to focus on the issues at hand and address my mother visiting me while I was unconscious later.

"She was. She brought important information concerning your well-being. She had to leave before her absence was noticed, but do understand she is desperate to see... I mean to say, meet you once again." I suppose after my reaction to the closet full of clothes he felt it best to tread carefully.

"If you'll excuse me so I can get dressed. And where are my clothes?" I waited as Anubis brought me a stack of my newly-washed and folded clothes and then headed out the door to give me privacy.

"I bid you a good day. I have work to do. Until next time." Thoth bowed to me and turned to leave.

"Wait." I hesitated as he turned.

"Yes?"

"Thank you. Thank you for being there for her." It was all I could say. I didn't know how else to express how I felt as I worked through these new emotions and memories that were still somewhat foreign to me.

"It was always my pleasure, as it still is." He smiled and turned to leave once again.

I sighed, looking around the room. Grabbing the stack of clothes, I dressed quickly and called for Anubis to come back in.

"What information did Aph-Aphrodite bring?" I couldn't bring myself to call her my mother at that moment and my voice broke just a bit on her name.

"Zeus is aware of your return and he is planning something. She wasn't able to get much information, but she knows he will come for you soon." Anubis looked serious and his eyes clouded as if he were far away.

"Why? Why after so many years would he still pursue me?" I was tired of their stupid games. Tired of waiting around until the big bad came for me and did god only knows what.

"He holds onto an idea that things will return to what they were long ago. He fears your prophecy, and fear makes people do things that are wrong in pursuit of something they perceive to be right." Anubis sighed and ran his hand through his hair, rubbing the back of his neck. He looked tired and stressed.

I realized then that this was a battle that he'd been facing for many millennia while waiting on me. Through all that time, was he still the same person? Once I remembered him, or once the other Jewel was fully alive within me, would she... we... still love him? Time can really change a person. I stood there awkwardly watching him, thinking to myself, *Do I want to love this man?* I knew I felt a strong attraction, almost like a compulsion towards him, but was it genuine? Was it just this other Jewel who kept trying to break through the surface of who I was now or was it me? All the questions were making my mind spin, and I was aware of Anubis watching me closely as I wrestled through this internal battle.

"What do I need to do to be prepare for this? For Zeus, for all of it? I need to know." I knew there was a pleading tone to my voice, but I didn't care. This was about survival, pride be damned.

"As we discussed before, there are two who wish to control you—or destroy you. My father, Set, and Zeus, your grandfather, wish to regain control over this planet and put up barriers between our species once again."

"When you say species, do you mean the Olympians, the Egyptonians, and mankind? Or mankind and...? Well, you know what I mean." It was one big complicated mess that made sense but didn't at the same time.

"Both. They want the lines drawn between us and them." He was adding me into the "us," which now that I knew I wasn't just a gifted human, I supposed I was indeed considered a part of the "us" he mentioned.

"Do you think I should worry that one of them is going to attack me soon?" I knew there was fear and worry in my voice. It wasn't so much the idea that they wanted me either dead or possibly something worse, but the unknowns of the whole situation were what scared me the most.

Before I could ask another question, Anubis closed the distance between us swiftly, throwing my discarded dress and shoes on a nearby chair and looking at me with such intensity it made my legs weak. He pressed my back up against the wall and looked me in the eyes, that intensity still there, fully focused on me. His face was mere inches from mine as he leaned in, brushing his lips against my cheek as he spoke into my ear.

"No one will ever hurt you, *ever*, while I am still breathing. I will protect you with my life and everything that I am till the end of my days." His deep, low voice sent a wave of sensations down my body. I wanted to rub my body on his and purr like a cat. His hands moved from my shoulders and up to my hair, which was in a side braid. He pulled the tie out and ran his fingers through the braid.

I looked down, trying to avoid the intensity in his eyes and the strange things he was making me feel. "I should probably be getting home."

He didn't listen. Instead he pulled my face up gently and kissed me. The kiss started off sweet but quickly filled with intense need as he deepened it hungrily. I felt powerless in that moment. I kissed him back, matching his intensity and raw need. I wrapped my arms around him, pulling him closer. In that moment, I let go of my reservations and concerns and just felt. This felt amazing, it felt real, and it felt dangerous. With that last thought, I pulled away. The disconnect of our bodies felt almost painful. I wanted him close, but I needed to regain control. There was disappointment on his handsome features. It was disappointment caused by me.

"I'll take you home. The dance you've been waiting for is tomorrow night and I don't want you to miss it." There wasn't any jealousy or malice in his voice as he said the words, but I knew he probably wasn't happy I was attending it with someone else. If it bothered him, though, he didn't say; rather, he picked up the dress and shoes and handed them to me. "Please, you alwa—you'll look beautiful in it."

Rather than argue, I took the dress and shoes. "Thank you."

We left then without another word. He pulled open a dark portal, and the coldness that usually stung my skin felt good as we stepped through. On the other side was my living room, where my father was waiting. He rushed to my side.

"Are you well, bunny? I was worried." My father hugged me, pulling me tight. It felt good to be hugged by him. His love kept me grounded in this world.

"Hi, Dad. Were you not able to see me?" It seemed odd to me that I'd been out for so long. It seemed like just a few hours ago I was in my room with my newly discovered sister and a splitting headache.

"I was but"—He looked at Anubis—"the travel arrangements didn't necessarily agree with me." I realized he was talking about Anubis's portal travel. It hadn't occurred to me that perhaps others would find that form of transport harder to deal with. I nodded understandingly, happy that he had at least been able to see me once.

"I shall leave you two now, if you'll excuse me." Anubis bowed then to us both, something I'd only seen him do a few times before, but it was a small reminder that he was a man who was indeed out of his own time, or slow to adapt to the changing times, depending on how you looked at it.

"Wait." I stopped, unsure of what I was about to say. "Will I—I mean, will we see you again soon?" I didn't know why I was concerned with him leaving, but I was.

"Yes." He smiled, as if pleased with my concern. "You'll see me later, but for now I have some things to deal with."

I nodded understandingly as I watched him disappear into the dark abyss that was his portal. The room felt surprisingly empty without him in it. I turned back to my father, trying not to think about it. Everything that had happened in the last few weeks seemed like an insane dream that I'd just become entangled in. Yet, I realized that even though I'd only known Anubis a short time, I didn't think it would be possible to ever forget him. But what was more surprising was that I was sure I definitely didn't *want* to ever forget him.

"Dad, if you don't mind, I'm going to spend some time alone in my room. I need to think about some things and process." I turned to pick up the dress and shoes, realizing I also still had the pendant necklace in my hand.

"That's a pretty dress you have there." He said *dress*, but I noticed his eyes were on the pendant.

"Yes, Anubis helped me find it… in a way." I didn't feel like explaining further. It was obvious he was still very interested in the necklace, but I tucked it under the dress. Why, I wasn't sure, but I could feel the pulsating warmth it emitted at my touch, and I felt I wanted it to be just mine for now.

"Good night." I smiled, kissed him gently on the cheek, and swiftly rushed off, carrying my golden spoils of the day with me.

CHAPTER FIFTEEN

Anubis

I STOOD THERE IN the room that Jewel had just occupied. It felt bleak and lonely without her presence. When she'd fallen unconscious I thought I was losing her again. I was lost and useless, yet I had coveted every second I was allowed to stay by her side. At one point Thoth had to run me off, and I'd hated him for it.

Having her here in this room again was more than I could handle. I realized in those moments of sitting with her that I had come to love her here, in this time as she was now, just as much as I had in the past. She was so similar to the old Jewel, yet there were many small differences in her personality. She'd always been adventurous and headstrong, but here she had developed an independence and passion that intrigued me. Her soul called to me, and the closer she came to transitioning the louder it became, till it was at a deafening volume that pierced right through me.

I ran my hands through my hair, sighing. I had things—important things—to accomplish before I returned to her. It bothered me that she was going to a dance with some teenage boy; however, I knew being overbearing and controlling would not only be wrong, but it would drive her away. Still, the desire to snatch her up and brand her as mine was so strong it was a constant struggle not to do just that.

Knock. Knock.

There was a gentle rap on the door that pulled me from my tormenting thoughts. I walked over to it, expecting to see Thoth standing at the threshold. Instead, there stood a woman who looked much like the woman I burned for every second of the day. It was her mother, Aphrodite.

"Hello again, Anubis." She didn't smile. Instead she stood there looking dire, waiting for me to invite her in.

"Hello, Aphrodite. Do come in."

She didn't even bother to pause as she swept into the room with a shuffling of silk and lace. She was always elaborately dressed. I noticed today she wore a dress the same shade of green as Jewel's eyes. It was one of their only differences. Jewel had sparkling green eyes that changed to a blue green on occasion. Her mother, on the other hand, had bright, pale blue eyes. Yet, they shared so many other features they could be confused as sisters.

"How is she?" She glanced at the empty bed. She had obviously chosen to arrive after Jewel left for a reason. She had come to visit Jewel earlier, when she was in her unconscious state, and helped care for her, only to leave with the plan to collect more information from the Olympians. She wanted to discover if they knew anything about Jewel's return yet. It was only a matter of time, and we needed to be prepared.

"I must say, Anubis, it would be alright to update the room. I'm sure she would understand." Jewel had been the last person to update the room and although I had changed things out and replaced them as they wore down, I had always replaced everything with an almost exact replica. The important things had gone into stasis, such as her closet. I'd gone into stasis as well, but I could only put myself in such a state for so long before having to come out for a period of time. This was the only way I had made it through the years without her: I would check on things while I was here and then go back in for another extended stay.

"I like it this way." I looked at the deep purple and brown bedspread and teal sheets. The remnants of the sea she had found on various excursions were still spread out here and there around the room. A tapestry she had been given by a fisherman's wife that she fell in love with still hung on the wall, tattered but intact. It was these things that I held so closely because they were hers. I'd never allow anything to be changed unless she was the one to do it.

"I see. You two were always something special." She stopped then, scrunching her face as if she was going to say something more on the subject but thought better of it. "I've information."

"Please share." She had my attention now. We needed to know what was being planned.

"As you know, Ares and I have not had such a pleasant relationship since... well, you know... what happened with Jewel. He and I have more or less cut ties." I nodded, understanding that Ares and she had been put on different sides of a conflict, causing severe stress on their relationship. "As a result, my information is harder to come by. Yet, I was still able to utilize a few resources."

"And what do they know? What are they planning?"

"They know she's here, which I told you before, and they're planning an attack soon. They want to do it before she transitions fully."

"Zeus is becoming scared. What about my father, have you heard any whisperings that way?" When I'd visited my father I'd learned very little that would help.

"As you know, Set doesn't feel as threatened by Jewel as my father does. His biggest concern has been his legacy, meaning you." She walked to the closet that Jewel had left open, looking inside it. A look of pain over things she'd once seen on her daughter crossed her features. "My father is concerned for his position and the future of his rule."

"So nothing from my father, then." I stated, rubbing my chin in thought. He wasn't a problem now, but he could become one in the future. If that problem did arise, we could deal with it then. With Osiris and Horus gone, he was left to rule in their place. Right now it was important to focus on Zeus and his plans.

"I do have news about another of my children." We had walked deeper into the closet and her hand stopped at the spot where the pendant necklace Jewel had taken had once been. "Eros has returned."

"I thought he was assumed dead after so long?" Eros had come back some time after Jewel's punishment was exacted, but he soon left and said he would return once again when it was time. It had been so long that I had forgotten all about his promise.

"He has returned, but where he is now, I'm not sure. I've just heard that they know his ship is near and he took a pod down to Earth." Aphrodite had been close to her son Eros. When she lost Jewel she, in essence, lost him as well.

"We'll find him."

"We had better because he knows how to save her." She stepped in close to me. "There's a good chance Jewel will die when she fully transforms because she has to transfer both immense power and a whole previous lifetime of memories into one vessel. She may not survive it. The transformation will come in waves; each eruption of power will increase. You'll see."

"How do you know this? No one truly knows what will happen. What they did to her has never been tried before."

It was then that Thoth entered the closet. "She is correct, my friend. It is a logical assumption that she would go through such a process." Thoth was using the logical tone he used when detaching himself from his emotions. I knew it was his own way of dealing with the infinite time he'd lived and his own past pain. "We must be prepared."

"So she could still die?"

"Yes," both Aphrodite and Thoth answered in unison.

"We need to find Eros. Where is he? And an even better question: How does he know what will happen?"

"Because he tried it on himself," Aphrodite said as she started to walk out of the closet.

"So he survived. She can too." I looked at Thoth then, hoping for support.

"It's not as simple as that." Obviously Thoth had already spoken to Aphrodite because he looked down, shaking his head in thought. "The process for him was different."

"He didn't go as far forward in time, and he found a way to complete the process without the age regression."

Aphrodite walked over to the bed and sat down. "Apparently after he left and accomplished his goal of establishing a colony on Planet Olympia, he began working on the technology necessary for the archaic science, despite it being banned. He was able to successfully send himself close to two thousand years in the future. After spending almost the same amount of time fixing our home planets."

"I must admit, I'm curious as to how and if he succeeded. And are there still people left on the surface of the planet? They must have changed somewhat through the millennia." As I said those words, I thought of the biggest failure of our two races combined. We left them behind. All of them. It was said that they had died, but some of us knew better. We left them to fend for themselves on planets that had been destroyed by our greed. It had been so long they would have forgotten about us. Most of the people who had come to Earth had forgotten as well, but not the few of us who held tightly to what we'd done. We had ultimately been punished by our greed, but truly there was not enough penance for the crimes we carried out against our own. That was why Eros had left. He couldn't bear the thought of how we left them there among wastelands.

"That is apparently where he 'ran off to' as you tend to say, but yes I am with you, Anubis. I would like to know how he succeeded and know how things are on that side of the universe after so long as well." Thoth paused, running his hand contemplatively along his chin. His respect for Eros was evident, but he too carried the same burden.

"Okay, well we still need to find him." I turned, directing my next words to Aphrodite. "I need you to focus on finding more information on what my father and Zeus are doing and when they're going to strike. I'm going to stay close to Jewel at all times, just in case." Even though I was doing this for protective reasons, any excuse to be near her made me happy. "Thoth, please try to see if you can find Eros's location." There was one other thing I'd wanted to say, so I paused, trying to remember it. *Ah, yes.* "Also, we need to find out what the hell Beroe and Poseidon are planning. Beroe has been in contact with Jewel."

"She can't be trusted." Aphrodite's words were cold. Beroe was also her daughter, but their history was less pleasant.

"I agree with you, but let us tread carefully on that one. She could be a strong ally if her intentions are good." Thoth put his hand on Aphrodite's shoulder to comfort her, something that was uncharacteristic of the normally distant man. She turned towards him, accepting the comfort and even putting her head on his shoulder. I realized this was something I would need to ask about later. They seemed to have gotten closer over the many years.

"I'm going to return to Jewel. In the meantime, if you need anything, just summon me." I quickly left the room cold as I stepped into my pitch-black portal, ready to see the one thing that drove out the cold from my life. My Jewel.

CHAPTER SIXTEEN

I HADN'T BEEN HOME for very long when Anubis returned. I felt the shift in the room when he arrived. My hair was wet from the shower I had desperately needed and I was lying across my bed on my belly. Although I'd obviously been asleep for a long period, my body still felt tired. The pendant lay on my nightstand and I reached for it. I waited, watching Anubis make himself comfortable in the chair in the corner of my room.

"Do you know what this is?" I myself knew, to a certain extent, but I was staring at the pendant intently now, trying to remember every detail of the memory.

"Yes, it was a gift to you."

"From Eros, my... my brother."

"Yes."

I scrunched up my nose at him. I hated that he knew so much and I felt I knew so little. "Do you know why he gave it to me?"

"I do."

"Tell me." I looked at him pointedly. I was being demanding, but he was being irritating, so I didn't feel so bad.

"How about we start with what you know."

I threw a pillow at him then, which he dodged without batting an eye. It made me want to throw another one, but I only had one left. I sighed loudly and with impatience. "I know he gave it to me." My words were laced with the annoyance I felt.

"He did. And what else?"

"He said it would show me the truth of what lay in people's hearts, their true intentions." I was surprised at how easily I was able to remember that. My annoyance was gone now, and I held the pendant up, letting it dangle freely. I felt a strong urge to put it on. I was about to when Anubis stopped me.

"I would wait to put it on. You have a strong connection to that necklace and it could cause you to have more... issues." I realized he was right. I should probably at least give it a day before I put it on.

"Okay, then what brings you back to invade my room with your cold hotness?" I laughed at the oxymoron, which fit him perfectly. Even though physically he was hot in practically every way possible, cold seemed to follow everywhere he went, especially with his portals. Luckily, he found it humorous too and smiled back. It was the kind of smile delicious fantasies are made from.

"I'm here to make sure you stay safe. I'll just stay here in the chair while you sleep and watch over you." He leaned back in the chair, crossing his long legs, as if preparing for the long haul.

I rolled over onto my back, placing the necklace in the

drawer of my nightstand. With him here with me I didn't think it was possible to fall asleep, but before I knew it I drifted off and was dreaming once again.

"I MANAGED TO *upgrade the thrusters, just like you showed me." I beamed up at my mentor, waiting for his approval.*

"Indeed, rather impressive. And we've enhanced the shield so that the pod is undetectable to any kind of probe or sensor. I was also able to upgrade the GPS and COM system. With what we've done together, it could easily be space flight ready with a few more upgrades to the shield, but only for short distances. It should do rather nicely." He examined the outside of the pod. He was an intense stickler for smooth lines and precision. "What name have you given it? It is customary for people on Earth to humanize objects."

"It looks to me like a great warrior, even though it has no weapons. It's smart and agile." I paused, trying to think of an appropriate name, but I couldn't come up with anything. I looked up at Thoth. "In your culture, who is the greatest warrior?"

He contemplated for a moment. "The greatest warrior would be a matter of opinion, as there are many that have been given that title in my 'culture,' as you put it."

"May I ask who? You talk so little of your people."

"Indeed, I do, for they remain the same whether I talk about them or not." He looked at me, but it seemed as though his gaze went right through me, as he was lost in his thoughts. He did this often, as if all his thoughts and ideas sometimes took hold of him.

"Thoth, please. Who are your greatest warriors, and in your opinion, who is the greatest?" I stood then, dusting off the sand that seemed to find its way into everything in this small,

hidden city.

"*Well there is Horus, Osiris, who now prefers peace, Set, Anubis, and many more. But as for my opinion on the greatest, well I suppose Anubis would hold that title. He was coined 'the bringer of death,' which was then translated to 'the guide of the dead' on this planet.*"

"*Well that sounds morbid, but it fits, in a way. I'll name it Anubis. Do you think he will approve?*"

"*I'm not sure, but it's time, my child. You must gather your things.*"

I sighed, looking out around me at the city. Poseidon and Beroe were gone, both at the same time, which never happened. This was my only chance to leave. I'd been here for four years, and I had learned of Poseidon and Beroe's desire to use me years ago. I'd kept to Thoth mostly, seeing as his intentions were true. He'd been my closest friend and ally. Now I finally had a chance to go. I had to take it.

"*I know you're right, but how do I know that they won't find me in the world of humans?*" *We had decided that the best course of action was for me to hide as a human in a coastal town close to the border. We weren't sure if, when the time came, I might have to flee.*

"*I'm going home to Egypt. If ever you need me, you can seek me there, where you are forbidden to seek. But you must only do this if times are desperate, because it is dangerous, Jewel.*"

"*I understand. I'll miss you.*" *He wasn't one to allow emotions to influence him, so I didn't expect a reply.*

"*I shall miss you as well,*" *he said with sincerity in his eyes.*

I felt my eyes well up with tears as I hugged him tight. At first he stood awkwardly but eventually returned the hug. "*We* shall see each other again, I'm sure of it."

"Indeed, my child, I'm sure we will." We turned to gather the supplies we had hurriedly put together. "We must make haste or this opportunity will leave us both."

"How shall you travel if I'm taking the pod?"

"I have my own ways of reaching destinations."

We didn't say much else after that because there wasn't really anything else to say. I finished loading the newly named pod, gave him one last look, and jumped into the seat of the Anubis. Thoth waved to me before disintegrating into a whirlwind of sand before my eyes. I set my navigation system and turned on the thrusters and was gone in a split second. As I took off, my hand went to my pendant necklace around my neck. It had always lived up to Eros's promise; it showed me the true intentions that lay in people's hearts. Otherwise, I would have still been stuck here as a puppet for my sister and Poseidon.

The ocean stretched out around me, far as the eye could see, and I easily pushed through the barrier that hid Atlantis. I remembered back to the day I had come, not realizing it would become my home. I had been fascinated with Atlantis at first, but the truth had slowly leaked its way to the surface. It was time for me to leave the city behind.

I traveled quickly; my thrusters were indeed a smart upgrade. Before I knew it, the tiny fishing village on the coast across from Thoth's people's territory came into view. I checked to make sure my shields were working properly and found an area outside of the village that was shielded by trees. I landed the pod and looked around to see if I was alone. There were a few sparse areas of green brush and trees, and then a sandy beach met gentle waves. I opened the hatch and I breathed in, tasting the salt and smell of ocean life. I could also smell the *faint smell of fish wafting from the fishing village.*

When I realized the coast was clear in all directions, I slowly stepped out of the pod. I assessed my dress. It was plain enough to blend in with the clothing of the area. I grabbed the change purse Thoth had procured for me and an apple to hold me over. It was time to find my new home. I had never felt more alone in all my life than I did in that moment. Yet, the excitement of trying something new took over and my loneliness dissipated.

Off I went, following the sandy beach towards the village and my new life among humans.

CHAPTER SEVENTEEN

I AWOKE THEN TO the sound of Anubis sleeping near me, breathing deeply. It was still dark outside. I lay back in the bed thinking of my dream. I could only imagine how difficult Jewel's life must have been. She was forced to live with people who wanted to use her, and she was in danger starting at a young age. As I started to process her memories, I found that I was gaining respect for the person that was me before this life. She was brave, fearless, and able to adapt easily as things changed around her. She was pretty amazing. It occurred to me that I might not be able to live up to her image.

I sighed, looking at Anubis. Suddenly, I couldn't hold back the giggles that escaped me. She had unknowingly named her pod shuttle after the man she would fall in love with. I wondered if she found that as hilarious as I did. The laughter caused Anubis to wake up, and he was now smiling at me.

"May I ask what is so funny?" The room was dark, but

even so, I could easily see his chiseled outline and his smirk. I smiled back, knowing I had to ask.

"Did the Anubis and Anubis ever meet?"

He smiled wider, and I could see the whiteness of his teeth in the dark. "Unfortunately, no. We did not get the opportunity to meet. The Anubis perished before I was fortunate enough to meet it." His voice was deep and teasing. It made me feel warm inside.

"That is unfortunate," I said, laughter still in my voice.

"You should go back to sleep. It's only been a few hours."

I looked at my bedside table and saw that he was right, but I felt wide-awake. So instead, I turned on the lamp next to me. There were seashells stenciled onto the lampshade so that, when the light shined through, it projected them onto the wall. It occurred to me then that subconsciously I had gravitated towards things that reminded me of my previous life. I examined my room, wondering what other little reminders I might find. I looked up at the constellations on my ceiling, trying to remember when I'd put them there and why.

"You know, when I was nine I studied the constellations. I decided to put the constellation that matched my zodiac sign on my ceiling. I told my dad it was so it would always remind of who I am and where I came from. I painted it and went over the stars with glow-in-the-dark paint. I was so adamant about it being perfect."

"That's interesting because, do you see that star there?" He pointed up to the only star I'd given surrealistic sparkle to, with light streaming from it like a Van Gogh painting. It was to the right of Orion and not really important in the scheme of the constellation, but my nine-year-old self had painted it that way.

"Yes."

"That one is our sun. From our planet."

"Shut the front door!" I would've thought I'd be more creeped out by this revelation, but I wasn't. I was intrigued.

"I would, but it's already shut." His response was so serious and dry that I burst out into uncontrollable laughter once again while he sat there with the funniest puzzled expression that just fed my laughter more.

"No, it's just an expression."

"Oh, well my apologies. The lingo changes so rapidly, it becomes hard to keep up."

"Indeed." I gave my best Thoth-mimicking response, suppressing my smile poorly.

"Again, you should go to sleep. Your body needs to heal." He looked at me pointedly.

"Okay, Dad, I'll get on that," I sarcastically teased.

He seemed appalled at my words. "I am *not* your father or anything like him." He leaned forward then, looking even more set to make me obey.

"Fine, I'll go back to sleep if you do something for me."

"Anything for you."

"Good, come lay with me like you did the other day." I moved over in my bed and patted the space next to me. He sighed, but didn't protest as he slid into the bed. He lay on top of the covers, probably to protect my dignity. I wasn't sure I wanted him to and so I pulled his arm around me and snuggled in close, his large body once again fitting perfectly with mine. I was soon fast asleep.

I woke in the late morning. Anubis wasn't in bed with me. I could hear him and my dad in the living room talking, but couldn't make out their words. I rolled over, staring up at my Van Gogh star on the ceiling. Today was the dance and my unofficial graduation. I stretched out like a cat and rolled over to where Anubis had slept. The pillow he'd used smelled just like him and I breathed in his scent. I could see why old Jewel fell crazy in love with this guy. He was pretty special, even if you took the popping through portals and the fact that he'd lived for like ever out of the equation.

I quickly got dressed and joined them in the living room. They were sitting at the counter drinking coffee together, as if it were a normal thing for them to do. It struck me as odd that they were so comfortable with each other. It seemed Anubis was more comfortable being in close proximity to my dad than most people at the compound were.

"Good morning." I rushed over to kiss my dad on the cheek and I stole a sip of his coffee.

"Good morning, bunny. Anubis and I were just discussing the fact that we feel it would be best if we come to the dance tonight for added protection."

"Wouldn't that be a little weird? You being my dad and all?"

"I suppose you're right. I'll stay out of view and Anubis can keep an eye on you."

I still felt awkward. I was going to the dance with Andrew. Having Anubis watching over me just made that seem wrong.

"The dance is actually starting in just a few hours. I slept the whole morning away. So I'll agree to this, but you two need to let me have my last bit of human normalcy for tonight," I insisted.

I danced around the kitchen, grabbing the milk, a bowl and spoon, and a box of Rice Krispies. Once again, I felt like I hadn't eaten in forever. I polished off three bowls of cereal quickly without talking while they sat there watching me.

With a mouthful of Rice Krispies I said, "Oh my god. I look like a freak right now, don't I?"

"No," they both said in unison. They were lying.

"You just look hungry." Anubis interjected this comment with a wink, and I felt the desire to sling cereal and milk at him with my spoon. Instead I glared at him as I continued to shovel the crackling bits into my mouth. Before I gave into the urge to pitch food at him and his smiling face after all, there was a knock on the door.

"Come in," my father called towards the door.

Teddy walked in, his hair wet, probably from a recent swim.

"Hey Teddy." I waved at him and set my cereal down. Teddy was glaring at Anubis, who was matching his stare. Teddy broke first and I almost swore I saw a slight twitch of a triumphant smile on Anubis's face.

"Hey, Jewel. I came as soon as I heard you were back." He walked towards me and spoke more quietly. "Are you okay?"

"Yeah, I'm as well as can be expected. Hey, I want to show you something. Come with me to my room." I waved goodbye to the two large men taking up nearly all the room in the kitchen. Teddy was a pretty good size for his age, but they still dwarfed him by half a foot or more. He seemed unaware or didn't care because he waved as well and followed me to my room. I didn't miss the look of disapproval from Anubis. Screw his opinion. This was my best friend. I flipped Anubis the bird as I shut the door behind me. I was turning towards Teddy as the laughter from my dad echoed in the background.

"Teddy, I'm so glad you're here. I am in serious need of

some normalcy, you have no idea." I flopped onto my bed with an exasperated exhale.

"So what really happened to you? I know you didn't go visit family because you can't actually visit them. At least not without consequences." I had forgotten for a moment that I'd told Teddy everything, and his words took me aback for a second.

"Ah right, you're right. Yes. No, I was with Anubis." I sat up and he sat next to me. "I was in a coma of sorts. They tried to subdue my memories to help my transition by exposing me to one memory and using it to suppress the rest, but it didn't work, and the machine went crazy, and I don't know what happened after that."

"Oh shit, Jewel that's crazy. Are you sure you're okay?"

"Yeah, I think I am. I finally remember a bit more, and the awful headache I had before it happened is gone." I thought back to the events of the day I'd fallen unconscious. My own sister had sat on this very bed. "You remember Allison, right?"

"Yeah, what about her?"

"She's Beroe, my half-sister."

"Seriously?" He laughed. "You have so much drama. We could do a reality television show about your life and no one would believe it was real."

"Heck yeah, I do." I stood then, walking over to the nightstand. "I have something I want to show you." I pulled the necklace out, feeling once again the warmth on my palm.

"What is that?" He moved closer to me, peering at the pendant. "It's nice. Where did you get it?"

I wasn't showing him the necklace to get a compliment. I wanted him to know what I knew. I needed someone to share in my crazy, and Teddy was my best friend and therefore my best option to share the knowledge burden with.

"It was hers. The other Jewel's. It was given to her by her brother Eros." As if in response, a low light pulsated from the pendant in my palm.

"Amazing." Teddy reached for it, but I pulled my hand back. The look of disappointment was evident on his face.

"Teddy, I'm not entirely sure what all it does. I'm going to wear it tonight, but I think it's best that I be the only one to handle it." I didn't trust it not to do something nefarious to him. He nodded in understanding, which elicited a sigh of relief from me.

"So, did you ask her?" I nudged him with my shoulder playfully. He'd been contemplating asking Monica out for weeks now but kept losing his courage.

"I did."

"What did she say?" I waited, ready to either give him moral support or share in his triumph. His smile gave me the answer even before he spoke.

"She said yes, but that I better not stomp on her feet." We laughed together, because it was so like her.

"That's great! I'm so happy for you," I said with as much honest sincerity as I could muster. She and I weren't each other's favorite people, but all I cared about was Teddy's happiness.

"What about you? What's going on with all your man drama, guuuurl?" He flipped his wrist with a snap and did his best RuPaul impression, and I lightly smacked him on the shoulder.

"It's complicated." I sighed and my back slumped as if the weight of the world were pushing me down.

"How is it complicated?"

"It just is." I was trying to avoid the question, but he wasn't going to let it go.

"So you like both Andrew and Anubis? Is that what's complicated?"

"Somewhat," I answered, standing up and pulling out the gold dress that Anubis had brought for me. "What do you think of this?"

"You'll look good in it, but stop evading the question."

"I'm not evading, more like I'm not sure how to answer."

"Okay, but you know eventually you'll have to make a decision."

I sighed heavily. I knew he was right and as I stood there running one hand over the soft fabric of the dress and clutching the pendant in my other hand I realized Teddy was the best person to help me work through my feelings.

"I like Andrew. I do. I like that he holds some sort of normal-ish opportunity for me—or at least the idea of it. I guess I feel like that's what he represents."

"But?" Teddy was so direct in his questioning. I felt like he understood me better than anyone. Well, almost. It seemed Anubis somehow knew me just as well.

"But it's different…." I sat there for a moment, working through my thoughts and feelings. "It's different with Anubis. I'm scared of what that means." I put the dress down and walked back to Teddy.

"It depends on how it's different."

"I have strong feelings for Anubis. I don't fully understand them. I feel a *need* to be with him, almost like we're two magnets being pulled towards one another. I find myself thinking about him when he isn't around. It's as natural as breathing but…" I paused again, looking towards the door, towards where Anubis was more than likely still sitting with my dad. "But I'm afraid these are *her* feelings and not mine. What if I lose me in the process?"

"Well that's some deep shit there." He patted me on the shoulder, trying to relieve some of the tension. "I guess the question is, what would you feel if he just disappeared from your life?"

I sat there contemplating Teddy's question with sincerity. "I don't think I want to think about that right now."

"Why?"

"Because I'm afraid." I looked pleadingly at Teddy, hoping he would let me off the hook. No such luck.

"What are you afraid of?"

"I'm afraid of several things. I'm afraid of losing who I am to this other Jewel, and I'm afraid that the only way to be with him is to become her. And then I'm also afraid I'll never see him again, like the sun will never rise for me again if he suddenly goes away." I let the words, raw and emotionally charged, just slip out in a way that surprised even me.

"So I suppose the real question is, do you—as in this Jewel, in this life—love him? And does it really matter that she did?"

"It's not that easy. How do I know that it's not her emotions influencing me?" I asked, letting my insecurities out in that moment.

"Jewel, I think it's time you come to terms with the fact that you and she are one and the same."

"We are not. I don't want to be her." I narrowed my eyes at him, feeling the conviction behind my words.

"You are her and she is you. You think you're going to

change, but I disagree. I think she's been with you all along."

I realized he could very well be right. I looked around my room, seeing the influence she'd had on it when I didn't even know it.

"Shit." I playfully punched him in the arm. "I hate it when you get all philosophical and right."

"Damn straight, because I'm awesome, guuurl." He did his RuPaul imitation again and we burst out laughing.

"Sometimes you get it right," I admitted.

"So I guess the next question would be: How do you feel about Andrew?"

"I don't know. I need to think about that."

I changed the subject by asking what he'd learned about his abilities lately, and I was happy he didn't fight me this time. We spent most of the rest of the day catching up and playing a few video games. Soon there was a gentle knock on the door.

"Come in."

Anubis opened the door and peered in. "I believe it's time for you to start getting ready for the dance if you want to make it."

Teddy popped up out of the gaming seat he liked to use and we turned off the console. "I should go get ready for my hot date as well." He winked at me as he ran out the door.

"Thanks, Anubis. Can you stay here while I get ready? I might need help. That zipper looks like it will be an issue."

"Of course." He nodded towards me and went to sit in the chair he'd occupied the night before.

I grabbed the gold dress and headed towards the bathroom. I took a quick shower and applied my makeup and fixed my hair, then I pulled the dress on. It fit just as Anubis said it would, perfectly. I walked over and opened the door, realizing that the zipper was too hard for me to zip up on my own, just as I'd suspected it would be.

"Anubis."

"Yes"

"My zipper, can you?"

He stopped short as soon as he stepped through the door. His eyes roamed my body and I felt myself flush. "Of course." He walked behind me as I faced the large vanity mirror. I watched him look down and felt his fingertips graze the skin of my back as he closed the zipper. I swear he took his time on purpose, and I didn't even care. I had a strong desire to lean back into him, and when I looked up to examine myself in the mirror, my eyes landed first on Anubis. He was looking at me like I was a big juicy steak and he was starving.

I tore my eyes away from him and went back to focusing on my appearance. The gold dress shimmered and looked amazing against my pale skin. I had pulled my hair to the side and pinned the back. I kept my makeup simple, but left my lips a red that made them look luscious and pouty in an old school Hollywood glam way, perfectly complementing my complexion. The dress was beautiful. It was long and had a slit up one leg. The bustline was low-cut but still modest enough for the dance. It had spaghetti straps that went over my arms, connecting to straps that crisscrossed along my sides. I turned around so I could see the back of the dress in the mirror. My back was bare except for the straps at the sides, and the dress dipped dangerously low just stopping above my round ass. I looked… I looked different, but good.

I grabbed the shoes and left the bathroom, leaving Anubis behind. I slipped the sandals on, grateful that they weren't high heels. I knew I wouldn't survive the night in heels. Then I remembered the last piece of the puzzle. The necklace. I turned once again to Anubis, who had followed me out of the bathroom.

"Do you mind?" I held the necklace up to him. He smiled at me as I stood to let him put it on.

"Of course." He helped me again, less strained this time as he clasped the pendant necklace around my neck and I felt it warm my skin. His hands brushed along my skin, leaving a trail of tingling warmth as well (or was that my imagination?), and I felt myself blush. The pendant heated up even more, then gradually cooled down. I thought I might have felt more of a powerful surge once the necklace was on, but no, that was it.

I turned back to Anubis. "How do—?" I stopped and stared at him. He was glowing a bright red, almost the same color as my lipstick. And he was looking at me with the same intensity he'd had in the bathroom. But the glow. Why was he glowing? "You… you're red."

He smiled and I swear that smirk was devious. "As for your first question, you look absolutely beautiful. As a matter of fact, you are the most beautiful woman I have ever had the pleasure of knowing." The red glow around him intensified with his words. "As for the glow, you can thank the necklace. It shows you the true intent of people's hearts. It does that with color, sort of like auras."

"What does red mean?"

He was smiling again devilishly, and he moved closer to me, so close he whispered in my ear. It sent chills down to my naughty parts. "Red signifies love. It signifies passion. It signifies true devotion." His words, I knew, were true. And I felt his love, his passion, his devotion. I also felt the need to have his hands on my body. I wanted him, in that moment, in ways that were driven by pure, instinctual need and desire. I gazed up into his deep brown eyes and saw that he felt the same. When his lips touched mine, they were hungry, needy, rough, and the kiss ravaged me to my very soul.

The knock on the door brought us both back to our senses, and I stepped back, touching my now-sensitive lips.

"Jewel, Andrew is here to take you to the dance."

"I'll be right there," I answered, my voice rough, my breathing heavy. I walked towards the door, looking back at Anubis, who was still enveloped in a bright red glow. When I walked through the door, Andrew stood there in the living room area with my dad standing next to him. Their eyes took in my appearance.

"Bunny, you look beau—" His words were cut short when he saw the pendant at my neckline. My hands went up instinctively to cover it. I noticed that his coloring was a mix between yellow and pink. Andrew was enveloped in a soft pink glow, but he didn't glow nearly as brightly as Anubis had.

"You look amazing," Andrew continued where my dad had left off. My dad was still staring at the necklace. Andrew was wearing a black suit; his tie was a blue that matched his eyes and his dark hair was tamed into a slightly less messy style than usual.

"Thank you." Of course, his comment wasn't as personal or intimate as Anubis's compliment had been, but it was sweet, and I noticed that Andrew's pink glow intensified just the teensiest bit. That had to mean something, right? My dad's clear distraction because of the necklace was something I would have to look into later. But for now, I wanted to enjoy my last night of teenage normalcy. "Alright, let's get out of here."

I walked over to Andrew and took his arm just as Anubis was shutting the door to my room. Andrew was already walking out the door and didn't notice, but I looked back and smiled. Anubis didn't smile back. He was glaring once again at Andrew.

Ugh, men and their testosterone-driven need to compete. I turned my smile into a matching glare and then turned my back to him. He could suck a duck for all I cared. I was going to have a fun night without stupid drama.

CHAPTER EIGHTEEN

EITHER ANDREW NOR I had our licenses, so I didn't expect either of us to drive to the dance. I also hadn't expected the stretch hummer limousine that pulled up to the front door as we walked through it. Yet, there it was, with bright purple undercarriage lights and the sounds of blaring music coming from inside. The driver came around and opened the door for us, and Teddy popped his head out.

"Get your butts in here and join the party!" His head disappeared back into the hummer.

We ducked our heads to step in. Inside Gale, Jeff, Teddy, and Monica were waiting for us. Jeff was in a black tux with a silver vest and tie, while Gale was wearing a sky-blue lace dress that was short and showed off her long legs. Teddy was also in a black tux with a silver and purple tie; they'd obviously gone shopping together. Monica wore a burgundy puffy ballgown with a corset that almost swallowed her tiny body, which would probably look very elegant on her when she wasn't shoved into a hummer. It was a beautiful color with her brown eyes and skin tone. Even though she didn't like me and was currently shooting looks of death my way, I held no ill will towards her.

"Monica, you look very pretty. I love that dress." Her glare softened for a moment and I gave her a delighted smile, only for her to glare suspiciously at me once again—small steps, small steps of achievement.

I felt the heat of the necklace touching my skin as I looked at Gale and Jeff, who were engrossed in only each other and both glowed brightly crimson red, though theirs still wasn't as deep as Anubis's red glow. Then I turned towards Teddy, who was looking at Monica. He was glowing a color similar to Andrew's. It was more pink than red. I had a good idea of what the different colors meant, but I still wished I knew exactly what they represented. I didn't like guessing games.

"Jewel, how was your trip to see your family?" Jeff asked. It was rare that any of us left Glen Delphi, let alone visited family on the outside. Sometimes Evols chose to live in society or on another compound, but not often.

"It was good." I smiled, hoping they believed me. I wasn't in the mood to explain to anyone else my screwed-up life. Luckily Teddy came to my rescue.

"Canada must be super cold this time of year. Did you get a chance to do any skiing?" Teddy knew I liked to ski on occasion. We would bug my dad until he finally relented and let us spend a short few days in Vail or Breckenridge hitting the slopes.

"No, I didn't want to use their crappy rental skis." Teddy and I laughed together at that. He knew I dragged my coveted pair of skis with me on each trip we took.

I noticed Monica giving me more glares, and I was sure it was because, once again, I was having a conversation with her date. I noticed in that moment that the color that surrounded her was a light green mixed with smoky-looking tendrils of pink. Did this mean she was starting to like Teddy? And did the green mean she was jealous of me? Seriously? She was actually literally green with envy? I found myself laughing so hard at this thought that the rest of my group looked at me with unease, probably trying to decide if I was crazy. I just laughed even harder.

After my crazy outburst, the rest of the car ride was pretty quiet as we waited to get to the school. I watched as Jeff and Gale snuggled into each other and Teddy and Monica politely sat next to one another. Andrew put his hand in mine and looked up at me to see if it was okay. I nodded, seeing nothing wrong with him holding my hand. However, the contact just didn't feel the same as when Anubis held me. I flushed, thinking about how Anubis had touched me earlier and sent shivers through my body.

"We're here," Teddy announced. He was sitting closest to the door, so he opened it. He helped Monica out with her poufy ballgown then turned to help me out as well. Monica became even greener around the edges. I smiled at her. Okay, I'll admit that there might have been the teensiest bit of satisfaction in my smile, but I really was trying.

"May I?" Andrew took my hand once again as we headed hand-in-hand towards the entrance. We could hear hip-hop blaring as we walked through the lobby and stood in line to get in. Many of the teachers were around, chaperoning or taking tickets. A few nodded or smiled towards me, but none said anything. I'd always been a pretty good student, but the stigma that surrounded me and my friends usually scared them off, so they weren't ever really close to any of us.

The cafeteria was empty of the tables and chairs that normally occupied the room, and instead the room was set up with muted lights, streamers, and lots of cardboard decorations that were reminiscent of a night out on the town. A few tables were pushed to one side of the room, decorated with tablecloths and centerpieces with green hydrangeas and a few black feathers sticking out. The events committee had really outdone themselves on this dance. It made me sad to think I wouldn't be here for prom. I supposed this was my prom, in a way. Most of the people were already on the dance floor. There was a DJ in the center of the room that was riling up the crowd. Then the latest Justin Timberlake song popped on over the speakers, telling everyone to dance.

"Ready to show me what you got?" I teased Andrew.

"Anytime, anywhere."

I smiled at Andrew and let go of his hand, running over to the dance floor. I'd never been shy and was ready to enjoy tonight as much as I could. Andrew followed me with an equally mischievous smile to match my own. Teddy and Monica followed behind him, but Gale and Jeff had disappeared. I threw my arms up and let the music flow over me, moving my body to the beat. Andrew followed me pretty well. I gasped when he grabbed me and spun me out then back into his arms. The whole time, I watched as his glow changed; it always had some pink, but sometimes it was mixed with orange or yellow. I wondered what those new colors meant. We laughed and smiled at each other, dancing to each song that came on until we began to sweat.

"Would you like something to drink?" Andrew shouted over the loud music and nodded towards the refreshment table.

"Yes!" I laughed my answer, realizing water was much needed in that moment.

"I'll be right back." He veered off to the right squeezing through the people that had crowded the floor.

It was then that Beroe bumped into me with her Allison disguise on.

"Jewel, you look beautiful." She looked me up and down, her eyes falling on the pendant around my neck. Her colors were such a strange mix, it was confusing. She glowed a mixture of blue, green, purple, and a tiny amount of pink. I really needed to find out what these colors meant.

I had once known an Evol with a similar ability who was able to read a person's emotions and connect empathetically with others, to the point that she could influence their moods. I really wished I had her with me so I could learn how these colors matched up with a person's emotions.

"What do you want?"

"Believe it or not, I *am* here to help you." She looked around, her eyes pausing on someone at the back of the room. I looked to see who'd caught her attention. It was Anubis and he was now headed our way. "They're coming. You will need to leave soon and not draw any attention to yourself."

"Who?"

"People who want to hurt you and won't care who gets in the way." Her colors changed again. She was like a swirling Grateful Dead tie-dyed t-shirt. I didn't trust her and her myriad of rainbow emotions, but before I could ask any more questions, she was weaving through the crowd in the opposite direction from the one Anubis was coming from.

Anubis stopped in front of me, a look of concern on his face. A slow song came on. I knew I should tell Anubis about Beroe and her warning, but in that moment with the lights down low and the look of hunger and need on Anubis's face as his eyes fondled me, I felt drawn to him. I was as desperate for his nearness as he was starving in his expression as he devoured me with one look. I was unable to resist him. I decided Beroe's veiled threats weren't going to ruin my night. I needed this. I needed to be normal for just one moment, with this man. I grabbed him and moved in close, looking into his eyes. At first, I caught him off guard and he gave a startled look, but he quickly recovered and pulled me close. I couldn't look away from his eyes and quickly forgot Beroe's warning until he leaned close to my ear and spoke.

"What did that girl want from you? You looked concerned." His voice caressed my ear and sent shivers of pleasure down my body. I wanted to melt into him.

"She said she was trying to help me." I knew I should have been more concerned than I was in that moment, but it felt good to be held by him. This was nothing like what I felt when I was with Andrew. Right now, dancing so close to Anubis, I wanted to stay here forever, in his arms. I wanted to wrap my body around him and feel his body pressed against mine. I wanted him to touch me. I wanted him to stay near me. I couldn't deny it anymore. No matter how much I tried to fight it, I wanted this man more than anything in the world.

"Help you with what?" he whispered. His words, again so close to my ear, turned me on to a point my knees almost buckled. I wanted him to kiss me so bad. I practically begged him with my eyes as I bit my lip. I couldn't focus on his question. He was so brightly red right now, but there was a little bit of green on the edges as well.

"Hmmm, oh yes, that's apparently my sister Beroe, and she said they're coming. I don't know who they a—"

Before I could finish, he snatched my hand and started dragging me through the crowd. "We need to go."

I pulled back, confused and desperate to hold onto this moment, but he didn't even budge. He continued to drag me along. The haze I was in earlier quickly vanished, and my stomach turned to ice. Something was very wrong. I realized then that I'd let my feelings and desire to be near him blind me to a very serious situation. We were in some serious shit.

"Hey, wait a minute!" I stopped, planted there, not budging. "It's Zeus and his hunting party, isn't it? I didn't trust Beroe. I thought she was lying to distract me." I tugged again, wanting to know what I was potentially facing before I ended up rushing into it headlong. "Tell me, am I right?" He paused, turning towards me. I was about to say something else when he picked me up and carried me out like a sack of potatoes. *What the hell?!* Okay, he was going more than a little overboard.

On our way out, I saw Teddy and Monica. They stopped dancing and went for Andrew, who was still waiting in the long line, trying to procure drinks.

"It's dangerous. We need to go now," Anubis said, his tone commanding and blunt. By this time, we were almost in the parking lot. Teddy, Monica, and Andrew were hurrying after us, trying to catch up.

When Andrew got close enough for us to hear him, he called, "Hey man, what are you doing? You'd better put her down."

Anubis ignored him. I looked to the right of the building and noticed Gale and Jeff. They had apparently been making out, but once they saw the scene that was starting up between Andrew and Anubis they disentangled themselves and quickly joined us. Anubis ignored everyone and walked faster. I decided I was done with being hoisted over his shoulder, so I swatted at his back.

"Listen, put me down! I'll go with you, okay." He dropped me to my feet, but I started to fall and he grabbed me before I face-planted. It must've looked like he was hurting me, though, because Andrew jumped to my defense again.

"Hey, seriously if you don't let her go, I'm going to torch you." Andrew stood poised to fight. His emotions were getting too riled up and the fire was in his eyes. He was about to go up in flames, quite literally. Teddy was the only one trying to first assess the situation, while Monica, Gale, and Jeff were all poised and ready to go.

"Yeah, he's right. I don't know who you are, but we are not the people you want to mess with," Jeff announced, moving his body in front of Gale as if to protect her. The wind around Gale began to spin in a tornado fashion, lifting dirt and debris up from the ground, her dark hair whipping madly around her face.

I looked at Anubis, silently pleading with him to let me fix this before it escalated. He nodded silently. "Listen, guys, it's fine." I put my hands out in a calming gesture. "He's right. You need to get out of here. There are bad people coming and they only want me."

"Jewel, what's going on? I'm not going anywhere without you," Teddy piped in from next to Monica. Teddy wasn't much use without a water source nearby, but he was still preparing for a fight.

"I'm not going anywhere either." Andrew planted his feet, glaring at Anubis as if he were the threat, and in a way, I suppose he was—to Andrew.

"Damnit." Monica stood straight and directed her words towards me with conviction. "As much as I really don't like you most of the time, you once helped me learn how to do what I can do, so I'm staying too."

"Us too," Jeff and Gale piped in together.

I was surprised and moved by their support, but I couldn't let them stay. Just as I was about to argue, a bright light appeared in the field and we heard sounds like something was landing there. Dust and dirt exploded into the air. As it cleared, three figures stood there with their backs to us. Anubis pulled a sword emanating some sort of purple energy out of what appeared to be thin air.

"Get ready. They're coming. Jewel, stay close to me. Do not leave me for anything." I nodded, but my eyes stayed fixed on the three figures across the field. They were turning. They saw us. They were coming.

"That's far enough," Anubis shouted across the field.

"Anubis, is that you?" the man in the lead shouted back. He was tall and his hair and beard were a dark auburn color. He held a similar sword to the one that Anubis carried, but his was blue. He wore what appeared to be a breastplate, much like what a Roman soldier would have worn.

Next to him were two opposites. One was the most beautiful woman I'd ever laid eyes upon. Her hair was pale and braided back. She also wore armor of some sort, only in a different style. The other was a pale, ugly creature of a man who looked at us with glee that somehow managed to look like an expression of disgust. He wore more modern attire. It was black and he held no weapon. Something told me he *was* the weapon.

"Ares, what are you doing here?" Shit, did he say Ares? This man in the lead who looked like a warlord was my real father.

"You know why I'm here." He pointed towards me. "I'm here to collect my daughter."

"Over my dead body." Anubis glared at him, and although he was sort of assuming I couldn't take care myself, I did appreciate that he was here to protect me—until he spoke again. "She's mine."

I ripped into Anubis for that, yelling, "Who the hell said I'm yours? Or anyone's for that matter?" I then turned my anger on the man that had provided part of my DNA. "And as for you, absentee dad, I'm not going anywhere with you. Call Maury because I'm pretty sure you don't deserve to call me daughter."

"Jewel, it's been so long I had almost forgotten how difficult and hardheaded you are. Since you refuse to come willingly, we will take you." He responded as if he were bored and talking to a small child. I wanted to bash his smug face in. The man with the face full of ugly disgust sent a chilling sneer my way, as if he was excited to try to take me by force.

"Bring it, asshole." I could feel everyone but Teddy drawing on their abilities with full force. The power was surging through me. I was channeling it and ready for my enemies to come.

The lady pulled out a bow and arrow and shot it towards us. It split into multiple arrows that were burning with what appeared to be some sort of smoking energy. Andrew stepped forward and let himself light up like a torch. He focused on the arrows and burned them while they were still in the air. A look of astonishment crossed Ares's and his lackey's faces when Andrew ignited. They didn't know about the Evols. I found that interesting and decided to ask Anubis about it later.

Right now I had a fight to win.

Everything happened so fast. Ares came for us, and I barely had time to think. He was on Anubis, their swords clashing. Anubis was pushing him back, but there were a few times that Ares almost had the upper hand. I watched them fight, trying to decide when and how to jump in. They were so fast I could barely keep up. Ares swung at Anubis and barely missed him; Anubis jabbed, only to be blocked. The fighting became more and more intense.

Ares leaped forward, swinging his sword and cutting Anubis deep on his forearm. Anubis lost his footing and fell back onto his back as Ares pointed the sword at his head, then raised it up as if to strike him a final blow. Anubis swiftly blocked his stab and rolled away from the deadly jab, which sliced through the Earth and not him. But the fight was still not over.

Fear gripped me so tightly, I couldn't move. I was afraid. Afraid I would lose this man. All I could think about was what if Ares stabbed Anubis? Or worse, what if he killed him? My heart literally skipped a beat and damn near stopped. I decided there was no way in hell I was going to just stand there. I let my borrowed powers wash over me completely. Ares might be my father but he was about to pay dearly for his mistakes. I gathered the energy into a ball in my hands and was about to release it onto Ares when I was knocked down from behind.

"It's so good to see you again, Jewel." The ugly man smiled at me; his teeth were sharpened to points.

"Not sorry to say I don't know who the hell you are." I turned my energy ball towards him, passing it between my hands, ready to aim it.

I didn't have much time to think when he descended upon me. He punched me in the jaw. It hurt, but I stood up, pissed, and punched him back. We began to fight in earnest. I blocked many of his kicks and jabs and even got a few in, but he was a much more skilled fighter than me, and I had a sinking feeling he was just playing with me. He hit me once and I fell to my knees.

"I find it interesting that you can't even remember one of your own brothers." He gave me a sarcastic pout, and I wanted to punch the sarcasm right out of him.

"Obviously you weren't important enough for me to remember," I shot back. Then I slammed my fist into his face and he laughed at me.

"Yeah, you always were scared of me. You preferred Eros, that sad excuse for a man." I don't know why but his comment pissed me off so bad. The memories of Eros had shown me the love I held for him. He continued, "You have too much love in you, just like he did. You never had enough war." He spat the word love at me. I hated him and it was more than just his words. I didn't know why but I wanted to squish the life out of his disgusting head.

I quickly stood up and decided it was time to use my assets. I pulled in Gale's and Andrew's powers. I combined them and made a firestorm. I didn't goad him or even speak to him anymore, and I didn't allow him to say anything that would distract me. I just let the power rush through me. I felt it lift me off the ground. In that moment, I wanted him dead. I let the power go. I surrounded him with the fireball and forced him to back away, but somehow he was able to step out of the fire without even being singed. I was in shock at first, but then began to pull the energy around me again. But before I could do anything with it, I was gripped by a piercing fear.

I was so terrified that I suddenly fell to the ground and couldn't move. I looked towards my friends and saw them fighting the lady warrior. Anubis was engaged in a fight with Ares, while I was lying terrified on the ground, paralyzed with fear. I was losing. We were losing. We were all going to die. My friends were going to die, and it would be my fault.

And then the terror stopped.

Anubis had sliced straight through the disgusting ugly man, who was now clutching his bleeding stomach.

"Jewel," Anubis called. "Jewel, look at me."

I looked from the bleeding man to Anubis. He was scared too, but it was obvious he was scared for me. I realized then that this man loved me more than I deserved, and damn it, I loved him too.

That was the thought in my mind as I watched Ares slice through him.

CHAPTER NINETEEN

A NUBIS BARELY FLINCHED at the slice through his shoulder, and he turned to fight off Ares's attack. He was able to throw him off balance and held his blade to his throat. Just as he was about to move the blade, he stopped.

"I will not kill you." His words were menacing, and I could only imagine the deadly looks he could give in his warrior state. "You will leave now."

"Not before we take a few things with us," the beautiful warrior lady yelled from behind us. I whirled around and saw that Andrew lay bleeding and clutching a wound in his side. The lady held Teddy close to her with a knife to his throat. She moved her nose to his neck and breathed deeply then licked him along the side of the face. If I weren't so terrified for him I would have been grossed out. "This one belongs with us."

I started running towards her, ready to kick her ass and get Teddy back, but she disappeared in a bright light before I reached her, and when the dust finally settled they were all gone, including Teddy.

I felt lost. I desperately looked around, as if I were hoping it was a joke and he was hiding. "Teddy. Oh my god. They took him."

Then I heard Andrew groan in pain. I decided then and there I was going to kill that bitch.

I ran to Andrew's side. He was bleeding out from a deep wound in his side. It looked like a stab wound, but deep, and it appeared to be burnt, in a way. He was trying to speak through gritted teeth. "She took me by surprise and shot an arrow at me. It exploded and somehow was able to penetrate past my fire." He moaned louder as I examined the wound further.

I looked up at the remaining three Evols. "He needs to get back to the compound quick. Monica, put pressure on his wound." I turned towards Anubis. "Can you do a portal for this many people?"

"Yes, but it will be difficult on them." *Why would it be difficult on them and not me?* I wondered. I pushed that thought aside and refocused once again on the situation. "Can he make it?" I looked concernedly at Andrew. He couldn't die for me. I wouldn't let him.

"The chances are good he'll survive, but he may have frostbite when we get to the other side."

I nodded, though I didn't fully understand. "Take him. The others can ride back in the hummer. I'll go with you and help you carry him." I turned towards Jeff, Gale, and Monica. "We'll get him back fast. We'll meet you there." They all nodded and took off.

I noticed as we hoisted Andrew up that Anubis was also bleeding, but he barely seemed to notice. I decided it must not have been too serious, even though I'd watched the sword go clean through him.

"Grab ahold of him and hold on tight." He made the portal and we stepped through, carrying Andrew with us. The portal was cold, but not cold enough to cause frostbite, at least not in my opinion. It was too dark for us to see one another, which was normal, but in just one extra step we were through. It wasn't until we got to the other side that I realized what Anubis had been talking about. Andrew was freezing.

"That was c-o-o-o-old." His teeth chattered the words out and he shivered.

I looked around. We were in my living room. "Dad!" I yelled as loud as I could.

He rushed into the room from outside, as if he'd already been on his way. The others must have called him. Behind him, two of the employees we hired to work in the basement rushed through as well. They grabbed Andrew and placed him onto a gurney. My dad draped a thick blanket over top of him, and they disappeared through the front door, my dad staying behind. He turned after shutting the door.

"Are you okay?" He was looking me over, assessing if I was injured. I remembered being punched in the face and decided I must look awful. I looked down at my torn and dirty dress and touched the pendant at my neck. At least that was still intact.

"Yeah, I'm okay. Thanks to Anubis." I remembered then the slice that Ares had made into the right side of Anubis's shoulder. It was bloody, but the bleeding seemed to have slowed down considerably for the wound that was inflicted on him. I moved towards him, intent on checking his shoulder.

"My shoulder is fine," he answered, realizing what I was doing.

"He cut clean through you. Let me look."

He froze and watched me as I tenderly touched his shoulder.

"I'll go check on Andrew." My dad walked out of the room and through the front door, allowing us privacy. Anubis and I barely noticed, as I was so close to him, and we were both fighting the effects of that closeness.

"Take off your shirt." My voice was rough, but I was trying to control the overwhelming desire bubbling up inside of me and focus on seeing if he was okay.

"As you wish." He pulled the black t-shirt over his head. He was magnificent. His chest was thick with muscles and he had perfectly shaped abs. I ran my hand down them, almost forgetting about his shoulder, and I watched him shudder. Then I looked up at his shoulder and stopped when I saw dried blood and what looked to be no more than a thin, angry red closed wound, already healing.

"What?" I couldn't say any more. I didn't know what to say. Did he have extraordinary healing abilities as well?

"Yes, I have fast healing abilities."

I looked at him then, wondering again if he was reading my mind. "Are you reading my thoughts?"

"No, I'm reading you. I will always know you. Neither time nor separation, not even death could change that."

I could feel the heat of his body so near to mine and I couldn't resist for another moment—I kissed him. Although my lip hurt and my swollen, bruised face was throbbing, I didn't stop the kiss, and the sensation of his lips on mine made everything else go away. For a moment. I wanted this man and knew I was powerless to even consider choosing another, but I pulled back from the kiss when a tormenting thought crossed my mind.

"Teddy." I felt the pain of his loss, of him missing from my side, straight down to my soul. My best friend, the one who knew my secrets and still loved me and stood by my side through all the years, was gone, taken by those psychos. Who knew what they had planned for him?

"He'll be okay. They won't hurt him. They want to use him." He tenderly touched my face, trying to be careful of the bruised and swollen areas.

"Why? Why do they want him?"

"They want him because he's one of them. I suspected that he was part Olympian, but wasn't sure. I think—but I haven't confirmed this—that Poseidon is his father. Possibly your sister Beroe is his mother and they gave him up for adoption for their greater good. They wanted him near you." His words floored me. I didn't know what to do or think in that moment.

Was this why we were so close? And they thought to use me by using their own son? This angered me beyond words. Why would anyone use their child to suit their own agenda? I was going to get Teddy back. I just didn't know how yet.

I looked down at my dirty and torn dress. It had survived centuries, only to be destroyed tonight. I felt the necklace warm against my skin again, and as I looked at Anubis I saw that he was watching me intently, and crimson red again surrounded him.

"When a person has an aura that's deep or crimson red, that means love, right?"

He smiled and pulled me close and leaned in. He did this

quite often and it turned my knees to rubber. "It means true love, passion, desire. The deeper the red, the more they feel it."

"So pink would be something more like affection or a crush?" I thought back to Andrew.

"It can mean that, or the love of a friend or family member, but it doesn't have the same depth and substance as red." He caressed my face and I was having trouble thinking.

"Oh, can you see them?"

"No, only a select few can who have the ability or tools." He ran his finger over the pendant.

"How did you learn this, then?" I watched him, interested in his answer but knowing in my heart what he was going to say.

"Because you told me." Of course, he meant the me from the past. At least I was learning to slowly accept this reality.

"Eros gave this to me?"

"Yes."

I thought about Andrew then, realizing I had forgotten about him for a moment. "I'm going to go check on Andrew." I noticed there was a hesitant look in Anubis's eyes. Jealousy perhaps? He did shimmer a bit green around the edges. "Is that a problem?" I almost dared him to say it was.

"Of course not. It's just, when I had to watch you dance with him… it was difficult."

"Good." I smiled and turned, walking towards the door. I felt Anubis create a portal. The air became colder. Then he and the portal were gone. I knew he'd be back. There was no reason for goodbyes. I headed out to visit Andrew.

CHAPTER TWENTY

"WELL YOU LOOK awful."

I laughed, knowing it was true. "Leave it to you to be as blunt as me. You look like shit as well."

"Thanks." Andrew sat on the bed, pale and hooked up to several different machines.

"You going to make it?" I said it with a playful tone, but I was just trying to hide my real concern.

"So they tell me." He moaned, though, and I rushed closer to his bed.

"Good, because I'd have to kill you if you didn't."

He laughed at the irony of my statement but winced in pain while he did it.

"Oh my, I'm sorry. Can I get you anything?" I felt bad that I'd made him laugh. I realized now that the feelings I had for Andrew weren't real, but I still cared about him as a friend, and if Anubis was right, he felt the same.

"No, just explain. Who were those people and where

is Teddy?"

I sighed, knowing I couldn't keep things from my friends anymore. It was time to have allies. I told him everything: who I was and why my people were hunting me. I explained about my race, leaving out, for now, the Egyptonians and why the Olympians took Teddy.

"Your bio dad is a dick. And who was the chick who shot me?" I realized that in the craziness that had occurred in the aftermath of our fight, I'd failed to ask Anubis. I was going to have to put that on my million-question list. It seemed I was always asking him questions. I needed to know the answers for myself, and that meant becoming her.

"I don't know, but I'm going to find out." One of the doctors walked in to examine him, so I said, "Andrew, I'll visit you again soon." He nodded as I left.

I rushed back upstairs to my room. I knew what I needed to do. I needed to get over this fear and I needed to become her. I was ready. The only way I could think to do this would be to see Thoth.

My father came home as I was waiting for Anubis to come back. He gently knocked on my door.

"Come in."

"How are you, Jewel?" He sat next to me, and I leaned my head onto his shoulder, wincing a little at the pain in a swollen area.

"I'm fine. I've just been thinking."

"Hmm, of what?" Sometimes he already knew since he had the ability to see certain futures if he chose to. I suspected he knew but was politely letting me tell him.

"Dad, I've been so afraid of becoming her. I was scared I would lose who I am now." I paused, trying to decide how to word my next sentence.

"And now?" he gently probed.

"Now it doesn't matter that I'm scared. It's a matter of need. I need to remember, and I think I need her."

He kissed my forehead. "Everyone has choices in life, Jewel. Sometimes the outcome of our choices isn't what we expect, but it ends up being what we need the most. I don't think you will lose yourself to her. I think you'll remember things from that life." He stopped and looked at me. "I think, in a way, your experiences here have made you stronger, but in your soul and your essence you have and always will be her. Memories won't change that."

I sat there thinking about what he said, and the tears began to flow. He was right. I was still me, and the memories were already invading my life. All my fear had been for nothing. The only thing that I was uneasy about now was the question of whether or not I'd like the other me. Would I want to know what really happened to me? And why had my family wanted to take me or, worse, hurt me?

"Do you know what happened to me, the other me?"

"Yes."

"Was it bad?"

"It wasn't good." He looked at me then and the look in his eyes told me I wasn't going to like it.

"But you aren't going to tell me?"

"My bunny, I'm sorry. It isn't my story to tell. You must discover it on your own." I noticed him glance at the pendant around my neck. He'd done that a few other times during the conversation as well.

"You know, it's interesting that you call me bunny. Someone else in my new memories used to call me that as well."

He smiled, about to say something, but he was interrupted by the sudden appearance of a black hole. Anubis stepped through.

"Robert, I'm glad you're here. I'm going to take Jewel home." He didn't phrase it as a question or even a request. "Jewel, pack something, we're going."

"Now wait a darn minute here, you can't just command me." I stood up and squared my shoulders, standing tall in front of him with my arms crossed.

"My apologies, Jewel. Please collect your things. It's safer for you at home." Home. He called it home for the both of us. As much as I liked the sound of that, I wasn't sure I was ready to just up and leave. My dad didn't argue with him; he was leaving the choice up to me. He knew I could stand my own ground when needed.

"Listen, I get it, you're a god almighty or whatever, but you don't command me to do jack diddly squat. I'm going with you, but only to see Thoth. You, on the other hand, had better really think about your words, because right now you're being a really big dick." My dad smiled. I kissed him and told him I'd be back soon.

"You will, bunny, and we'll have much to talk about." I didn't know what he meant, but him calling me bunny reminded me again that someone else had once used that nickname with me. I was going to make it my mission to ask my father about that when I returned.

Before we left I slipped the pendant into my pocket, noticing my father's eyes still glanced at it oddly. I felt the familiar warmth of it in my pocket, but it was slowly cooling and I couldn't help but slip my hand in to feel it on my skin. It lost its receding coolness and became warmer at my touch.

I pulled my hand out and allowed it to cool. It was odd that even though I'd only had the necklace for a small period of time, taking it off seemed as if I were cutting off a part of myself.

Anubis and I walked through another of his black, lightless, cold portals. He held my hand as we popped onto the other side, directly in the middle of Thoth's laboratory. He was, as usual, hunched over some equipment, studying something.

"Good to see you, Jewel." He didn't look up when he addressed me.

I dropped Anubis's hand and went directly to him, and the urge to hug him was so great. The memories of the time I'd shared with him in Atlantis brought up emotions I didn't fully understand, but I was starting to. He was startled by my hug, but after an awkward moment, much like the hug we'd shared in my last memory, he embraced me back.

"I see you are starting to remember things."

"Yes, but I need to remember more."

He pulled back from the hug and looked me directly in the eyes. "No."

"Please, I'm ready. I need to know why. I'm tired of asking questions and not fully understanding."

"It's too dangerous." His voice had lost its monotone indifference, and there was fear and harshness to his words.

"I'm ready. I'm ready to start to become more of her." I looked at Anubis then. I thought I noticed a mixture of resolve and gratitude cross his features. Yet, when he walked over towards me I realized he was also worried. I found it interesting how I could so easily read him, even without the help of the pendant.

I think I found the issue that caused you to go into a coma last time." Thoth stopped and went back to the microscope, where he had another blood sample on a slide. "There was a substance in your blood that was accelerating the process. Only it didn't work properly; it only made you lose consciousness for a long period of time."

"Will I be okay now?" I knew whatever the substance was, it was from Beroe. She had hightailed it out of the dance after warning me.

"Let me test your blood and we will see." He walked over to a cabinet full of supplies, bringing with him the tools to collect my blood. Anubis walked over and grasped my free hand in his. The contact felt good. He quietly watched with me as Thoth collected and examined my blood. "It appears to be free of the substance."

"Then we're ready to party." I started to walk towards the back where the machine was when Anubis tugged at my hand and pulled me towards him. He wrapped me in his arms and put his face close to mine.

"Before you do this. I need to say something." His lips were so close to mine I tilted my face up, almost begging to be kissed.

"Yes?" I breathed out.

"Whatever you remember. Whatever you learn, just remember I love you as you are now as I loved you then, and nothing will ever change that." He paused, ready to say something else, but nothing came.

"And what else?" I brushed my lips on his cheek, unable to resist.

"And I'm sorry."

That startled me. Why was he sorry? I backed away then,

looking at him. There was anguish in his eyes.

"For what?" My words were harsh and direct. Had I made a mistake to trust him?

Thoth interrupted us. "It's ready." He had set up the machine as we'd stood there in each other's arms.

"For what?" I asked again with more desperation.

"For not protecting you."

I sighed with relief, realizing then that he was just carrying guilt, guilt that he'd carried for thousands of years.

"I don't know yet what happened in its entirety, but please unburden yourself. That's why I'm here, to find out what happened to me."

I turned from him and walked towards Thoth, the machine, and my past. It was time for my past and my present to become one.

I was ready to finally meet this other Jewel.

I was going to save Teddy.

I was going to take my life back.

The hum of the machine started, and I gave in to it. I let her in.

And my life would never be the same.

ACKNOWLEDGMENTS

There have been many great people in my life who have supported me; I have truly been gifted to be surrounded by such amazing people. I'd like to thank my grandfather for reading to me when I was too little to remember so that I now have an unhealthy love for all things fiction and my grandmother for not saying no. As well as my mother for putting up with me through my horrible teen years. Really, I was absolutely a pain. And for always being my support person, the one that I can always count on. My husband because he is my best friend and second half. My in-laws, Karen and Jim, for their continuous positivity and support. And, most of all, my very first beta reader Monique Carranza, who read the first 10,000 words and said she needed more. As well as the friends who suffered through my earlier novels, Christa Allen and Jessica Coffey. Also, J. L. Mac for her advice.

My editor Nicole Hewitt, who took something of a jumbled up, hot mess of my imagination and turned it into something readable. You are amazing and I am so glad to have found you and to learn from you! And cover designer Robin Harper, who took my ideas and made them real. Their websites can be found on the cover page of the book.

Thank you!

Made in the USA
Lexington, KY
08 December 2017